Love Me Forever

DONNA FLETCHER

J

JOVE BOOKS, NEW YORK

This is a work of fiction. Names, characters, places, and incidents either
are the product of the author's imagination or are used fictitiously,
and any resemblance to actual persons, living or dead, business
establishments, events, or locales is entirely coincidental.

LOVE ME FOREVER

A Jove Book / published by arrangement with
the author

PRINTING HISTORY
Jove edition / February 2003

Copyright © 2003 by Donna Fletcher
Poem in dedication used by permission of Marc Fletcher
Cover art by Danny O'Leary
Book design by Julie Rogers

Visit our website at
www.penguinputnam.com

ISBN: 0-515-13464-3

A JOVE BOOK®
Jove Books are published by The Berkley Publishing Group,
a division of Penguin Putnam Inc.,
375 Hudson Street, New York, New York 10014.
JOVE and the "J" design
are trademarks belonging to Penguin Putnam Inc.

PRINTED IN THE UNITED STATES OF AMERICA

10 9 8 7 6 5 4 3 2 1

For my best friend,
Greg Romanow

The waters of time sweep by me
I see my youth and loves gone by
I remember times of great sorrow
I see faces long since past
I grow cold thinking of lost friends

The pain of those memories
have haunted me these many years
But a soft voice beckons me back
It slows the waters just so
Showing me smiles
Showing me the love my friends and I once shared

A small ember that remained grows inside of me
The fires of my memory stoked by the sights I behold
A smile crosses my face as I watch my youth from a new view
No longer sad or cold, but happy and filled with love

Midnight walks under the moon
Car rides that lasted all night
Three A.M. dinners
Friends' parents who were all named Mom and Dad

The voice whispers that these are my memories
I must take them with me
I hold them close and walk from the waters
A small tear rolls down my cheek as I leave for this I know
Memories are all I now have of those days of youth gone by

—MARC FLETCHER

I

∽

Scotland, 1513

I AM SORRY, BRIANNA, YOUR HUSBAND IS DEAD.

Those words resonated in her head and echoed in the depths of her soul. She had shed not a tear when her brother, Ian, had delivered the startling news. She had simply stared at him in silence. What else was there for her to do? Was she not waiting on this news? Had she not prayed for this?

Ian had not approached her nor had he offered her any further condolences. He appeared at a loss as to how to comfort her and had turned a helpless look on his wife, Moira.

Her remark had taken her husband completely by surprise. "You will be late to the village if you do not leave now."

Thinking back, Brianna appreciated her sister-in-law's directness. She had helped her to face a difficult moment. Now, sitting alone in the coach a good distance from her brother's keep in Glencoe, she was glad for the solitude. Her brother had protested her departure, insisting she should not go, insisting that she should not be alone at this time. But solitude was her friend and she needed this time alone. This time to think and reason and recall all she had been through.

Moira thought his suggestion nonsense. She insisted that Brianna had healed nicely over the last six difficult months and that the villagers were eagerly awaiting her arrival. She would be instructing them in the making of new dyes and proper food preparation for the winter, which was but six weeks away. This trip was necessary not only for the villagers but for Brianna.

Her sister-in-law had been well-schooled at the convent where she had spent seventeen years of her life before marrying Ian. A monk had educated her in mathematics and science, and Moira had never lost her interest in knowledge; she continued to educate herself as well as those who wished to learn.

Brianna had wished to learn. Her studies had helped her to heal. It had taken time and she had shed endless tears in the process, but she had succeeded with Moira's help in facing the truth about her husband and her marriage.

Arran had been a handsome and selfish man. He had cared naught but for himself and in the end his own greed had been his destruction. He had plotted to murder Moira, the babe, and then Ian, leaving himself to lead the clan Cameron. He had managed to escape in the end, though not before threatening to kill his own wife.

She wiped at a single tear. It was not shed for Arran; he did not deserve her tears. It was shed out of relief that her ordeal had finally come to an end. She was free, no longer wed, nor ever wishing to wed again.

She had given her heart only to have it broken. She had

thought love could heal all and survive all. She would not make that foolish mistake again. She would trust no man, particularly a handsome man, and besides, she found it difficult to believe in love. She had thought when she fell in love it would be forever. She was wrong and she would take no second chances.

There was, however, one man in her life she knew truly cared for her, and that was her six-month-old nephew, Duncan. He had captured her heart and she was madly in love with the tiny lad. And since she was barren, never in her four years of marriage having conceived a child, she would give her love to her brother's son.

The wooden coach hit several bumps in the road, and Brianna grimaced, knowing it would be a sore bottom she would suffer upon her arrival. But it mattered little to her, for she was looking forward to teaching the village women all that Moira had taught her. Ian had sent two men along with her for protection. Usually she had many more around her, but with Arran's death there was no longer any need for concern and she was pleased.

She had felt a prisoner. She was now free.

"Free," she said softly, smiled, and hugged herself. It was a good feeling.

Another hard bump had her almost tumbling off her seat, and when she heard the crack of thunder in the distance, she assumed the men had hastened the pace in an attempt to make the village before the storm made the roads impassable.

Autumn was fast giving way to winter and it was an unusually cold day for November. She wrapped her red and green plaid around her, her soft green wool tunic and underdress keeping her warm, and there was a fur wrap in the coach in case the weather worsened. She felt well-protected.

The coach gave a leap and a bump, and Brianna took a

peek past the leather hide window coverings. She did not like what she saw. They rode dangerously close to the edge of a hill, and while it was not a far drop, it was nonetheless a drop that could prove fatal to them all.

She sat back in her seat and recited a silent prayer for their safety. In a few minutes the coach slowed, though the pace remained hasty, and Brianna sighed with relief.

The sigh was but brief. At that moment the coach suddenly tilted, sending Brianna smashing against the door. She tried frantically to grab the window strap for support or to right herself, but it was a hand's length from her reach. The coach then toppled over and she screamed as her body was thrown senselessly around the toppling coach. It turned over and over and over, and before it came to a crashing halt on the ground, Brianna had mercifully slipped into unconsciousness.

Darkness was all she could see and pain was all she could feel. She dared not make a sound, for that might disturb the throbbing pain that already resonated throughout her body. She lay silent in the darkness wondering how she had gotten here and where here was.

It took several agonizing minutes for her to regain her senses and realize what had happened. The coach had run off the side of the road and plunged furiously down the hill, rendering her unconscious and quite possibly killing the two men with her. And if that was so, she was now helpless. There was no one to offer her help or protection, and she was in no condition to protect herself. She kept slipping in and out of consciousness, and that made it more difficult for her to focus. Her one constant thought was that she needed to open her eyes and see to her whereabouts. If she could determine the extent of her situation, perhaps then she could determine a solution.

She thought she heard the crunching of leaves as if someone approached, and at first she felt relief, though fear quickly followed. If one of the men had survived the crash, he would have called out to her to let her know of his approach. A stranger would remain silent.

Robbers and villains were well acquainted with this area and would waste no time in claiming what they could from the damaged coach and the bodies they found.

Fear raced through her and only caused her more pain. She hurt so badly that she could not determine her injuries. Pain at the moment was in complete control of her body, and she could only maintain her presence of mind sporadically.

The heavy footsteps moved closer, the crunch of the leaves sounding louder to Brianna's ears. There was naught that she could do. She was defenseless. She could but wait and meet her fate.

Being a Cameron, she felt the need to react with courage since she was unable to defend herself, and she struggled to open her eyes and meet friend or foe.

With great difficulty she managed to lift her eyelids enough to see the shape of a dark figure. Tall and broad were the only distinguishing features she could determine, for her eyes warred with her to close.

The mysterious figure bent down beside her, and in an instant she felt herself being lifted into powerful arms, but the pain that the movement caused her so overwhelmed that she slipped back into the blessed darkness.

A stab of pain brought Brianna back to consciousness. Only this time she rested on soft bedding and a comforting warmth penetrated her aching body. Her first thought was to remain still and linger in this heavenly bliss, but it was a brief consideration and one she could not take seriously. She had to know where she was and who had brought her here. And of course she had to determine if she was in danger, though there was little she could do to defend herself.

Still, she could not remain ignorant of her situation no matter how much the soft bedding eased her pain.

She opened her eyes slowly and it took several agonizing minutes for her vision to clear enough for her to determine her whereabouts. She lay in a good-size bed with a layer of coverings over her. And in an instant she realized she lay naked, not a stitch of clothing on her.

Worry seized her and with great effort she made a cursory glance around the room. It was a one-room cottage of fair size, and it smelled fresh as if tended to regularly. She fought to keep her eyes open and fought to focus them on her surroundings, but the relentless throb in her head made it a battle hard to win.

She allowed her eyes a brief rest before forcing them open once again. This time she caught sight of a table and two chairs in front of the hearth. She kept her eyes steady on the stone fireplace. It was large, taking up a good portion of the wall with a rough log mantel across the stones, a good head's height above the flames.

A sudden stabbing pain to her ribs forced her eyes shut, and she attempted to take several deep breaths, which only worsened her pain. She wondered if she had broken any bones, and while she wished to know, she was too much of a coward to discover for herself. She felt as if she had suffered a bad beating. Every part of her ached or throbbed, and if she attempted to move a mere inch she quickly found herself slipping into the depths of unconsciousness.

She could never see to her own care in this horrendous condition, but how then could she allow a stranger to tend her? Tears threatened her eyes and she fought hard to keep them away. It would do her little good to shed senseless tears. They would serve no purpose and only manage to hamper her already hampered sight.

Courage.

She needed the courage of her heritage. She was born of a strong clan, and no matter the difficulties or challenges, the Cameron clan faced all adversaries with pride and honor. She had only recently regained that pride and honor in herself after having surrendered it to a husband who was not worthy of her. She had promised herself she would never do so again. She would maintain her rich heritage and face life's challenges with courage as only a Cameron could.

The pain subsided enough for her to focus once again on her surroundings. She thought she caught sight of a single window but could not be certain, and the delicious scent in the air told her that something tasty roasted over the hearth's flames.

The well-maintained condition of the cottage told her that a caring heart resided here, and that thought gave her pause to sigh in relief.

Her eyes drifted shut once again, and she almost slipped back into the blissful relief of the darkness when she heard a movement and her eyes sprang open, causing her to grimace in pain. She did not moan, for she had found that even the slightest sound caused her discomfort.

Where had it come from?

She listened to the silence, hoping to hear the slight movement again, but she heard only the crackling of the hearth's flames. Someone was here with her and she knew not who. The thought that a stranger lingered nearby made her grow fearful.

How could she protect herself? She had not the strength, nor the means to defend herself. She could do nothing but rely on the kindness of a stranger.

But was it kindness he offered?

She searched the room, her glance going from corner to corner, and she could see nothing, but she had heard.

What had she heard?

The sound came again.

It was a shuffle of sorts, as if someone moved, but it was a brief movement, a barely noticeable or audible one.

Did he not want her to detect his presence?

She remained quiet, not moving, only listening. She fought the darkness that reached up to capture her. She could not surrender to it even though it removed her from the constant pain and offered her relief. It was a false sense of relief, for she would wake to the pain once again and realize her plight.

Strength was her ally and she could not surrender to her pain.

She battled with herself and forced her eyes open, forced herself to glance once again around the room. She thought she caught a movement in the corner next to the fireplace, and she allowed her glance to settle there.

She thought it a shadow, a large shadow that dominated the corner, the width and height of it overpowering and intimidating like a dark angel who hovered in wait.

She swallowed her fear and remained focused on the shadow. It moved, only slightly, but it moved.

She waited to see if it would move again.

It did.

It moved away from the fireplace slowly, as if hesitant, and with even slower steps it approached the bed where she lay.

Brianna tried to take a deep breath, but pain rushed into her chest and she gasped as relentless arrows of pain stabbed repeatedly at her body.

Her distress caused the shadow to move faster, and it reached the bed in an instant.

Brianna stared in horror at the sight that hovered over her.

She thought the face that of a man, but she could not be sure, for a freshly stitched scar, red and raw, ran from his forehead over his eye, down his cheek to his jaw. His other eye was badly bruised and swollen almost shut. His lower lip was in the process of healing from a severe split. His multiple injuries had swollen his face grotesquely out of shape so much so that he resembled a demon from the depths of hell.

Her response was natural.

She screamed herself into unconsciousness.

2

BRIANNA MADE HER WAY OUT OF THE DARKNESS. A nagging thought warned her to remain in the shelter of the darkness, but that was not possible. The light would bring her knowledge, and Moira had taught her that knowledge was important to survival.

She opened her eyes slowly and her surroundings rushed back to her, filling her with an anxious fear. The hideous face she had last seen before unconsciousness claimed her loomed in her mind's eye. And the realization that the grotesque man shared this lone cottage with her made her tremble with dread.

Was he merely a hapless victim of unfortunate circumstance? Or was his beating a justifiable punishment for a crime? She would not have her answers or ease her fear if she did not ask, but she found it difficult to speak. She was not certain if the lack of her voice was due to her injuries or her fear of hearing unfavorable answers.

"I mean you no harm."

His soft, deep voice startled her. It was much more gentle than she had expected, but still she knew little of this man.

"I apologize for my appearance. I do not wish to frighten you."

He offered her an explanation in a tender and caring tone and made no move to approach her. She had not expected thoughtfulness, and her anxiousness calmed, though it did not vanish. It lingered nearby along with apprehension.

He continued, his voice filled with a confident strength yet touched with a soft concern. "I have recently seen a harsh battle and my wounds only begin to heal. Again, I mean you no harm. I but wish to help you. While your body shows no signs of broken bones, you have sustained a severe bruising to your chest and legs and need care."

The thought that she was helpless upset Brianna, and tears trickled from her eyes, though she fought to keep them under control. It would do her no good to show this stranger weakness.

"My name is Royce and I ask your permission to tend to your needs."

That he spoke the truth to her was obvious. She could not move without pain stabbing at her. But how could she allow this strange man to see to her every need? How could she bear the thought of being so vulnerable in front of him? Could she do nothing for herself?

Her Cameron pride made her attempt to at least sit up in the bed without any assistance. If she could accomplish that menial task, perhaps then she would not feel so helpless and dependent on this stranger.

She stubbornly moved her arms, though her chest ached from the effort, and when she attempted to brace them on the bed and move herself, a vicious stab of pain knifed through her and forced a scream from her.

She did not, however, count on the scream being his name.

He rushed to her side and took her hand, holding it gently while his other hand tenderly stroked her forehead. "It is all right. Calm yourself and the pain will subside. I am here and will care for you and protect you. Think naught but of my hand soothing your head and my voice that reaches out to you in concern. Tell me your name? I have wondered over it."

She concentrated on his strong voice, and his confident touch comforted her. "I am Brianna." She made no mention of her clan, for she knew not of his clan distinction, and there was much friction amongst Highland clans.

"A gentle name," he said and stroked her face.

She kept her eyes closed, gaining the courage to look upon him. It was not that she thought him horrendous, though his fresh scars made him appear so. It was that she felt for his plight. He had suffered horribly, and the scars that remained attested to his horrific ordeal.

"It is kind of you to look after me." Her pain was slowly ebbing and she breathed more easily, though she would not surrender the comforting strength of his hand.

"I do not mind. You need me."

She instantly responded, "Aye, I do, though I do not mean to be a burden."

"I do not think of you as a burden and I tend you most willingly."

She was relieved to hear his truthful words. "I am grateful for you, but I must ask of the two men who were with me."

A moment of silence preceded his answer. "I am sorry; they did not survive."

She felt a sense of sorrow for her companions. They

were good men and free of family so there was no particular person who would mourn their loss, though the clan would. All members of the clan were considered family and all mourned a passing.

"They were good men."

"Then they will be missed."

"Aye, they will," she said softly and offered a silent prayer for their souls.

"Are you hungry?" he asked, his hand remaining firmly locked with hers.

She thought a moment, for food had not been a thought and she simply felt too weak even to consider attempting to eat. "Nay, I have not the strength."

"Which is the very reason you should eat something, to regain your strength."

She sighed softly, knowing a deep breath would only bring her pain, and before she could respond he spoke.

"The broth I have made would suit you well."

Brianna knew she could not lift even a simple spoon, and her disappointment was evident when she repeated, "I have not the strength."

"I will feed you, you need not worry."

A single tear trickled from her eye. The idea that she was completely dependent on this stranger upset her. She had no choice but to rely on his kindness and to trust him. She realized that trust was the most difficult for her. She had not been able to trust her husband; how was she ever to trust this man she did not know?

With a gentle swipe of his finger he removed the single teardrop from her cheek. "You need not fear me. I mean you no harm, Brianna. I will care for you as long as is necessary. *Trust me.*"

She had shut her eyes and listened to the soothing lilt of his voice. If she had not known his features, she would have thought of them as gentle, a smooth complexion, tender eyes, soft lips. This vision of such a man she could trust, but the man who stood over her possessed no gentle features.

Her eyes drifted open. He looked down at her with an intense dark green eye; his other eye was too badly swollen shut for him to open. The color reminded her of the forest in the winter, cold and empty yet content in its solitude. His hair was long, a burnished brown, as though fire and light mixed with the color of the earth, and it looked to be well tended, for it shined with a silky radiance. One braid hung down on the right side of his head, a brown leather strip entwined in the strands. His lip swelled from the severe spilt and made it impossible to determine the true shape of his mouth.

And one look at his body left no doubt that he was a warrior. He wore a dark shirt over a broad and heavily muscled chest. His plaid was of dark colors and wrapped snugly around a narrow waist; below that she could not see, for he leaned over the edge of the bed, blocking the rest of him from her view.

"Now that you have looked me over, will you trust me?"

"Have I a choice?" Brianna asked, feeling justified in blatantly taking stock of him.

His hand gently pushed a stray strand of hair off her face. "Nay, Brianna, you have no choice but to trust me."

An unexpected cough seized her and she cried out as pain stabbed at her chest. Without thought she squeezed at his hand that held firm to hers, and his other hand instantly reached out to gently cup her face and force her to rest her glance on him.

"Look at me and breathe calmly," he ordered in a tone that he must have used to command men in battle, for she immediately obeyed him without question.

"Calmly," he repeated when she fought the breath that

followed. "If you struggle you will only worsen the pain and bring yourself more discomfort. Ease your breathing."

She followed his words and took short shallow breaths and realized the pain lessened, though her hold on his hand remained firm.

"Time and rest will heal your bruises."

She nodded slowly, knowing he was right.

"I will get you some broth and you will eat."

"A command?" she asked with effort, the pain not having completely subsided.

"If it is necessary."

His response warned her that he was a man accustomed to having his command obeyed, and being that she had no choice at the moment, she wisely chose to defer to him.

For now.

"Nay, I will eat what I can."

"It is good that you try, but first I must raise you up more on the pillows so that you may eat more comfortably."

Her eyes rounded, the thought of pain filling her with dread, and he understood.

"I will move you as gently as possible."

He did not wait for her to respond or object. He removed his hand from hers and slipped his arm beneath the wool blanket.

Her eyes grew even wider.

He offered an explanation. "I had no choice but to remove your clothes. They were torn and dirty. And I needed to see how severe your injuries were. I could carry only you and thought to return later for your chest, but I have been reluctant to leave you alone."

She said not a word but gave him a brief nod, letting him know she understood.

"Relax," he said softly, his hand slipping slowly beneath her back. "I will not hurt you."

The strength in his arm was remarkable, for he moved her with the gentlest of touches, his other hand pushing the pillows beneath her back and head so that she lay reclined. She suffered only the slightest discomfort and paid it no heed, for her new position eased her aching body.

"That feels much better," she said, sending him a brief smile. "Thank you, you are most kind."

He stared at her a moment with an intensity that could frighten; she, however, slowly raised her hand to gently touch his swollen lip. "I wish I had the basket of herbs my sister-in-law Moira had sent along with me. I have something that would help relieve your swelling."

He eased his hand out from beneath her back and adjusted the blanket around her. It had slipped down when he had moved her and near exposed her naked breasts. But then he had already seen all of her, and that thought disturbed her. What had he thought of her body? Every time her husband had made love to her, he had told her that her body was undesirable. He had made her flaws known and had made it known how inadequate a lover she was. But what did that matter now? This man was not interested in her in such an intimate way.

"Something troubles you?" he asked, his confident voice assuring her he could ease any concern.

She stared at him, uncertain how to respond.

He seemed to understand her hesitation. "Trust me. I will not hurt you."

She continued to stare at him, wondering over the battle that had caused such vicious scars. He had fought hard and suffered. She wondered if the battle had been victorious or if he had suffered defeat and if his scars would always remind him of that day. And she wondered why he had chosen to reside here in this cottage alone. Why had he not returned to his clan?

With so many questions and not one answer, she wondered how she could trust this stranger. The answer was simple, for it had repeated in her head too often.

She had no choice.

He understood by the resigned look on her face. "I will get the broth."

She watched him walk off. If he suffered any other injuries, they could not be detected, for he moved with strength and confidence. It seemed his face had taken the brunt of the battle, and she could only imagine the horror of it all.

Her eyes grew heavy as she watched him ladle the broth into a bowl from the black pot over the open flames, and try as she might she could not force them to remain open. She thought to rest them for a few moments, just a few, but as soon as they closed, she slipped into a restful slumber.

Royce returned with bowl in hand to find her sound asleep. He had not the heart to wake her. She needed as much rest as possible, and while the food would help aid in her recovery, he could always feed her later when she woke.

He returned the bowl to the table and then returned to the bed, adjusting the covers over her to make certain she stayed warm. He had come upon the coach by accident. He had not planned to take that trail when out hunting for food, but now he was glad he had. It was obvious that the two men had been thrown from the coach and died on impact. He was surprised to see that anyone inside the coach had survived. When he had discovered her body, he had thought for certain that she had suffered fatal wounds. She had not, though her body was badly bruised and her pain considerable.

He had not realized the extent of her bruising until he began to undress her and the faint purple marks began to surface, and they would only grow worse over the next day before they subsided and began to heal.

She was a beauty that he could not help but notice. Her long dark hair fell in a riot of curls down her back and around her face. It mattered not how many times he would push them off her face, the stubborn curls would return with a bounce and determination—much like her personality, he realized. Her features were soft, her complexion a creamy pale, and her eyes were a vivid blue that put the color of the sky to shame.

She stood a bare three or four inches over five feet and she possessed a body that captured the eye and melted the heart. She was stunning. She had full breasts, with large rosy nipples and a narrow waist that gave way to curving hips. Her skin was soft and silky, the type he could touch forever and never grow tired of.

He had not, of course, touched her intimately. She was injured and required aid, and he tended her in such a manner, keeping his thoughts from straying, though not always successfully. He had been too long without a woman. He had never found it difficult to find a willing woman, and being he lacked a wife, women were his to enjoy.

Of course, if he had such a beauty as Brianna as a wife, he would look no more; she would forever be in his bed.

He ran a careful hand over the scars on his face and shook his head slowly. How would women see him now? Would they scream in fright as Brianna did? Would they turn away in disgust where before they eagerly joined with him?

The battle he had fought had been victorious and a necessity, but he had suffered greatly, losing many men and leaving him with horrendous memories and scars that would never truly heal.

He had decided to heal alone. He needed this time of solitude, this time away from his clan. This time to think.

He had not counted on a companion and one that required tending. He had his own wounds to heal and there were many. How would he ever help another when he had difficulty helping himself?

It did not really matter. She needed him. She was helpless, alone, and dependent on him for her care. Why that made him feel good he could not say. He only knew he wished to protect and care for her. Perhaps in caring for her he cared for himself, and they would heal together.

She stirred and came out of her sleep, his name on her lips. "Royce?"

"I am here," he said softly and took her hand.

She grasped on to him. "You are not a dream."

He kept the smile from his swollen lip. She actually thought him a dream and not a nightmare. She did possess a courageous heart. "Nay, I am not a dream. I am real."

"Can I trust you?"

He wondered if she had meant to voice her question, for it was filled with doubt.

He leaned down close to her ear and whispered, "Aye, Brianna, you can trust me with your deepest darkest secrets. I will never betray your trust. *Never.*"

"Promise?"

"Promise," he whispered and brushed a tender kiss across her cheek.

She sighed contentedly and turned, tucking herself against his chest.

She was warm and soft, and though he had wished for solitude, he suddenly ached for the nearness of her. He stretched out beside her and wrapped a gentle arm around her, and for the first time in days he fell into a restful slumber.

3

Royce slowly spooned the broth into Brianna's mouth. With the first delicious taste she realized she was hungry, and she eagerly waited for each spoonful. He was patient with her, taking his time, not forcing her to hurry. She had not expected that of him; he was, after all, a warrior. She did not think patience was a warrior's trait. They seemed ever ready to charge into battle thinking little of the consequences.

She was discovering that he was a far different warrior than most.

"Tell me when you have had enough," he said.

She kept steady eyes on him where he sat beside her on the bed with bowl in hand. His ravaged face was familiar to her now, and she did not think to look away in horror. "It is good."

Royce tried to smile, but his mending lips allowed but

a brief curve before the pain forced compliance. "It is a simple broth and will help you to gain strength."

"You need to gain strength as well," she said, acknowledging that she was not the only one who required healing.

"We can mend together."

"But I can do nothing to help you mend."

He heard the disappointment in her voice and was surprised that even in her painful state she gave his wounds concern. "You provide me with companionship."

"A companion who must have constant care."

"Enjoy my attention, for I am not known for it."

She caught the gleam in his dark green eyes and realized he teased her. She smiled before accepting another spoonful of broth.

A sudden wind whistled outside the small cottage and was followed by a clap of thunder. Raindrops fell hard after that, and soon the steady downpour took on a soothing rhythm as darkness covered the land.

She relaxed and found it easy to ask him, "What are you known for?"

He could not help but grin and suffered the price. His swollen lip throbbed with pain and he winced.

"Are you all right?" she asked anxiously.

"I am but reminded that pride is a sin."

She laughed softly. "Tell me of this pride."

The gleam in his eye remained. "I think it wiser that I do not."

She took no offense to his refusal. She understood that he teased her, though she was also aware that he did not volunteer information on himself. Was he guarding secrets? Was he reluctant to trust her?

She yawned, fatigue creeping up on her.

"Time to rest." He stood, the bowl he held near empty.

"You like giving orders."

It was as if she understood his way and thought nothing of it; perhaps she was familiar to obeying, and then the thought struck him. Was she wed? She had traveled alone with but two men to guard her. Was she going to join a husband? Or had she been promised and yet to wed?

His immediate response was to ask—and yet he held his tongue. In time he would learn all about her—the inclement weather would see to that, making the roads difficult to travel and covering their tracks so there would be no trail to follow.

She would belong to him if only for a while, and he would see that she was well tended, well protected. This need to protect her haunted him. She appeared fragile, but he did not assume she was delicate. There was courage and a tenacity about her that sparked strength in her. She was by no means a weak woman.

He returned to the side of the bed and spoke bluntly though gently. "I need to examine your bruises and see how they fare."

Her eyes rounded, her fatigue faded, and she tensed, a look of fright crossing her face.

He ran a tender hand over her warm cheek. "You need not fear me."

Fear of him was not on her mind. Fear of being naked and vulnerable in front of him weighed heavily on her mind. But those were her fears to contend with and caused by a selfish husband, and presently she should be more concerned about her injuries than being naked in front of a man. But old habits could not help but haunt her, and she saw no way out of her dilemma. She had no choice but to allow him to tend her, no matter how uncomfortable it made her feel.

She did attempt, however, to put off the inevitable. "I am tired."

"It will take but a moment." He reached for the edge of the blanket.

"I am very tired," she said with an urgent fright.

Royce sat down beside her on the bed and brushed a stubborn strand of hair off her cheek. When it would not remain where he placed it, he tucked it gently behind her ear. "Tell me, Brianna, are you wed?"

"I am a widow."

Was that relief he felt? "Then you have known a man."

"Only my husband."

He heard disappointment in her voice, not sadness but disappointment. Did she not mourn her husband? He would find out more in time. "Then you have felt a man's touch and mine will not be foreign to you. I may not be your husband, but I am a man concerned for your well-being and only wish to see to your care."

She believed him. Though he was a stranger and a warrior who probably wielded a sword more deftly than a gentle hand, still she believed him.

He recognized the resignation in her eyes, and he slowly slipped the blanket down to rest at her waist. He kept his look impersonal, though he could not help but admire the swell of her full breasts as his fingers gently probed the bruises on her ribs. His fingertips unintentionally brushed beneath her breasts, just a faint skim across her soft flesh.

She stiffened and turned her face from his.

He immediately thought he hurt her, for his intentions were not of intimacy. "I am sorry, I do not mean to cause you pain."

She could not explain her pain to him, for it was an emotional scar she had yet to deal with, so she chose to present a false bravado. "I am all right."

He moved the blanket farther down, exposing her completely.

She was about to shut her eyes when she thought better of her cowardly actions. It would serve her well to know the full extent of her injuries. She forced her eyes to follow his hands.

His fingers ran over the lower part of her stomach, and she felt a slight discomfort. He then ran his hand over her right hip, and she winced in pain.

"That wound seems to be one of your worst," he said and moved his hand down her right leg.

From his touch she could tell that her right side had suffered the most damage, though her left ankle was badly swollen. She suddenly recalled being thrown against the inside of the coach, her right side slamming viciously against the door, and how soon after she had lost consciousness. She thought him done and was surprised when his hand traveled slowly back up her leg.

"Can you move your legs apart, Brianna?" he asked, giving her an encouraging glance.

She looked oddly at him.

"You have a bruise on the inside of your thigh that I did not notice when I first examined you."

She accepted his explanation and attempted to move her legs but choked on the pain that gripped her.

"Easy," he cautioned, his long, lean fingers stroking her thigh gently until her pain subsided. "I will move them for you. Relax and do not worry. I will not hurt you."

Brianna listened to his soft yet strong voice, which soothed her, and she did as he instructed, though when his hand spread her legs and slipped close to the warmth between her legs, she stiffened and caused herself pain.

He thought he had caused her pain, and he attempted to rectify his mistake by gently stroking the bruised area, which ran completely around to the back of her thigh just beneath her backside.

"I am sorry," he said softly and continued stroking her.

Surprisingly, she found herself relaxing and all her worries fading until her eyes drifted shut and she thought of nothing but his tender touch.

He did not wish to disturb her, she looked so content, but he did need to turn her on her side so he could take a look at her back. And he needed to stop stroking her for his own sanity.

"I need to turn you," he said a bit more sharply than he intended.

She seemed not to notice and simply nodded her approval.

He slipped his arm to rest between her full breasts, and with his one hand on her shoulder for support he eased her over on her side with his other hand.

She winced and her delicate hand grabbed hold of his arm, giving it a squeeze.

"I will hurry," he said and saw that her back held fewer bruises than the front of her. A touch here and there told him what he needed to know. He then carefully eased her over on her back and covered her with the warm wool blanket.

Her sigh was deep and she shivered.

He tucked the blanket around her. "Are you comfortable?"

"Aye, and tired." She yawned.

"Sleep."

His word sounded like a whispered command, and she smiled, her eyes drifting shut. He was a warrior but a gentle one. How very strange.

Royce watched the smile light her face, and he thought her the most beautiful woman he had ever laid eyes upon. Sleep claimed her as soon as her eyes closed, and her body relaxed beneath the blanket.

She had been uncomfortable being naked before him

and why not? He was a stranger, and how did she know if she could trust him? But she handled herself well and hid her fear and doubt, demonstrating a false courage, which took bravery.

He wondered over her husband. Had she loved him and favored his touch or had it been an arranged marriage that brought her no happiness? The sound of disappointment in her voice when she had mentioned her husband left him curious. He wished to learn all he could about her, though that thought struck him as odd. He had never bothered to learn much about the women he had known. He had cared only for the battles he fought and won, and they had been endless, one after another. And he had always been victorious.

He had lived for those battles, ached for them. He raised his hand to carefully touch the scar on his face. Now he would always have a reminder of his victory, though he no longer ached for the battles. He shook his head, chasing away the bitter memory.

Brianna sighed and winced in her sleep, and Royce instantly soothed her with a gentle hand to her face. She calmed with his familiar touch. In her sleep she seemed to respond to him without hesitation or fear.

She sighed and turned her face into his hand as if she needed the comfort of his touch. He rubbed her cheek and her slim neck with the back of his hand in a soft steady rhythm, and she once again settled into a contented slumber.

He stared at her long and hard, lingering on her delicate features. Her lashes were long, dark, and curled perfectly over her eyes and against her creamy pale skin.

He shook his head. Lord, but she was beautiful.

The thought struck like lightning. He had been sent an angel. Was she here to save his soul from the fires of hell? Was she to rescue him from the depths of despair?

He laughed silently inside himself. How could she help save him when she could not help save herself? She was presently vulnerable, forced to completely rely on him for her every need.

Yet she did so with courage and strength.

He saw the spark of fear that lighted in her eyes every now and again, and yet she faced that fear and conquered it each and every time. She shed not a single tear for herself but for the pain she bore bravely.

He had admired different women in his life, his grandmother in particular. She had raised him upon his mother's death when he was but five years. She was loving and strong, instilling within him the necessities of survival, and he would forever be grateful to her for the many lessons she had taught him.

She could give him a hug as quickly as she could give him a slap for not paying attention. She taught him that awareness was everything in life and without it he would be as blind as most. And she had been right; that awareness had kept him sharp in battle and when dealing with friends and enemies alike.

She had been his strength until she had forced him to face his own strength. She was a remarkable woman, and he missed her every day since her passing two years ago. But she had whispered prophetic words to him before she died.

She had told him that a woman of courage and tenderness would enter his life when he needed her the most and that she would give him one daughter and four sons. She would teach him what it meant to truly love, and his warrior skills would be necessary to keep her from harm. They would live to an old age and he would die in her arms, she following two days after him, for their love was too strong for even death to separate them.

His grandmother had never been wrong in anything

she had predicted for him or the clan, and he always paid heed to her advice.

Now he wondered if Brianna was this woman. She fascinated him, but he could not say why. He wanted time with her. Time to know her and time to understand her. He would care for her as long as necessary; he after all needed to heal as well, not only his physical scars but the ones that festered within him.

They would help each other, as strange as that may seem, and he looked forward to the healing. He needed it; he yearned for it.

She whimpered in her sleep, and without thought to his actions he stretched out beside her and gently took her in his arms. She went without protest, snuggling against him as though he could protect her from the pain, and he wrapped strong yet tender arms around her and settled her snugly in his embrace.

He felt the emptiness inside him that had seemed to forever linger fade away and be replaced by a gentle acceptance, as if he had finally arrived home, as if he was welcome and could remain as long as he wished here in her loving tenderness.

He slept knowing that he protected her and that an angel protected him.

4

❧

Royce watched her sleep. Sleep was what she mostly did these past two days. She would wake and talk with him for a short while and then drift off to sleep once again. It amazed him how often she would smile at him when her eyes slowly opened to find him beside her, and at times she would drift immediately back to sleep as if she had opened her eyes only to make certain he was nearby.

That they had established a trust between them was obvious, but it extended only so far, and he realized the wisdom of her ways. He was after all a stranger, and she was vulnerable in her weakened condition. He had made certain to treat her with gentle hands and with respect, never once touching her intimately, though it was difficult. After all he was a man.

A man who needed to heal.

Brianna stirred in her sleep and he moved swiftly to

her side from where he sat near the table. He adjusted the wool blanket around her and then ran a soothing hand over her forehead. He had worried about a fever setting in, though she had no open wounds, and usually festering wounds drew a fever. While bruises were painful, they were not always life-threatening, though he had seen men die from a single bruise.

He sat on the bed beside her and ran his hand along the side of her face.

She sighed and snuggled her face against his touch.

He had gone and retrieved her satchel from the overturned coach, and he had searched for the healing basket she had mentioned, but he could not find it. He had thought she would feel more comfortable in her night shift, but the movement required to slip into it had proved too painful for her, so she remained naked beneath the blanket.

Questions haunted him, questions he wished to ask of her, yet he knew now was not the time. He had come to realize that while she may have been married, she was not comfortable with a man's touch, which led him to believe that her marriage had not been a loving one.

He did wonder who now watched over her, for she had two clansmen with her on her journey, a sure sign that someone offered her protection. Who was it? And was he now searching for her?

She had offered no information on her clan, but then he could not fault her for that, for the Highland clans were forever at odds with each other, one minute calling one a friend, the next minute a foe.

He had time to discover more about her even if someone was out searching for her. The cottage he had brought her to was tucked away deep in the woods with no direct path leading to it.

And it seemed that Mother Nature herself wished Brianna to remain with him, for a light snow had started in the late morning and turned heavier as the hours passed. It was near to nightfall now and several inches covered the ground, concealing their footsteps and preventing anyone from finding them.

They were tucked away from the world for a while and he liked the idea. Brianna needed time to heal from her wounds, as did he.

He watched her eyes drift slowly open, and her soft, faint smile forced him to smile in return.

"I feel chilled." She shivered and attempted to burrow further beneath the covers.

Royce silently cursed himself. He had gone hunting earlier and had left his heavier tunic on when he returned, being in a hurry to clean the fat rabbit and prepare a stew for supper. He had felt she needed more solid food than just broth. He had not realized he had allowed the fire to burn low until he placed the iron pot in the hearth. He had added more logs immediately, but the logs were damp and taking time to flame. He had since moved a stack of logs inside knowing that if the snowstorm continued, a blazing fire would be essential to their comfort.

He retrieved another wool blanket from the chest at the end of the bed and placed it over Brianna. "We can try again to dress you in your night shift. You would be much warmer."

She seemed to give his suggestion careful thought, then slowly shook her head. "I know I must sound a coward, but it is just too painful." She paused, taking a light breath. "Perhaps in another day or two."

"A coward you are not." He sounded as if he scolded. He wanted her to realize her own bravery. It took courage to bear pain and to trust a stranger to help.

She paid no mind to his gentle scolding, her smile

growing stronger. "My brother tells me that I am stubborn; my sister-in-law tells me I am determined."

"I like your sister-in-law." His own smile grew along with hers.

"She is a woman I much admire." Brianna sniffed the air. "Is that rabbit stew I smell?"

"Hungry?" He had hoped her appetite would improve, and while he knew she probably could not stomach much, it was necessary to her healing that she eat more. She needed to regain her strength, for she remained weak, unable to do for herself, and he knew that upset her, being vulnerable.

"Aye, I am. I think perhaps I could even feed myself this time."

She seemed determined, but he thought of how slight movements left her in pain. A few of her bruises had worsened, and two new ones had slowly made themselves known. Her recovery would take time and patience.

"We will see."

Before he could stand, her hand slowly crept from beneath the covers to touch his arm. "Really, I feel stronger."

He held his hand to hers. "Squeeze one of my fingers."

She looked ready and confident to prove her point, and she grasped his one finger. Her eyes shut tight instantly from the stab of pain that shot through her, and she felt herself grow faint. His name was but a mere whisper on her trembling lips. "Royce."

He cursed beneath his breath for foolishly offering her a choice. His hand closed gently around hers, and his other hand softly stroked her face while he soothed her with tender encouraging words.

"The pain will pass. Relax and think only of my touch." His voice softened to a whisper. "Your skin is so smooth and warm, and it blushes when I touch it."

Her eyes remained closed, but a faint smile touched her lips. "I am not accustomed to such a gentle and caring touch from a man. And you are a caring man, Royce, for a warrior."

He did not wish to reveal himself to her, but he did wish to keep her talking and thinking about anything but her pain. "My scars betray me?"

"Not only the scars."

"What, then, besides the scars?"

"Your sheer size, the thick, hard muscles in your arms and chest, the confidence with which you carry yourself. And the pain within your eyes."

He was impressed with her observations. Not many bothered to look and actually see the truth of a person. As a warrior, he had learned the skill of observation at a young age and used it to his advantage. He had, however, never met anyone who could do the same until Brianna.

"Battle must leave heavy scars on the soul." Her eyes opened slowly and she looked at him, waiting for a reply.

She challenged him in conversation and thought, something he had never experienced with a woman, yet something that titillated in its own way. "One needs a soul to have it scarred."

Surprisingly, she laughed gently. "Everyone has a soul, Royce."

"Not warriors."

"Especially warriors."

He shook his head.

She would not let him deny her words. "Aye, warriors have the strongest of souls. They protect the weaker souls and do what must be done for the sake of freedom. Life can be cruel without warriors; complete chaos would reign and no one would know peace."

"You speak with wisdom for one so young."

"I am not young." Her smile faded. "I am old from my experiences."

"Like a warrior?"

She nodded slowly. "Aye, a warrior who faced a different type of battle."

She suddenly seemed uncomfortable and attempted to move.

His arms instantly locked her in place, preventing her from making the slightest movement. "Do not, you will only cause yourself pain. I will move you."

She looked about to object, but he would not have it.

He was firm and adamant. "I will move you until you are well enough to move yourself, is that understood?"

A flash of concern crossed her face.

He was glad he saw no fear there, and he hurried to ease her concerns. "I will not harm you. I do not wish to see you in pain. In time you will be able to do for yourself, but until then allow me the honor of seeing to your care."

She did not understand what it was about, this man who made her trust him. She only knew instinctively that she could, and that puzzled her. Why did he seem different to her? She knew nothing about him, and yet she felt safe and protected by this stranger.

"You wonder over the truth of my words."

"Nay," she said softly. "I wonder why I believe you."

"My charm?" He grinned.

Her smile bordered on a laugh, but then a laugh would have caused her pain. "I think it more your caring soul."

He would not deny her the safety of her thoughts. If she assumed him a caring soul, then so be it. The truth would only upset her, and while he was not without a caring soul, he was also a man who abandoned his soul when necessary.

"Then it is set; I will care for you, and you will do nothing until I determine you well enough."

She was quick to speak. "I think not. It is necessary that I rely on you for my care, and for that I am grateful, but I will determine what I can and cannot do."

"We shall see," he said, sounding as though he ignored her words, and gently slipped his arm beneath her back. Before she could protest, he easily moved her to rest more comfortably on the pillows he added behind her back and neck. "Now for supper."

She thought to admonish him, but then wondered over the wisdom of it. He would ignore her and do as he felt. Her only course of action was to grow strong and independent, then she would have her way. She would see to that, most certainly she would. She would not have another man dictate to her and most certainly not a stranger.

He stood and walked over to the hearth.

Royce could see that she was annoyed, but she refrained from objecting. Was her marriage one of strict obedience? Was her husband's every word a command meant to be obeyed regardless of her own desires? He went about preparing the meal with many questions haunting him.

"You eat first," she said to him when he sat on the bed beside her ready to feed her the delicious-smelling stew.

He placed a clean cloth beneath her neck and over her chest, guarding her and the blanket from spills. "I thought we would share it, if you don't mind?"

It did not disturb her to eat from the same spoon as he. "Nay, I have no objections. I just do not wish to see you go hungry while feeding me."

"You barely eat a mouthful," he teased. "It is not I who will go hungry."

He offered her half a spoonful and she eagerly took it.

"It is delicious," she said with a lick of her lips after finishing the small portion.

He had a mouthful, having helped himself to a spoonful.

"You cook well."

He prepared another small portion for her. "I was young when I was forced to prepare my own meal. After spitting out the awful concoction, I swore that I would not suffer such a heinous fate again. I learned to cook for myself."

Brianna eagerly waited for another bite. "I am glad that you did, for now I do not have to suffer such a fate."

They talked of their younger days and the freedom and joy only a child possesses. He discovered that she had a brother she adored and who treated her well, and from this he assumed her parents had passed on. She discovered that he guarded his privacy well and sparingly gave her clues to his life.

But through it all she watched his eyes, and deep within their dark green depths she realized there was a part of him he kept hidden. And she wondered over it.

"A little more," he urged, feeling she had not eaten enough, but she protested.

"I grow tired from all I have eaten." She yawned to prove herself correct.

"Then you will sleep well."

Her sleep had not been without interruptions. Her pain seemed to increase at night while nightmares haunted her. Royce had joined her in bed, comforting her in his arms and assuring her that she was safe and that he would allow no harm to come to her. She did not wish to think of the night without him. She had come to rely on his presence beside her and the safety of his arms.

She did not worry about him being intimate with her. He had assured her often enough that she was safe with him and she believed him. What other choice did she have but to trust him?

He finished cleaning and added extra logs to the fire. He took a quick peek out the door to check on the weather, and to Brianna's surprise she saw snow falling heavily outside.

"When did that start?" she asked.

"Some hours ago." He slipped out of his shirt and boots, leaving his leggings on.

Her glance settled on his bare chest. She had seen it before, though today she was much more alert than the last two days. The pain had consumed much of her waking time, and sleep was a friend she sought often. When she had first seen his bare chest, it had been through a hazy fog, and even then it was an impressive sight. Now she looked with remarkable awe at his form.

He had to be a warrior of tremendous skill, for his arms and chest were thick and hard with muscle. His strength she knew of firsthand, for he lifted her effortlessly, as though she weighed no more than a feather. His waist was slim, though also thick with muscle, and his legs could easily support his firm bulk.

She glanced over the length of him quick enough, and while she had no interest in his manhood, or so she told herself, she couldn't help but notice he was well endowed. Her husband had often boasted of his remarkable size and how she was not capable of satisfying a man so powerfully built. From what she could see, Royce looked to put her husband to shame. Surely she could never please a man like him. But then, she need not worry about it. He had no interest in her and she had none in him.

Why, then, did she think of it?

His words caught her attention. "It was a gentle snow at first but turned heavier fast enough."

Would her brother ever find her if there was no trail to

follow? She wondered over her fate. How long would she remain with Royce? Could she trust him as she thought she could? Could she trust herself to remain strong and fearless? She shivered, not knowing the answers.

"Are you warm enough?" he asked, leaning over the bed to once again slip his arm beneath her back.

She nodded and tensed when he lifted her off the pillows.

"Relax," he said softly. "You will only cause yourself pain."

He spoke the truth, but for some reason her situation suddenly seemed hopeless and her misgivings made her feel all the more vulnerable.

He adjusted the pillows and gently laid her down, moving her over ever so gently so there would be room in the bed for him. He thought she might object, since he caught the look of doubt in her eyes, but he thought it better to do as he had done for the last two nights, and that was climb in bed with her and soothe her troubled sleep.

He slipped in beside her beneath the covers, and it took barely minutes before she managed to ease herself slowly against him, her head resting on the top of his shoulder.

"Comfortable?" he asked.

"Aye, I am and thank you."

"Nay, there is no need for thanks. It is good to have you here beside me. It is less lonely." He kept his hands to himself, though he would have preferred to slip his arms around her and give her a gentle kiss. He would wait, for nightmares seemed to haunt her, and it was then that she eagerly went into his arms and remained until he released her upon rising. He was growing accustomed to her there nightly in his embrace and he liked it.

What, then, would happen between them when she grew stronger?

He had no answer; he would wait, have patience, and allow nature to take its course.

She was barely asleep when she grew restless and began to whimper as if being hurt. He wondered if she continued to relive the accident or if more painful memories haunted her.

He took her in his arms, held her close, and soothed her with gentle kisses to her face. She settled as she always did, and together they slept, both healing in their own way.

5

It was time to find out about this stranger, especially since she had been sleeping beside him these last five days.

That he was a man of his word was true. He meant her no harm. His intentions were to see that he helped her to gain back her health and strength. That he was accustomed to having his way was also true. He would not allow her to do for herself. He fed her, moved her, and did much too much for her.

She felt she could keep no secrets from this man, and yet she had many secrets. They talked, but it was of common things and she slept much. She needed the rest so that she could heal properly; her body demanded it. He was always nearby when she woke, and she was always grateful to see him.

His scars were healing as slowly as her bruises. She wished she were well enough to move about on her own, for she recalled the pouches of dried herbs in her satchel. If she combined certain herbs to make a poultice and applied it to his scars, they would heal more rapidly and leave less scarring. She vowed that when she grew strong enough to, she would do just that.

Now, however, she must be wise and allow herself time to heal. It would do no good to impede her healing by being stubborn. Besides, with the substantial snowfall, no one would be coming to her rescue anytime soon.

Actually, if Royce had not found her, in all probability she would have died. The elements, wild animals, or thieves would have seen to her demise. She was in no condition to defend or help herself. How ironic that would have been—to have gained her freedom only to have perished without having lived at all.

She did worry over her brother. He was probably upset and at this moment raving at the weather ... or was he? He would not know that she did not reach her destination. He would only know her missing when she did not return at her designated time, and that would be a week or more.

The thought concerned her, for it meant she would spend more time with this stranger than she had anticipated. That was all the more reason she attempted to learn more about him.

Who *really* was he?

A warrior? A man running from his pain? A man hiding from someone? He was a mystery that needed solving.

She looked to the hearth where he knelt, feeding the fire more logs. The dancing flames cast a reflection on his face, giving his wounds a ghastly glow. Not many would be able to look upon him without disgust. The swelling around his eye and lip was just barely beginning to subside. She could detect the difference since her glance had settled on him often these last few days. The blows he suffered must have been fierce, and she wondered how he had survived the ordeal.

He was a man of considerable size, strength, and determination, which told her he was a force to be taken seriously and at times feared, but at all times respected.

She noticed he had turned around and stared at her with as much interest as she at him. They both had questions, but who first would have the answers?

"Hungry?" he asked, breaking the silence between them.

"Nay," she answered softly.

He stood and walked over to her, his frown one of concern. His hand went to her head. "You feel well?"

"Aye, I feel fine, just not hungry."

He sat beside her on the bed, his usual perch throughout the day. "You did not feel hungry this morning as well."

She yawned, though she had slept well last night and had slept again only two hours after waking. It had been but an hour's sleep, and now after only a couple of hours she felt tired once again.

She grew annoyed thinking of all the time she spent sleeping. "I sleep too much."

"You heal."

"I grow sore and useless from the constant use of this bed." She grew brave. "I need to move around more on my own."

"Nay!" He was firm and stern in his response.

She raised a brow without realizing it. "You cannot dictate to me."

He grinned, holding back a laugh. "You think not?"

Silence and thought would have been a wise choice, but she was not feeling wise at the moment. Her forced confinement, her lack of mobility without pain, and his dictatorial manner caused her temper to flair. "You have no right."

He could not contain his laughter. "Aye, but I have the strength."

She had the need to prove her own strength, perhaps more to herself than him. She braced her meager weight on her elbows and attempted to pull herself up off the pillows. The pain surrounded her, captured her senses, and set her head to spinning. This time, however, she intended to fight it. She had to gain her strength back. She could not remain in bed day after day. She had to grow strong.

He watched the struggle on her face, the way her eyes squinted against the pain, the way her slender arms trembled from their effort to support her, and he wasted not a moment. He reached out to her.

"Nay!" she shouted at him, but had not the strength to avoid his reach.

His arm went quickly around her, and her body sagged in relief against the thick muscle of support. Her head rested in the crook of his shoulder.

"You are a stubborn one," he said, annoyed at himself for allowing her to behave so foolishly.

"Determined," she corrected with a labored breath.

He needed to make certain she would not be foolish again, for he suffered along with her and he would not see her suffer needlessly. "You will do as I tell you."

She laughed this time, softly but enough for him to hear.

"You think me humorous?"

"We make a strange pair, both of us needing healing and both ignoring what is necessary."

"I do what is necessary for me to heal."

"Hiding away is necessary to your healing?"

He took affront to her remark. "I do not hide. I chose solitude as a poultice for my pain."

"You chose solitude so that you would not have to face your pain."

"You speak foolishly." He arranged several pillows so that he could brace her in a comfortable sitting position. He eased her up against the pillows, making certain the soft wool blanket remained covering her breasts. He then grabbed for the white wool shawl that hung on the square bedpost where he had placed it if needed. He draped it around her bare shoulders.

She placed a gentle hand on his bare arm, his shirt-sleeve having been pushed up for him to work more safely with the fire. "Tell me of your scars."

"You have no need to hear of them."

He tucked the shawl around her, concentrating on his task, but she could tell that her question disturbed him. "You have need to speak of them."

"And what of your scars?" he challenged in defense. "You hide them within you. Why do you fear a man's touch?"

She was too tired to react defensively, so she answered as honestly as she could. "I had a husband who treated me poorly, and I simply do not know how to react to a man's touch be it gentle"—she paused, weighing her words, then spoke without hesitation—"*or intimate*."

He was impressed with her courage to admit such an intimate truth, and he was angry with the fool husband of hers for having made her so fearful of a touch that was meant to give comfort and pleasure.

"An intimate touch is gentle."

"I knew no such gentleness"—she paused again, giving thought to her words—"I knew obedience."

"Intimacy has nothing to do with obedience. It is about caring and sharing, smiles and laughter, pleasure and satisfaction."

"You sound as if you possess much experience. Are

you married?" She laughed at her own remark. "I forget that a man has no need for marriage to gain experience."

"True enough."

"A man has a freedom that a woman does not, and now that I have tasted that freedom I intend to keep it."

"You do not wish to marry again?" he asked.

"Nay, I wish no marriage. I wish to retain my freedom."

"You have a man's protection?"

"My brother," she answered but gave him no more.

"He does not mind you remaining with him?"

She smiled. "Nay, my brother wishes only my happiness, as does his wife. He will let me live my life as I choose."

"And you choose loneliness?"

"You think me lonely because I have no man?"

"Nay," he said seriously. "I think you lonely for you have never truly known a man."

"I was married," she said, not understanding him.

"To an idiot."

She could not help but grin.

He smiled along with her and encouraged her to continue. "Tell me about your husband."

"Will you tell me about your wife?"

He admired the way she diverted his remark. "I am not married."

She raised her hand slowly, her fingers gliding ever so gently over his swollen lip. "You have no one to care for you."

Her words affected him more than he cared to admit. He had no one special who cared for him, who worried over his safety, who prayed for him when he faced battle. He had only the occasional woman who satisfied his needs, but no one who was always there for him. No one who would reach out and touch him in his time of need like Brianna had just done.

"And yet you have a caring soul and give without thought to its return." Her hand fell slowly to her side.

Her tender touch left a tingle on his lips, a tingle that spread slowly through him. And his thoughts were anything but caring. "My soul is not what you think."

"I do not think you know your own soul."

"Teach me," he challenged and was not surprised by the sparkle that shone in her eyes.

"Aye," she said on a yawn. "I will do that."

He wanted to ask her more questions, especially about her husband, but she was tired and needed to rest. They had time to talk, time to learn about each other, and he looked forward to the many talks they would share, but for now she needed rest.

"Rest and then you will eat."

"I have rested enough and I am not hungry."

"You persist in having your way."

"As do you." Another yawn attacked her and she grew annoyed.

"Why fight your need to rest?"

"How can I grow strong if I do nothing but lie in bed?"

"The first few days you did nothing but sleep and moved not a finger. Now you sit up, move your arms, your legs, and remain awake longer. You heal, slowly aye, but you heal. That is what is important. And you must eat, for the food fuels your body."

"You are wise in ways I would not expect a warrior to be."

"A warrior sees much, much too much." His voice grew soft as though he did not wish to hear his own words.

She thought to ask him what he saw, but now was not the time. He did not need to relive such harsh memories.

She found the strength once again to raise her fingers to his lips. "If you look in my satchel, you will find a pouch of herbs. I can make a poultice from them that will help heal your wounds."

He realized it took great effort for her to hold her hand up, and he realized he wanted to continue to feel her tender touch. His hand went to her wrist to gently give it support.

She was pleased that he did not mind her touch. She had reached out to him without thought, wanting only to offer comfort. A strange reaction for her, for she was taught never to touch her husband without permission, yet she gave no mind to touching him. And he gave no mind to her action.

"When you are stronger," he said, his warm breath a gentle whisper on her fingers.

"The sooner the poultice is applied to the fresh wounds, the better the healing."

"Then you will instruct me how to prepare it and I will make it."

She pouted like a child who was disappointed in not having her way. "I wish to make the poultice."

He took her hand and held it lightly in his. "Squeeze my hand."

She understood he intended to prove his point, and she intended to prove him wrong. She eagerly did as he directed, mustering all the strength she possibly could.

She focused on her hand, took a deep breath, and with all her might she squeezed. She paid dearly for her effort. Her hand throbbed and her arm trembled and a vicious pain stabbed at her side.

Her eyes fluttered and she whispered in urgency, "Royce."

"Damn," he mumbled. He soothed her with comforting

words, kissed her forehead, her hand, her cheek, and she turned her face to rest her cheek to his.

"I feel so safe with you, so very safe."

"Always. You will always be safe with me. I will allow no harm to come to you, *ever*."

"You do have a good soul," she whispered and kissed his cheek before her eyes fluttered closed.

It was a silent *nay* that echoed in his head.

How could he have a good soul when he had no soul at all?

6

"YOU WILL BE AS YOU ARE WHEN I RETURN."

"That sounds like an order." Brianna smiled and watched Royce make ready to leave the cottage.

She had such a pleasant smile that he could not help but return it, though he had come to realize her smile could precipitate her stubbornness. "It is a wise edict."

"I am feeling better." She actually was feeling stronger and had managed to move herself around in the bed. Her bruises, the ones that she could see, were healing nicely. It was the bruise she could not see that gave her the most discomfort. Her sleep had calmed considerably, but then she had Royce to thank for that. His arms were always there to ease her restlessness and she had grown accustomed to seeking them even when not necessary and the thought troubled her.

"When I return I will help you into your night shift, and if you feel able I will help you to stand." His look was stern, or as stern as it could be with his features so distorted. "For only a moment and then it is back to bed. Until then you stay as you are—in bed."

"You will not be long?" she asked, not worried about remaining alone but wishing time to perhaps attempt to help herself.

He walked to the bed, looking twice his size, his shoulders and chest encased in leather and fur. "Does it bother you to remain alone?"

His voice was full of concern and it touched her heart. He had been and continued to be so very good to her, and she wondered why. She was a stranger to him and yet he cared.

"Nay, I will be fine. I but wonder how long the hunt will take you."

"The snow has stopped and the animals are as hungry as we. It should not take me long." He reached out and tucked her dark hair behind her ear. "You will be safe here. The cottage is in a remote area with no distinct path leading to its door, and with the freshly fallen snow no one will be about. And I will not be far off."

She smiled and nodded.

He hesitated as though he thought to say more, and then without a word he turned and walked out of the cottage, closing the door firmly behind him.

Brianna thought she would feel a sense of relief when he left, instead she felt an emptiness descend over her. She could not possibly miss him, she barely knew him, though he was no longer as much a stranger. He kept much to himself but actions oftentimes provided information about a person's strengths and weaknesses.

In her present condition she had much time to watch him. He was methodical in his movements and always aware of his surroundings. He paid heed to all words spoken to him. And he had a caring soul, which was important to Brianna, for that quality allowed her to trust him or perhaps to trust her instincts.

She felt that she had been unwise in her judgment of men. She had thought most men were like her brother and his friend Blair. While both strong men, their tongues could charm and their smiles could steal hearts. They treated her well, though teased her much when they were young, and they were always there to defend her.

Not so with her husband. He had charmed her to get what he wanted, and then abused the very person he professed to love dearly. She had felt so very foolish having been so easily fooled by him. And she vowed never again to trust a man so easily.

She had, however, no choice but to do just that with Royce. And as the days passed, he seemed to win her trust more and more. He tended her with gentle hands, and never once had she felt threatened by his touch. Actually of late she found his touch more soothing than she had ever realized a man's touch could be.

He showed concern for her pain even when she knew his own wounds must cause him just as much discomfort. He never complained of his own suffering and was immediately at her side if she issued the slightest moan or sigh.

He was like no man she had ever met, and the thought brought a smile to her face. She quickly forced it to fade. Whatever was the matter with her? She was acting as if she had an interest in this man. She wanted an interest in no man. They were not worth her time or effort. She was presently content with her life, and she wished to keep it that way. Her brother cared not if she married. She was welcome to live with him and his wife Moira, as long as she wished. And she decided that she wished to remain with them until her dying day. They were her family and she would have no other; after all, she could have no children. She was barren, as her husband often reminded her.

Her hand slowly moved across her flat stomach. She would never know the joy of a child cuddled safely in her womb or the pleasure of creating a child with someone who deeply loved her as she did him.

She wondered what Royce thought of her body when he tended her. He saw more of her naked body than her husband ever had. Arran would insist they make love in the dark, for her body displeased him and he did not wish to look upon her.

She had noticed that at times Royce diverted his eyes from her body. Was she that displeasing to a man? But there were other times his eyes would linger over her. What, then, was he thinking?

"It matters not," she said and slipped her hand out from beneath the blanket. "I need no man. I want no man."

She sighed. Why, then, did this empty ache grow in her and why did her thoughts linger on Royce?

"Stop this, Brianna," she scolded herself and strained to sit up on her own.

It took some effort and pain that eventually subsided to a dull ache, but she succeeded. She felt victorious and courageous. If she could sit up on her own, why could she not stand? And if she could stand, then she could reach her satchel at the foot of the bed and slip on her night shift.

The thought of gaining back her mobility excited her, and she moved back the blanket so that she could slide her legs to the edge of the bed. She took her time, for she realized that if she rushed, the pain would return. With slow movements her body had time to adjust, and while there was some discomfort, it was nothing she could not endure.

She was grateful Royce had added logs to the fire before he left. The cottage was heated well, and she did not worry about a chill. She grew eager to stand but tempered her enthusiasm, giving her body time to acclimate to each movement.

Her feet finally rested on the thick carpet of rushes that covered the earthen floor. She felt a slight pain begin to throb in her lower back and paused to allow it to subside. It persisted and she decided to ignore it. She was doing well and she intended to retrieve her night shift, slip it on, and return to bed. She would deal with Royce when he returned, though with the task accomplished, what could he say to her?

She took several fortifying breaths and gently began to ease herself to stand on her own two feet. Her smile grew with each successful movement, and her smile spread wide when she finally stood to her full height, allowing her legs to accept her weight.

The pain shot through her lower back so fast and furious she had no time to respond before she fell hard to the ground, the breath knocked completely from her. She was braced on her hands and knees, gasping for a breath.

The room suddenly became like an oven, and beads of perspiration dotted her face. She felt faint from the intense pain, and she did not know what to do. Her arms grew weak and would not be able to support her much longer, and her knees trembled. The one thing she was grateful for was that she had regained her breath.

She focused on her breath, diverting her attention away from the pain, and she did not know how, but she managed to ease her backside to the floor and brace her back against the bed. It took effort and it wore her out, but it relieved the pain in her lower back.

She gave herself time to breathe and think of nothing else, for if she gave her situation thought, she would grow upset, and she was close to tears at the moment. Tears, however, would do her no good. A clear head was what was needed for her to evaluate her dilemma and decide on a course of action.

Fool.

The word echoed loudly in her head and she agreed. She *was* a fool. Sitting up in bed and moving around was a grand accomplishment for her, but she certainly had been foolish attempting to stand on her own with no one about to help her.

This was one time her determined nature got her into a difficult situation.

She began to feel a chill creep over her body and realized that a draft of cold air came from beneath the front door and hovered on the floor. Her bottom was getting cold quite fast.

She reached up and over her head and pulled at the blanket on the bed. She managed to pull it down around her, but she did not possess enough strength to get the warm wool blanket beneath her to where she needed it the most. And she knew for certain that she did not have the strength to return herself to the bed.

Her only option was to wait until Royce returned. He told her he would not be long. She could manage to sit there and wait. She had no choice, she had to, and she intended to convince herself that she could. She had courage, she had strength, and she had a relentless throbbing pain in her back that began to move down her leg.

She lost track of time; she did not remember when her tears began, she only knew she could not stop crying. Her cries turned to sobs, and that is when the front door opened.

She had no intentions of calling out to him. She did not wish to embarrass herself any more than necessary. But the open door brought a rush of cold air, the pain had grown unbearable, and she ached for the comfort and safety of his arms.

She called out to him through her sobs. "Royce."

He shoved the door shut at the same moment he dropped the gutted rabbit he held. He rushed to her side and lifted her up into his arms, the blanket falling off her and her cry of pain tearing at his heart.

"My back," she said between labored breaths.

He placed her gently on the bed, turning her so that she rested on her stomach and he could examine her back. The dark bruise on her lower back and hip was taking its time healing, and it had spread down her leg. He ran tender fingers over the discolored area and she flinched.

He wanted to yell at her for being so foolish, but now was not the time, though he intended to have his say.

"It hurts," she said, her tears continuing to fall. "And I am so very cold."

He ran a slow hand over her backside and down her leg, brushing off the rushes that stuck to her tender skin, skin that felt like ice. "I am going to move you to rest on your good side so that the pressure will be taken off your injured side, and then I will get you warm."

She nodded and allowed him his way with her. She simply did as he asked of her. She placed her arm around his neck as he directed, held on to him until he finished bracing pillows along her back, and did all that he asked of her without objection. He was easing her pain and his warm hands felt so very good against her chilled skin.

The pain faded slowly, but she was grateful that it faded, and she knew soon, very soon he would take her chill away.

Royce slipped his fur cloak off and covered her naked body with it. He then piled three wool blankets over her, covering her up to her chin and tucking the blankets in tightly around her so that no cold air could penetrate her warm cocoon.

He wiped at her tears, his heart aching for her, and it

was with a firm voice he told her, "You will listen to me well, for you do not wish to see my wrath."

Her eyes rounded with an ounce of fear, and she paid heed to his words.

"From this moment on you will do as I say without question. You will not move in or from this bed without my permission. You will do nothing for yourself without my permission. You will eat what I tell you to eat; you will sleep when I tell you to sleep. Is that understood?"

Brianna felt the need to defend her actions, foolish as they were. "I only meant to—"

"—be foolish," he finished for her.

"Aye, that I was," she whispered and turned her glance from him, shamed at her own foolishness.

He cursed himself. He had not meant to discuss this with her until he had calmed down, but he was enraged more at himself than her, for he should have never left her alone. He should have realized she would have attempted such a foolish feat. She was too damn stubborn, not *determined,* but stubborn.

He did not, however, wish to make her feel worse, though he did intend that she obey him, as angry as that may make her. He sat beside her on the bed and wiped again at the fresh tears that fell slowly down her cheeks. "The bruise on your back and leg is far from healed. Until it heals significantly, you will not move around on your own."

"Is that an order?"

"Must I make it so or will you realize the wisdom of my way?"

He did not speak harshly, though his voice was firm, and if she gave it thought she would realize that he was being wise in telling her to remain abed until strong enough to stand, while she was being stubbornly foolish in wanting to stand when she felt herself ready.

"I will do as you say—for now."

"Your word on this?"

"Aye, my word," she agreed without hesitation. She had trouble keeping her eyes open. The more comfortable and warm she became, the more tired she felt. Her ordeal had robbed much of her strength, and her body ached for a restful slumber.

"Sleep," he said softly and with concern.

"I am tired."

Her eyes drifted closed and his hand reached out and stroked her cheek.

He was with her and she was safe. She need not worry; he would look after her, ease her pain, keep her warm, protect her from harm. This she knew and did not doubt. He would be there for her always.

Why?

She spoke, thinking she was in a dream. "Why are you so good to me?"

Her question startled him, and her next question startled him even more.

"Why do you care for me?"

7

WHY DO YOU CARE FOR ME?

The question echoed through his mind as he prepared the rabbit stew, and he thought of many answers to the simple question, though one answer haunted him.

He cared for her because he *cared*, actually cared for her as a man would for a woman. The thought troubled him. He had not allowed himself to care for any woman. His life had been one of constant battle. He had learned to fight at a young age, his clan expecting it of him. He had known he would follow in his father's footsteps one day, and he would be no less the great warrior than his father had been. His father had often told him that he, his son, would surpass him in strength and courage.

He had worked hard and women were of little importance to him except to satisfy a need. He had no time to give women, no time to care for them. He had a responsibility to clan and family, and he had taken it seriously.

Until this last battle.

The battle had forced him to seek solitude and reconsider his own beliefs. His thoughts had tormented him, and he wanted nothing more than to be alone with his own agonies.

Then he found Brianna.

He could not say what it was about her that made him want to care for her and protect her. He only knew that he needed to, he had to, he wanted to. She seemed as alone and lonely as he did, and he felt he found in her a kindred spirit.

She relied on his tenderness, his gentle touch, and she sought the comfort and safety of his arms nightly. She did not fear him, though his face could cause fear.

He touched his fingers to his lips. The swelling had subsided and the wound had begun to heal. It would not leave a scar. He was, however, not as lucky with the other wounds. He would be left with a reminder of a battle he wished to forget.

He placed the pot of stew over the flames to cook, then sat in the chair near the hearth. His thoughts were chaotic, he could not seem to focus, and he grew tired of the warring in his head. It took only minutes for his eyes to grow heavy, and without thought he walked to the bed and stretched out beside Brianna, falling asleep instantly.

Brianna woke to a delicious smell and a comfortable warmth. She snuggled against the warm bundle, and arms wrapped around her and squeezed her gently. She looked up to see Royce, his eyes opening slowly. When he saw her he smiled and brought his lips to her forehead.

It was a loving kiss he placed there, and she sighed with the comfort it brought her. His arms remained firm around her as though he did not wish to let her go, and that was all right with her. She felt good in his arms and she had no wish to leave them, though her stomach rumbled to let her know otherwise.

"You are hungry?" He kissed her forehead again.

"My stomach protests, I do not. I like where I am."

"You like my arms?" He sounded as though he did not believe her.

"Aye, that I do," she said and rested her head on his shoulder. "I feel safe in your arms."

My arms will always keep you safe. His silent response startled him. He knew her but a week's time and he thought of her as his? He was being foolish in his thinking. He was merely lonely and she filled a void.

Foolish.

Was he being more foolish than he realized?

"You are safe in my arms. I will allow no harm to come to you."

"I believe you," she said on a sigh and cuddled closer to him, wedging her body against his. "And I"—she paused briefly, thinking over her next words—"trust you."

He made to answer, but she continued.

"I know you dictate to me out of concern and tend to me because you care. Your touch is respectful and you do not dishonor me. I am grateful that you are such an honorable man."

Honorable.

He had questioned honor of late, and here she told him of his honor.

He answered as he felt. "You can always trust me."

Her stomach rumbled loudly.

"You need food." He attempted to move her away from him so that he could get their meal.

She would not allow him to. "Nay, I feel warm and comfortable. I do not wish to move just now."

"Your stomach disagrees," he said, though his arms remained firm around her.

"I will eat soon enough. For now, I wish to enjoy where I am."

He did not argue with her, for he enjoyed where she was, and the thought that she wished to be there filled him with a sense of peace. He liked sharing the bed with her, he liked that she relied on him, he liked that there were only the two of them. He liked her more than he wanted to admit.

When both their stomachs began protesting, it was decided that they should eat. Brianna felt well enough to feed herself, but after her ordeal Royce would not hear of it. And she had agreed to follow his edicts—for now.

They talked and laughed and shared a pleasant meal together, but then all their meals had been enjoyable. They had formed a bond of friendship that grew stronger day by day, much stronger than either of them wished to acknowledge.

After Royce cleaned up from their meal, he returned to her bedside, leaned down, and with a grin asked, "Would my lady care for a bath?"

Her eyes rounded in wonder. "You tease me."

"Nay, there is a half-size wooden barrel outside the door that I could bring in, and it would serve as a perfect bath for you. I can heat the water to a pleasant temperature, and without effort I can carry you to the tub. Besides, I think the wet heat would help ease your pains."

Brianna desperately wanted a bath, but he had done so much for her and he was recovering from his own wounds. She raised her hand to his face, gently running her finger over his swollen lip. "You must be tired from all you have done for me."

Her touch was like none he had ever felt, feather soft, and it tingled his lips, masking the pain of his wound. If she could ease his physical pain so easily with a simple touch, what, then, if her touch turned intimate? Would her hands hold the magic to ease his anguished soul?

Not thoughts he should be having at the moment, and he made haste to chase them away, though they lingered in his consciousness. "Nay, I need no rest and I heal—"

She pressed a gentle finger to his lips. "Slowly. You need a poultice for a wound or two, and rest would serve you well."

It did his heart good to think that she actually cared for him. "When you are well enough, you can prepare a poultice for me, and after *your bath* we will sleep and I will rest."

"Is that an order? My bath, that is." She smiled, feeling a comfort she had never thought to feel with a man.

"Need it be?"

It pleased her that he made it seem she had a choice. "Nay, it need not be, a bath sounds much too inviting to deny."

Her hand slipped down over his chest to the blanket. It was a lingering descent, and one he felt through his shirt. He wished—he stood abruptly, forcing his thoughts away from where they insisted on drifting. He was about to give her a bath. He damn well did not need to be dwelling on intimacy.

"Rest, I will prepare everything."

She snuggled beneath the covers, her body feeling a sudden chill. It was from no draft or cold drift of wind. It was from the anticipation of Royce holding her naked in his arms and helping her to bathe.

The cottage door closed quietly behind him, and in mere minutes he would return with the tub. She so wanted a bath, just the thought of the heated water soaking her skin made her sigh with pleasure. And why should she concern herself with thoughts of how he viewed her body? He was not her husband.

She cringed at the thought. Here she was alone in a cottage with a man who was more stranger than not and who looked after her and touched her with the intimacy of a husband.

"Nay, not intimacy," she whispered. He touched her with respect, not once laying an intimate hand on her. Why, then, had she thought of intimacy when his hand touched her of late?

The door opened, Royce entered, and immediately went about preparing the tub for a bath.

"It will take a while to heat enough water for the tub," he said, moving the table to the side and placing the tub in front of the hearth.

Brianna was surprised at the size of the half-barrel. It would hold her comfortably, and it would hold Royce if he bent his knees. The thought startled her, for she was not certain if she thought of them taking separate baths or bathing together.

Her remark surprised her even more. "Do you not wish a bath?"

"When you are done."

"The water will be cold." Whatever was she saying? It sounded like an invitation to her. Did it to him?

His brief pause warned that he might have thought the same. "I have taken cold baths before."

"When necessary I assume." She continued sounding as though she wished him to join her. Whatever was the matter with her?

He turned after setting a large pot he had filled with snow to heat. "Aye, when *necessary.*"

She bit her tongue so she would say no more. The accident must have given her a good knock on the head and a degree of courage, for she would have never suggested such an idea to her husband, let alone a man she knew but a week's time.

She decided it was best to talk of a safer subject. That subject, she decided, was him. "Is this your home?"

He was waiting for specific questions to start. With her returning strength came courage, not to mention curiosity. He would tell her only so much. "Not my permanent home."

"Where is your permanent home?"

"A bit north."

He evaded direct answers, but bits and pieces of a person once put together could tell much.

"The battle you recently fought was near your home?"

"Nay," he answered and then poured the heated water into the tub, filling the large pot once again and setting it to heat. He gave her no chance to continue her questioning. "One more pot after this and there will be enough water for me to put you in the tub. I will continue to add hot water so that your bathwater does not chill."

"You are most considerate."

He made no comment. How could he when his mind was being anything but considerate? She had placed a suggestion in his mind that had taken root and insisted on growing. The idea of joining her in the tub was too tempting to ignore, yet ignore it he must.

A cold bath was definitely *necessary*.

Brianna remained quiet, her own thoughts worrisome. It had not been difficult having him tend her when she was completely incapacitated, for she could barely think clearly. And she could not move without pain. Now, though it was different, while the pain persisted, it was a level of pain she could handle, and her mind was clear now and her eyes open. They would not drift shut while she bathed as they often did when he looked after her.

Now she would see clearly his reaction to her nakedness, and the thought troubled her.

He arranged a large towel on the floor and placed another on a small bench he had brought to rest beside the tub. "It will be ready soon."

Soon.

Soon he would remove the blankets and take her into his arms. Soon. She trembled, her legs felt weak, and her heart thudded in her chest. She was being foolish, so very foolish. He would place her in the tub and it would be done. The water would cover her, and he would look away from her.

Was that what she wanted?

She silently scolded herself. Whatever was wrong with her? Why was she having intimate thoughts of this man? She had not thought of a man and intimacy in a very long time. Her husband had destroyed all her girlhood dreams of love and being loved. She had closed her heart off to protect herself from the pain of a loveless marriage. She had sworn to herself that she would not ever care for another man and never would she love again.

"Ready?"

Royce stood over her, his large size intimidating, though she felt no intimidation from him. It was her own insecurities that caused her to tremble.

She nodded, fearful her voice would betray her nervousness.

He hesitated a moment as though having a second thought, then he stepped back away from the bed, slipped the strip of plaid that ran over his shoulder down to hang at his waist, and hurried out of his linen shirt as though he might change his mind.

He approached the bed again, this time the size of him intimidating.

She had seen his chest before but not nearly as clearly as she did now. He was twice the size her husband had been, and his muscles were much more pronounced, almost as if his flesh were carved around the thick muscles.

His chest was broad, his stomach hard, and his arms powerful. He was an opponent most men would fear and a man that women would admire.

"I do not want a wet shirt," he said, as if he felt it necessary to explain his partial nakedness.

She nodded again and sent a silent prayer to the heavens for strength.

He eased back the blankets. "You may feel a chill."

She remained silent, not trusting her voice, and kept her eyes on him. She told herself to look away and not watch him. That was not possible; she was compelled to keep her eyes on him.

He eased the blankets off her all the way down to her feet.

"You are cold, you tremble."

She trembled from her nervousness, but this she would not tell him.

He was quick to effortlessly snatch her up into his arms and hold her close to him.

She noticed that his eyes did not linger nor did they avoid her body. He simply did what was necessary. His focus was on his task, and his eyes?

They caught her own glance as he leaned over to place her in the tub. "Tell me if the water is a comfortable temperature for you."

He lowered her toes in and she sighed, a smile following. "It is heavenly."

He laughed softly and lowered her further into the tub. "I will hold you until you can rest comfortably on your own." He wanted no repeat of the early day's incident. He intended to make certain that she felt no pain, only pure pleasure.

The heated water evaporated her nervousness. It was not lukewarm or unbearably hot, but seemed the perfect temperature for soothing her aches and pains. She sighed again and relaxed against his arm that wrapped firmly around her back.

Her eyes drifted closed for a moment and his glance drifted over her. She possessed a beautiful body, all curves and mounds in just the right places. And pale skin that was blushing pink from the heated water.

He shook his head. It was time to let go of her; her warming flesh was beginning to feel much too pleasing to his touch.

"Do you think you can sit on your own?"

She heard the reluctance in his voice, and she mistakenly thought that he assumed her too weak. Her courage surfaced. "Aye, that I can."

"Sure of it, then?" he teased, hearing the bravado in her voice.

"Let go and we will see," she challenged.

He accepted, though it was with a slow hand he released her to rest on her own.

It was barely a minute and her smile was wide when the pain in her back began. Her first thought was to ignore it, but she had made that mistake earlier. She would not be foolish enough to repeat it.

Her hand went out to him. "Royce."

His arm wrapped around her back and beneath her breast, taking her full weight. "What is it?"

"The pain in my lower back worsens when I place pressure on it."

She sounded upset and he understood. She had hoped to relax in the bath and now she could not. Not without his help. "You can rest against my arm."

She produced a weak smile. "You will grow tired of holding me."

"Never," he said without thinking.

"You are too kind to me. I should wash and get out right away so that I do not burden—"

His firm voice cut her off. "You are not a burden. You will enjoy your bath."

"How can I when you must kneel here and hold me? It is not fair." Her voice was just as firm.

"You will do as I say and enjoy the bath." He thought his direct remark would end the matter; after all he had warned her of obeying him.

"I will not enjoy the bath if you must remain in such an awkward stance to tend me."

"I do not mind."

"I do."

"There is no other way," he said adamantly.

"Aye, there is," she insisted. "You can join me and I can rest against you."

8

BRIANNA'S REMARK STUNNED HIM SILENT. HER RE-
mark that followed stunned him even more by making
sense.

"It is *necessary*."

He did not wish to admit that she was correct, that her
suggestion made perfect sense. And that he was going to get
what he wished. He was going to join Brianna in the tub.

"I can manage to sit for a moment on my own if you
can undress with haste."

He wanted to laugh, nay maybe cry at her words, for
he could disrobe within seconds knowing he would ease
his naked body behind hers. Instead he remained calm
outwardly while inwardly his emotions turned chaotic.

His warrior skills had taught him the art of remaining
calm under extreme pressure, and he called on those skills
now, or else he feared he would lose this battle with himself.

"Let me add more hot water first. Then I will ease your weight for a moment and then undress."

"Aye, I can manage that."

"Tell me when you feel comfortable enough for me to release you."

She nodded, took several deep breaths, and grabbed hold of the sides of the tub. "Now."

Her voice sounded unsure, but it was better that he did not question her, for courage sometimes disappeared when questioned. He released her slowly then quickly set to work, adding the heated water to the tub. His arm was around her again before the pain could trouble her.

"The heat feels so good. You must come join me and enjoy it."

He thought it would have been wise to douse himself in the snow before joining her in the tub, but that was not possible. He had to remember how she trusted him to keep her safe, but damned if he knew how long he could keep her safe from him.

She took several deep breaths again. "Ready."

He let go of her, stood, and flew out of his clothes. He noticed she had shut her eyes, and that brought a smile to his face. Wait until she leaned back against him; he wondered then if her eyes would remain closed or widen.

He hurried into the tub, though with care, for he did not wish to send the water splashing. He eased his legs around her and slipped his one arm around her to rest beneath her breasts, then after situating himself comfortably, he drew her back against him.

She rested her head on his chest and placed her hand on his arm. "I have never been naked in a tub with a man before this and never thought to be, especially with a stranger." His laughter was a soft rumble in his chest, and she enjoyed the sound of it.

"I am no longer a stranger. I tend you, touch you, and

sleep with you. We have become familiar with each other in more ways than many husbands and wives do."

"Aye," she agreed, "that is the truth. Many husbands would not do for their wives what you have done for me."

"How could I not? You are a gentle soul and so very beautiful."

Her eyes rushed open. She had kept them closed not knowing if she could look upon him after feeling the length and strength of him behind her. He had pulled her close, and she knew how very much of a man he was, and to her surprise the thought thrilled her. But him telling her she was beautiful shocked her.

"You think me beautiful?"

"Aye." He kissed her temple. "I have known no woman as beautiful as you."

"You tease me."

She did not believe him, and he found that odd. Women enjoyed being told of their beauty, though her beauty went beyond the common. She defined beauty and that was rare.

"Nay, I tease you not, I mean what I say. You are beautiful to look upon—all of you." He gave her an affectionate squeeze.

She simply did not know how to respond. She was stunned silent.

He sensed her discomfort and attempted to make light of it. "Are you not now going to tell me that I am beautiful?"

She giggled softly; she could not help it. She knew he but teased her. But then, he did not realize that a man's looks meant naught to her. It was what was in his heart that mattered, and his heart was beautiful.

"I think you the handsomest of men."

Royce could not believe that she spoke with such conviction. She actually sounded as though she thought him handsome. He could not help but say, "Has the accident left you with poor sight?"

"I see more clearly than I ever have, and it is clear to me that you are a handsome and caring man."

He was about to object when she gently squeezed his arm. "Please allow me to feel as I do."

There was a tender ache in her voice that touched his heart. He leaned his head closer to hers. "I am glad you think me handsome."

"And caring, do not forget caring."

"I care for you."

His words were a soft whisper one strained to hear. Brianna heard them, for they drifted over her and settled in her heart. She did not question them or give them thought, but simply held them close and made them part of her. This man was like no other she had ever met, and if she was not careful she could lose her heart to him.

"You are comfortable?" His arms remained firm around her.

"Too comfortable."

He understood, for he felt *too comfortable* himself. He had grown much too fond of her in much too short of a time and yet why did he feel it was so right?

"The water will chill fast. It is best we wash before it grows too cold. Let me start with your hair."

"You will wash my hair?"

"I will wash all of you."

She looked at him with disbelief. "The heavens surely smiled down on me when they sent you to my rescue. And when I am well, I will tend you."

He grinned. "You will wash me then?"

She liked his teasing manner. She had never imagined being playful with a man, but she felt like a carefree young woman with him. "I give a good scrubbing; you may think otherwise afterward."

"I will take my chances. Now let us get you finished and back in bed." He reached over the tub and retrieved a wooden bowl that he used to scoop up water and pour over her hair. He then lathered it with soap and scrubbed her head until she sighed with pleasure.

"Your hair?" she questioned when he had rinsed her hair clean.

"I will dunk my head after our bath and have done with it."

"The water is cooling—we need to hurry."

He grabbed the soap and it slipped out of his hand down onto Brianna. She grabbed it and lathered her hands. He thought she would wash herself and deny him the pleasure, but to his amazement she began to scrub his arm where it rested across her.

He took the soap from her, lathered his own hands and proceeded to scrub her shoulders. They worked well together, each scrubbing the other. With his support Brianna could reach his legs and her own. He did her back and down her arms, then gently scrubbed her breasts, lingering just a bit longer than he should have but keeping his touch as respectful as possible.

She shivered, and while the water had chilled, it was not the temperature that caused the shiver. Her nipples had turned sensitive when he ran his hand across them several times. She had not expected to respond, had not expected her nipples to harden—had not expected to want more.

"Enough! I am getting you out now before you catch a chill. Can you brace yourself for a moment?"

She nodded, her focus on her throbbing nipples.

He stood in haste, the water splashing over the sides, grabbed for a towel, reached down, and scooped her up with one arm. Bracing her against his wet body, he draped the towel around her and began to rub her dry.

He saw to both of them as he worked, being methodical in his strokes and making certain to cover every inch of her. She warmed and relaxed with every soothing stroke. He snatched up two more towels before scooping her up into his arms and carrying her to the bed.

"Hold on to me," he ordered after resting her on the bed.

She did and he wrapped her wet hair in the clean towel before laying her back against the pillows. To her relief the other towel he quickly wrapped around his waist. She did not wish to think that her glance purposely drifted where it had no place going, but then she had done many things of late she had never expected to do.

She lay still and allowed him to tuck her safe and warm beneath the blankets. She had not realized until she was comfortably tucked in that he had not helped her into her night shift. She thought to mention it, but he wore a stern expression, and she wondered over the change in him.

Without a word to her he walked over to the tub, kneeled beside it, and dunked his head in the water. She panicked when he did not raise his head after several minutes, and then in a flash he drew his head up and out, water flying out around him.

He took a great breath of air and released it with a force almost as if he were releasing a demon within. He then proceeded to scrub his hair quite vigorously. Another dunk of his head, this one not as long as the first, then a forceful rub with a towel over his wet hair, and he was finished.

He approached the bed, his stern expression gone, and she felt more relaxed in asking him, "Did that not hurt your wounds?"

He shook his head. "Nay, they sting but a moment, and the cleansing is good for them."

She raised her hands to her head to see to drying her hair, but he captured both her wrists in his one hand. Instantly she recalled the way her husband would grab hold of her like that and then begin to torment her with his free hand.

"Nay, please." She hated hearing the begging in her voice.

He instantly released her. "I meant you no harm. I will see to drying your hair."

She swallowed hard the lump in her throat, and it took her a minute to find a strong voice. "I am sorry."

"There is nothing for you to be sorry about. I should not have grabbed you like that."

"Nay, I know you meant me no harm—" She shook her head, not knowing what to say, or if she should offer an explanation.

He made it easy for her: he simply reached up and removed the towel from her head. "Let me see to your hair."

She raised her hand to his wrist and took a gentle hold of it. "Why? Why are you so very good to me?"

He looked puzzled, as if he had no answer for her, and then he softly whispered, "I care for you."

9

I CARE FOR YOU.

Those words had haunted Brianna for the last week. She had not been certain how he meant them. He sounded as though he actually cared for her, not *took* care of her, and she had wondered over it these many days.

She was up and about now and grew stronger day by day. Her steps were slow and sometimes laborious, the pain in her lower back refusing to completely subside. In time she was sure it would, but for now she would pay heed to its annoying presence and rest when necessary.

Her thoughts, however, continued to drift to Royce. Try as she might he was a constant presence in her mind, but then they spent almost every moment of the day together. The only time they were apart was when he went hunting for food, and he was never gone long.

They slept comfortably together like lovers long familiar with each other, and though they were never intimate, his hands forever touched her and his arms constantly embraced her.

He had dressed her in her night shift with the tenderness of a man who cared, and he looked after her every need like a man who . . .

Loved?

Nonsense, pure nonsense. He did not love her. He simply cared.

What was love anyway? She had thought herself desperately in love with her husband, and she had foolishly been mistaken. She did not wish to repeat the mistake, and while Royce seemed caring, so had her husband. He had been courteous and oh so charming.

She smiled. Royce was not charming, he was direct in his manner, and she believed him a man of his word. Odd that she should believe him after she had sworn never to believe another man again.

If she gave this situation serious thought, she might consider that she felt as she did because Royce had rescued her from certain death. He saved her life, and therefore she was grateful to him.

He did save her life and she was grateful, but another emotion haunted her, and she was uncertain of its origin. And until she could reason it, she would keep her feelings to herself.

The cottage door opened and Royce entered, followed by a flurry of snow.

"More snow?" she asked with the excitement of a child.

"A fresh coating, no more, I think." He hurried out of his fur cloak and to the fireplace, holding his hands out to warm them. "You like the snow?"

"Aye, especially when it is freshly fallen."

"Freshly fallen snow covers tracks." His remark was left for her to think on.

Brianna needed no time to think—her response came quick. "When the weather permits, my brother will have men out looking for me. He probably only recently discovered that I never arrived at my destination."

"He will wait for the weather?"

"Would you not?" she asked curiously. "It would be wise. You said yourself that freshly fallen snow covers tracks."

"Aye, it does; the more snow, the heavier the cover. It would be best to attempt a rescue even with a snowfall, for if more snow follows, it will make it nearly impossible to find any trail."

She asked the question that had been on her mind and tongue. "Will you return me to my brother's home if he cannot find me?"

His decision had already been made. "Aye, that I will."

She smiled. "Then the snow can keep falling."

"You will be stuck here with me."

"I am not stuck with you. I visit with you and I enjoy your company.

"I enjoy yours," he said in turn, adding his own smile.

His lip was no longer swollen, and the wound was healing nicely. The swelling around his eye had faded, though a slight discoloration lingered, but the scar on his face looked as though it had barely healed. It was red and swollen in spots, and while most of the wound had crusted, one or two spots refused to close completely. His face was not a sight many would wish to look upon, but Brianna had grown accustomed to him, and his distorted features did not disturb her at all.

She wondered occasionally what he looked like before his face had suffered such a horrendous assault. His looks mattered little to her. Her husband had been a handsome man and she had to admit she had been drawn to his stunning features; perhaps that was what had blinded her to his true character.

Royce's face was so badly distorted that she could barely make out normal features. Because of that she concentrated on the man within, not the horrendous face that had brought a scream to her lips when she had first looked upon him.

"Brianna? Are you all right?" His concerned voice roused her from her musings.

"Lost in thought."

"Share the thought with me."

She rested back against the pillows and did not think twice about sharing her thoughts, for she trusted Royce to understand. "I thought of your face compared to my husband's."

He felt no insult and he did want to know more about her marriage.

"Tell me," he said beside her on the bed.

"He was a handsome man."

Royce watched the way she drew the covers up around her. She looked for protection, not warmth.

"I cannot say that I am a handsome man," he said with a grin, hoping to ease the deep frown that crossed her face.

Her bright blue eyes grew wide. "Nay, you are handsome in ways my husband could never have been. And I was a foolish young woman thinking myself in love. He used his false charm to capture my naive heart but never truly loved me."

Royce listened: he wanted to hear it all, every word, every emotion, every hurt she had suffered. And he wanted to make certain she would never suffer again.

"Arran was only interested in me because of my brother being laird of our clan. With a marriage to me he would secure his importance and a keep to look after."

She continued on in a rush, a need for her to tell him and a need for her to admit the truth. "He had dreams of the clan gaining power and he gaining status. I learned quickly that I meant very little to him, and what he wanted most from me, I failed to give him. He found constant fault with me and belittled me, telling me how worthless I was. Of course, in front of everyone else he was a loving husband."

She took a much needed breath and realized how she had gone on without thinking. "You do not wish to hear this."

"Aye, that I do," he insisted, or he needed to hear it as much as she needed to talk of it. He reached beneath the blanket and gave her hand an encouraging squeeze.

"Sometimes I think you are a dream."

"You are telling me that I am too good to be true?" He winked at her with his good eye distorting his features even more.

She smiled and slipped her hand from beneath the blankets to lay a gentle hand to his cheek. "I think you so very handsome."

His heart thumped in his chest and his blood raced, flushing his face, a most uncommon reaction for a warrior.

"You are blind," he said, laying his hand over hers.

"Nay, for the first time in many years my eyes are finally open and I see clearly. And it is clear to me that you are handsome."

He attempted to protest.

"Nay," she said firmly, "you cannot order me to feel differently about you."

Feel.

She had said *feel.* Did she feel for him? Or was it simply pity?

"Besides," she continued, "you think me beautiful and I think you handsome—that makes us a fine pair."

Pair?

Did she think them a pair? A pair was a match, two of a kind. A pair could not be separated.

"Beautiful and handsome it is," he agreed, pleased that she thought them a pair. "Tell me more of your husband."

Her frown returned. "He was more selfish than I had thought. In his desire to gain status and wealth, he attempted to hurt those I loved—my brother and his wife. He escaped before he could be punished for his crime."

"His death?"

"My brother spared me the details, though my husband's ring was returned to me as proof of his demise. I chose not to take it from my brother, and I care not how my husband met his end. It is over and I am glad. When he escaped, he took me prisoner, threatening to kill me so that my brother would not follow."

"Coward." Royce almost spit the word out in disgust.

"My brother's opinion as well. Arran soon discarded me, for I was a nuisance and slowed him down. He shoved me off the horse, dumping me on the road. He cared naught for my fate, only his."

"He shoved you off his horse?" Royce asked, not believing he had heard her correctly.

She nodded. "My brother's best friend, Blair, found me and returned me safely to the keep and my brother's care. He then ordered that Arran be found at any cost."

"Your brother did not go after him himself?"

"His wife had barely given birth to their son, his place was by her side, and besides, there was not a clansman who did not wish to see my husband caught and punished."

"So your brother lacked no volunteers."

"Nay, there were many," she said with pride. "Unfortunately Arran could not be found, so my brother placed a guard around me. The guards were only removed after my brother was certain Arran was gone and no longer a threat."

"Your brother takes good care of you."

"My brother loves me."

She spoke with pride of her clan and with love for her brother.

"And you him."

"Aye, though he teased me often when I was young, he never failed to be there for me when I needed him. And I have tried to do the same for him. I realize now that if I had not allowed my pride to interfere and had spoken to my brother of the troubles in my marriage, he would have helped me."

"What of fear?"

She stared at him for several silent moments. "I do not remember when I began to fear Arran and did not even realize that I did until it was too late. I made myself a prisoner."

"You escaped—that is all that matters."

"I did escape," she said with a sense of pride.

"May I ask you what you failed to give him that appeared to anger him?"

She turned her head away briefly before returning her glance to him. "I could not give him children. I am barren."

"Barren because he told you that you were?"

"I conceived no child the four years of our marriage. I must be barren."

"Perhaps, perhaps not." He did not add his thoughts, for they might upset her. He wished very much to prove that she was not barren. He had no doubt his seed would flourish within her and he had no doubt that she would find pleasure in their coupling.

Intimacy with her had been on his mind much of late, and it was becoming more and more of a challenge to remain a gentleman.

"Have you any children?" she asked.

"Nay, I have no children." He paused and decided to add, "And no wife."

She smiled before she could stop herself.

His grin surfaced on purpose. "You are pleased that I have no wife?"

She attempted a reasonable explanation. "I would not want your wife upset over you tending me."

"You are in need. I would expect my wife to understand."

"You would not be unfaithful to your wife." It was a statement of fact. Somehow she knew that a wife would mean much to him. Nay, love would mean much to him.

"I intend to marry for love and love my wife until the end of our days and beyond."

His words touched her heart, for she had felt the same when she had married. Her smile faded with the thought of never finding such an enduring love.

He understood her concern and wished to ease it. "You will know love."

Strange that he had not told her she would love *again*, simply that she would love. "I had thought I had. I made a foolish mistake. How do I know I will not make that mistake again?"

He took her hand, his thumb softly stroking her warm palm. "The mistake would be not to try."

She stared at him, a tear tempting the corner of her eye. "I do not want to feel that pain again."

He locked his fingers with her slim ones. "You would give up love because of the fear of pain?" He shook his head as if he attempted to understand. "Yet I have watched you bear pain with courage."

He gave her words to think on and a challenge to meet. "My body heals."

"The heart also heals."

"Does it?" Her fingers tightly gripped his. "I have wondered—once a heart is broken, can it ever heal?"

"The heart can heal only if you allow it to."

Had she allowed her heart to heal or had she protected her heart by not facing the truth? She decided to speak of what was most worrisome to her. "I thought he loved me as much as I loved him."

He heard the pain in her voice and encouraged her to release it. "You cannot blame yourself for loving him more. We do not always love wisely."

She sighed, her fingers remaining tightly locked with his. "I wonder if I will ever love wisely."

"It matters only that you love."

She slowly shook her head. "To love is to hurt."

"To love is to know the fullness of life."

"I knew no such fullness."

He leaned down and kissed her cheek. "Then you knew not love."

"I was in love," she protested.

"A young lass's innocent love."

"Innocent, aye, but no more," she said with regret.

He wiped at the unshed tear that pooled in the corner of her eye. "You are more innocent than you know."

"My innocence has been taken from me. It is long gone."

"Nay, I do not agree. You are innocent." Before she could protest, he asked, "Have you ever been kissed?"

"I was married." She sounded as if his question was nonsense.

"I do not think you have ever been kissed." He brought his lips close to hers. "Would you like to be kissed, Brianna?"

She felt warm and her body trembled. She stared at him, a face that held its own pain and lips that had not fully healed, and yet she wanted that kiss more than anything she had ever wanted in her life. And he was giving her a choice.

"Aye, Royce, I wished to be kissed."

IO

ROYCE LOWERED HIS LIPS TO HERS AND BRIANNA stiffened.

He smiled, stroked the side of her face gently, and whispered, "This will not hurt."

She looked at him with concern, her body relaxing as she brought her finger to tenderly touch his lip that had not yet fully healed. "It will hurt you."

"It will be worth it."

Her lips parted to speak, though words escaped her, and he took advantage of the moment. He gently captured her mouth with his.

She winced instead of him when she felt his slightly swollen lip; she thought how it must pain him even with a gentle pressure. And then she began to sense the taste of him upon her own lips, and she suddenly found herself thinking only of his kiss.

He was in no rush and took his time. Kissing the cor-

ners of her mouth, her upper lip, playfully nibbling at her
lower lip, and then once again settling his mouth over
hers. This time he eased his tongue between her sensitive
lips and gently introduced her to a kiss she had never
known existed. It stole her senses, raced her heart, and
soared her passion. A passion she had never known she
possessed.

Her sigh mixed with a moan when his lips finally left
hers. While she certainly experienced pleasure, there was
also regret that the kiss had ended much too soon.

She spoke truthfully to him. "I liked that."

"So did I."

She knew she was being much too direct and much too
improper, but at the moment she did not care. "I do not
mind if you wish to do it again sometime."

He was just as direct. "What if I wish to do it often?"

She grinned. "I would look forward to every moment."

He laughed softly. "I love your honesty."

"I have no patience for deceit; I lived with it far too
long."

"I am honest with you in all we have discussed," he assured her.

"I do not question your honesty."

"Why? I am really a stranger to you."

She rested her hand on his arm. "Tell me about yourself, and then you will no longer be a stranger."

He was not ready to do that, and he doubted she was
ready to hear the truth. "There is nothing to tell. I am a
warrior. I fight for my clan and its honor."

She stared at him for a brief moment. "Then you are an
honorable man and a trustworthy one."

"Trustworthy enough to kiss you again."

Her eyes rounded with excitement. "Most definitely."

Her hands grasped his arms when he leaned over her to
share another kiss. They lingered in the kiss, lost in a haze

of tender passion, each wondering where this kiss would finally take them.

It took them both into a restless slumber. Where usually they slept with ease beside each other, this night they both were uneasy.

Brianna wanted to draw closer to him. It was an unrelenting ache and it startled her. She wanted so badly to feel his body against hers. She sighed as quietly as she could so not to disturb him. Her hands simply itched to touch him, and in places she thought she would never want to touch a man again. Instead she kept a distance from him. She thought it safer and much more proper, though she wondered if her fears made the decision for her.

She sighed again and turned away from him to rest on her side.

He in turn turned on his side and faced her back. He had given himself a sound silent thrashing since they had gone to bed. He had been a fool for kissing her the many times he had. Now he could think of nothing but touching her and kissing her in far more intimate places.

He was a man who took pride in controlling his emotions, his passions. But at the moment he felt like a young lad who was eager to taste a woman for the first time. That would not do. Not do at all. So he kept his thoughts neutral, fighting the urge to reach out and draw her to him, touch her, kiss her . . . and make love to her.

Damned, if he was not in trouble.

He moaned in frustration and turned his back to her back.

The night continued on, and it was not until they both fell into a deep slumber that they drifted into each other's arms and settled there for the night.

• • •

THE WEATHER TURNED FRIGID, AND ROYCE ADDED extra logs to the fire. Still there was a chill to the cottage from the incessant wind outside. It seemed to creep through the cracks and crevices and slip past the fire's warmth to torment the flesh.

Brianna had been up and about that morning with Royce's help. She was steady on her feet and suffered only minor pains and aches, though on occasion her lower back would trouble her. Royce had told her that the bruise had been severe and was continuing to heal. He insisted she not stand too long, for prolonged periods on her feet caused her back great discomfort.

She was, however, becoming bored with her confinement and lack of mobility. She simply wanted to do for herself without asking permission from Royce. He continued to make certain she did as he directed, and though she understood he did so from concern, she wanted her freedom returned to her.

After Arran had run off, she tasted freedom like she had never known before. She had been grateful to her brother, Ian, and her sister-in-law, Moira. They both had helped her through a difficult situation. And Moira had helped her to rebuild her self-esteem and gain her freedom. Brianna had grown accustomed to making her own choices, and she intended to keep it that way.

She did not want to seem ungrateful, for Royce had done much for her, but she wished him to understand how she felt.

She sat in bed, the pillows tucked firmly behind her back, the wool blankets tucked around her and his fur cloak thrown across her legs. Her blue shawl was wrapped around her shoulder for added warmth, and she had pinned her hair up with a comb.

She felt comfortable and confident when she turned

her attention to where he sat at the table working on his arrows. She was not prepared for the way her heart jumped at the sight of him. The firelight reflected off his dark hair and cast a partial shadow across his face, concealing his scars and making him a man of mystery.

She thought the shadows not only concealed his face but his identity as well. The shadows kept him well hidden from prying eyes and perhaps from himself. Why, then, did she find this mystery man so very appealing? Why did the shadows not disturb her? Why did she feel she understood him? And why did her heart pound so strongly in her chest when she gazed upon him?

"Did you need or want something, Brianna?"

"I would like to talk with you."

He did not hesitate. He placed the arrow he worked on down on the table, wiped his hands with a clean cloth, and walked over to the bed.

She watched him. He moved with purpose, as though every step were orchestrated, every motion intentional. He was a man of confidence with a touch of arrogance, yet he possessed a tremendously caring heart.

He sat beside her on the bed. "I am at your service."

She had not thought of him that way, but he was actually at her service. When she needed something, he was there. He looked after her every need, and here she was about to do what? Be selfish when he was being unselfish. He wanted her to follow his orders because of her own foolishness. If she had not attempted to get out of bed on her own he would never have ordered her to obey him. And he really did not order her about and he gave her choices. He had asked her when she wished to do things. He had never really forced her to do anything, not even kiss him.

"Deep in thought again?" he asked and leaned close to steal a faint kiss.

Her heart simply melted and she felt guilty for her selfish thoughts.

"Tell me what troubles you, for the worry is clear on your face."

She bit at her lower lip, no longer feeling the urge to discuss the matter with him and wondering what to say to him.

He smiled. "Thinking twice about what you wished to say?"

She loved his smile; even with his wounded lip and swollen eye his smile remained magical. His smile always lightened her heart and was contagious. It was a genuine smile, never forced, never deceitful. He smiled because he felt it in his heart.

"I have changed my mind; I do not need to talk with you."

His laughter was a soft rumble. "You think now that I am not curious."

"It is not important."

"It was important enough only moments ago."

She shrugged. "I have changed my mind."

"I wish to know." His smile remained, though his tone was firm.

"I do not find it necessary to discuss with you."

"Have you lost your courage, then?"

She bristled at his accusation, though he said it in a teasing manner. "Nay, I told you I have changed my mind."

"Then what will it matter if you tell me?"

She was annoyed at him for pressing the matter and annoyed at herself for having allowed the matter to trouble her. And would it really matter if she did discuss it with him, or was it her own stubbornness that caused her this worry?

"I am patient. I can sit here for the remainder of the day—and wait for an answer."

She stubbornly remained silent.

He ran his lips over hers ever so lightly, sending a shiver through her. "Talk to me, Brianna, I will listen."

His understanding often confused her, though it was more her own misunderstanding that brought on the confusion. She expected him to be like most men, and he was not like any man she had ever known.

She sighed in resignation. What else was there for her to do but talk with him? "I had wished to discuss my not having to ask your permission to move about and such. I am feeling much stronger and not so foolish."

He chuckled beneath his breath.

She poked him in the arm and doubted he felt it, for it was a solid wall of muscle she hit.

He brushed his lips over hers once again. "It takes courage to admit the truth."

He was right about that. It had taken her courage to admit the truth about her husband and marriage, and once done it had taken her courage to go on. Now was not the time to dismiss all she had gained.

"I know I had foolishly taken a chance that day I attempted to stand on my own. It has taken time for me to regain my strength, and once I did I never wanted to lose it again. So now I stubbornly hold on to it so that it can never be taken away from me."

His expression turned serious, for he clearly understood what she was attempting to tell him and he admired her courage. "You are stubborn, courageous, and beautiful, and I have no doubt that your strength will forever be with you. And if you feel well enough and"—he cleared his throat with a laugh—"no longer foolish, then I see no reason why you need my permission to do anything."

She smiled like a child who had just received an astonishing present.

"I but ordered you to obey me out of fear, Brianna. When I saw you in pain on the floor, I was angry with *me* for leaving you unattended."

"Nay, it was my fault," she insisted, her hand going to cup the side of his face.

He loved when she touched him; her skin was so warm and soft. "It seems that we both are stubborn."

"Then we will better understand each other."

"I think we already understand much about each other, and I like what I understand," he said, turning his face into her hand to kiss her palm.

She sighed as his tender kiss sent a ripple of pleasure cascading over her. "I am confused at times, for these emotions are not familiar to me." She shook her head as though her own words added to her confusion. "I thought I had but now—" She shook her head again. "I do not know."

He understood what she did not, but she needed to learn herself. He clearly understood how she felt, for he felt the same way, only he did not question it. He wished to experience every feeling, every moment, every thought as they fell in love together.

"You do not need to know right now—simply feel." He encouraged her with another kiss to her palm.

"I feel when you kiss me." She sounded breathless.

"What do you feel?" He wanted her to speak of it, understand it, and respond.

"Your kiss washes over me, touches all of me, and makes me more sensitive to my senses."

"Do you like the feeling?"

She giggled softly as though she did not wish to betray a secret. "Very much."

"Would you like to know how kissing you makes me feel?"

She nodded with enthusiasm. "Aye, I very much would."

He took her hand from his cheek and held it, bringing his mouth close to hers. "When your lips touch mine, a tingling warmth begins to spread through me. It starts slow, but as our lips mate the heat grows and rushes through me. My flesh grows hotter, my heart pounds, and I fight the ache to become intimate with you."

She fell silent at his words but only for a moment, for she had felt as he did, and she wished to be as honest as he. "I am familiar with the feeling."

He stared at her for several silent moments. "So this feeling is mutual?"

"Aye, it is." Her answer was brief, for she was not certain how to respond or where her response would take them.

He ran his lips over hers once, twice, paused, then kissed her gently. He looked into her eyes and asked, "What, then, are we to do about this?"

II

THE ANSWER WAS CLEAR, THOUGH BRIANNA COULD not bring herself to say so. She remained in silent thought, staring back at Royce.

"I will have an answer from you, Brianna," he said without demand.

She found her voice without difficulty. "Will I have an answer from you?"

"Aye, at this moment if you are ready."

Was she ready? Since she asked herself that question, she wondered if she was. "I need to talk of this with you before I can answer. Is that all right with you?"

"Of course, I do not expect you to hurry into something so very important if you are hesitant about it. Talk with me, talk with yourself, and when you feel comfortable enough to answer, then answer me."

"Can we talk now?"

"I would like that."

She gave his hard chest a slight shove. "I cannot think clearly with you so close."

He accommodated her. He sat back, resting his hands in his lap. "Enough distance?"

"I do not want you far away from me." Her words gave her pause to think, for she did not wish him a distance from her. She wished him near.

"I will never be far away from you, Brianna. I will always be close by in body, mind, and spirit."

His words brought joy to her heart and a smile to her face. "Then I will never feel alone."

"Nay, for I will always be with you."

She asked a question that would challenge them both and could put a distance between them. "Do you wish to know love?"

"Does not everyone?"

"Aye, I suppose, but I wonder if I or anyone else really truly knows what love is, and if we do not know it, how then can we find it or know that we have found it?"

He gave her question thought before answering. "I do not think that we need to find love. I think that love is part of each one of us, and that when we learn to share that love with a special person, then we truly know love. Until then we take chances, possibly make mistakes, and learn more and more about love."

"So then you think that mistakes help us to discover love?"

He nodded. "As strange as it may sound, I do. You have known the strong love of family. If you had not known that love, you would never have recognized the cruelty and selfishness of your husband. You would have believed him to love you."

"But I thought I loved him."

"You did love him; that is what makes what he did to you so much more difficult to accept. You understand the goodness of love, your husband never did. You cannot be sorry that you loved him, and you should be grateful that you understood enough about love to let go and suffer no blame for it."

"If you have not known love, how can you understand so much about it?" she asked.

"I knew the love of a caring and wise grandmother. She taught me skills of the mind and heart, and it is because of her that I have waited to know the love of a special woman. Tell me, though, Brianna, you talk of love; what of intimacy?"

"They are one to me."

"Then what you are telling me is that you cannot share intimacy without love."

She gave a hefty sigh, as though giving heavy thought to his remark. And since there was no avoiding a response, she intended to choose her words wisely. "I have shared intimacy without love and it repulsed me. I could not do that again. So, aye, I cannot share intimacy without love."

Royce charged forward like a warrior into battle. "Then do you question if you love me or if I love you?"

She challenged him without a sword or shield, her weapon his and her heart. "Both. We know each other a mere three weeks and we speak of love. Is it love or our forced confinement, or your tender care of me? Do I feel obligated to you? Do you want me because there is no other here? My heart and mind war with questions."

"And you fear making another mistake."

"Aye, I do and because of that I must have answers that satisfy me before I make a choice."

"Are you asking me if I love you?"

"Have you asked yourself if you love me or if you feel as you do because I am here when no other woman is?"

"What you are asking is if it is love or a need that I feel."

"I ask the same of myself. Do I love you or do I need you? Is it that I see in you what I wished in a husband, a caring man? Or is it my dreams and wishes that fill my head with these feelings? I need to know this before I go further than a kiss."

"You have uncommon strength for a woman. Most women would not give it the thought that you do."

"I know the consequences of not clearly looking before I leap."

"Are you suggesting that I look clearly before I leap into something—"

"You may regret," she finished. "We know little of each other."

"Untrue, I know much about you." He continued before she could protest. "I know how you feel about love, men, family, children. I know you are strong and endure pain with courage. I know you are not demanding when someone tends to your care. I know you have a generous heart, for you concern yourself with a stranger and his wounds. I know you are beautiful and that your skin is soft and wonderful to touch. And I know how very much I enjoy kissing you."

"I have opened myself to you more than I realized."

"Does it frighten you to think that I should know you so well?"

She nodded. "It leaves me vulnerable."

"You are only vulnerable if you allow yourself to be so."

"I was helpless and vulnerable when you found me."

"True," he said, "but you made your strength known and fought through the pain with courage. You protected yourself through mind and spirit. You were not as vulnerable as you thought."

"You were a gentleman. I was lucky you found me. Someone of less dubious character could have come upon me. Then what of my fate?"

He smiled. "Somehow I think you would have survived no matter the circumstances."

"You have much faith in my strength."

"You have not enough, and that makes me understand you more than you understand yourself."

She laughed. "I do so enjoy talking with you."

"There, you know something about me."

"I think I know some things about you. You are kind and caring, strong and brave. You have a loving heart that you keep closely guarded, and you dearly loved your grandmother."

"You do know me," he insisted.

"I know not of the battle that left you so badly scarred."

He grew silent, his dark eyes staring at her but not seeing her. When he responded, it was blunt. "I do not wish to speak of it."

She simply nodded.

"There is much for us to think on."

"I agree, but"—she grinned like a child not sure she should ask a question—"will you still kiss me?"

His grin was as childish as hers. "I was hoping you would want me to."

"I do," she said with excitement.

"Now?"

"Aye, now would be good," she said, a brief nod confirming her own words.

He wasted not a moment. He brought his lips to hers with haste, too hasty for a wounded lip. He yelped and drew quickly away from her, his hand hurrying to his lip.

"You have hurt yourself," she said, her hand rushing to his.

"I am fine," he stubbornly insisted, though he felt the blood begin to drip on his hand.

"Let me see." She was as adamant as he was stubborn. She tugged at his hand. "Let me see." She was no match for his strength; try as she might, she could not move his hand.

He attempted to move away from her, not wanting her to see the blood, but he was not quick enough. His blood slipped between his fingers to slowly run down his hand.

"You are bleeding!" Brianna cried out as though he suffered a fate worse than death. She shoved the blankets away from her and scrambled to climb out of bed.

"Stay where you are," he ordered firmly.

"I certainly will not. You need help." She tried to climb over him.

He stopped her, his strong arm going around her waist. "Stay put."

His words were mumbled, and she looked at him with alarm. The blood was running rapidly down his hand, and soon he would have trouble containing it.

"Please." She sounded as if she begged. "Please let me help you."

He thought to deny her, but her eyes pleaded with him and he could not help but surrender. "I will gather what is necessary for you to tend me."

"Nay," she said anxiously, "you will sit and I will gather what I need."

He was about to object, but she shook her head and a finger at him.

"You will not move. I will see to this. Now release me before you bleed to death."

He wanted to smile but knew that was not wise. He released her with an order, and though his words sounded mumbled from his hand covering his mouth, they were clear enough. "Any pain and you return to bed."

She nodded and slipped out of bed, his arm finally leaving her waist completely when she was steady on her feet. She felt a slight discomfort in her lower back, but she thought it more from being abed so much. It felt wonderful to move about, though she took ease with her steps.

He directed her to the clean cloths, and she managed without difficulty to scoop warm water from the pot near the flames into a bowl. She found her pouch of herbs and crushed a few in a small bowl.

Royce stood, intending to help her move the bowls to the small chest beside the bed. She would not have it.

"Stay where you are. I can manage."

His dark green eyes questioned her, and she understood what he wished to hear.

"I have no pain."

"None?" he mumbled, then winced; his lip was beginning to throb.

She was honest. "A small discomfort due probably to my lack of movement, which I intend to rectify beginning now."

She had all the items she needed moved to the chest in a moment's time, and without hesitation she proceeded to tend to his lip. She stood in front of him and eased his hand away from his mouth. The blood was smeared all around his mouth and covered his chin. She thought it probably looked worse than it actually was and went to work cleaning him off.

She immediately determined the problem. "The wound is deep and must heal within before it can properly heal on the outside. I am going to bathe the wound with the herbs that I crushed. It will lessen the soreness. Tomorrow I will make a poultice that I will place on your lip at night before you go to sleep. It will help it to heal more quickly."

He made to respond and she stopped him.

"You must limit your talk at least for the remainder of this day and—"

His eyes widened, for he knew what she was about to say.

"There will be no kissing until this lip heals." She looked directly into his dark eyes. "And do not think that it does not upset me to say that."

He looked about to smile.

"There will be no smiling, either."

She seemed to be able to converse with him by looking into his eyes. Somehow she understood what he was not able to speak.

"Aye, I am the one who gives the orders now, and I expect to be obeyed." She had to smile. She knew it was not fair to him, but the urge was too strong to ignore.

She was amazed to see that his eyes appeared to smile at her, and she proceeded with her task, working like a diligent healer. She did not realize that as she worked, she paused on occasion to rub her lower back and stretch to ease her discomfort.

Royce noticed her actions and paid close heed to them. He hoped she would be done soon, for he was not going to allow her to stand much longer. She did appear happy to be out of bed and on her feet, which he had allowed her to do, though he had made her sit in the chair by the fire. Perhaps it was time for her to walk about more and strengthen her back.

She rubbed her lower back again, but this time it was with a slight sigh that she did not even notice.

"Back to bed," he ordered when she turned to drop the cloth in the bowl of water.

"I am fine and I have yet to finish tending you. Your hand needs cleaning and you should not be talking. The bleeding has finally stopped—"

"Back to bed," he said before she could finish.

She was about to argue when she realized that it would do her no good and that he would be the one to suffer. He would continue talking and cause his lip to bleed again.

"You are stubborn."

"We are alike."

"Let me at least clean your hand," she said, "and then I will return to bed."

He could clean his own hand, but he saw that she wished to complete her task. It was important to her, and he did not wish to deprive her of the satisfaction. He held his bloody hand out to her.

"I need clean water."

He raised a brow.

"I really am fine," she assured him. "It feels so very good to walk about."

He nodded with reluctance, and to his surprise she gently kissed his cheek.

"This is good for me. I need to be out of bed."

He actually wanted her in bed, but that would have to wait. Not that he needed a healed lip to make love to her, but she needed to know for certain that she wanted him. He would not have her otherwise, for once he did he did not intend to let her go.

She dumped the dirty water in a bucket by the door for Royce to discard later, and then scooped clean warm water into the bowl and grabbed a clean cloth before returning to him.

He closed his eyes for a moment, enjoying the pleasure she brought him as she gently wiped at the dried blood with the warm cloth. How cleaning his hand could feel sensual he did not know, but his body was certainly responding. When he opened his eyes, he watched her movements. She made soft long strokes with the cloth over his fingers, then when all the blood was gone, she rinsed the cloth, turned his hand over, and went to work on his palm.

He wondered how he would keep his sanity. Her touch was light and she rubbed in a circular motion, round and round and round. Up his fingers and back again to go round and round and round.

Damned if he was not growing hard, and damn her for moving her body closer to his and leaning against him.

He thought her sigh was caused by the discomfort in her back, but there was a second and then a third, and by the fourth he understood that she was feeling the affects of her touch on him as strongly as he.

He took the cloth from her hand and she surrendered it without protest. He dropped it to the ground and slipped his arms around her waist, drawing her in between his legs.

"I—" She could not seem to find words to express her feelings. So she did what she most wanted to do. She began to kiss his face.

12

❧

BRIANNA SOFTLY KISSED HIS COOL CHEEK UNTIL IT
warmed from her lips, then she traced a trail of delicate
kisses up and around the fading bruise that circled his injured eye. She moved along his forehead, enthralled by
the sweet yet salty taste of him, and without thought she
ran the tip of her tongue down his temple to his cheek,
where she returned to spread kisses. She settled in the corner of his mouth and ever so gently let her tongue play
with the taste of him.

She could not seem to get enough of him, and with
warm wet lips she moved down to nibble at his neck. She
thrilled at the joy she felt nipping, licking, and kissing,
and she would have continued enjoying herself if he had
not grabbed her by the shoulders and gently shoved her
off him, holding her a safe distance away.

"Continue this and I will not be able to stop myself
from making love to you."

Her common sense returned like a splash of cold water to the face. She was startled more from her actions than his remark.

"I did not think."

"Your actions were intended for pleasure not thought. There was no reason for you to think, only feel."

She seemed even more startled. "You tell me that my intention was pleasure?"

"A kiss or two is pleasing; more than that ignites passion and pleasure."

Her eyes rounded like full moons.

"Your reaction surprises you." He wished to lift her and settle her on his lap, for she favored the side that gave her discomfort. But his arousal would be too evident to her and her bottom nestled on him would not help matters.

"I have never felt such an overwhelming urge to kiss a man."

"You mean to seduce a man."

"Seduce?" She stood straight, her eyes remaining wide.

"Aye, and a fine job you were doing of it."

She shook her head in disbelief, then stopped and asked, "Was I?"

He took her hand and slowly, so that the choice was hers to follow, brought her hand to rest over the hard length of him.

"Oh," she said and kept her hand on him, her own desire soaring at the thought that she could affect him so. She did not intend to stroke him, but it felt so natural and he felt so very good to the touch.

"You really are going to be in trouble if you keep that up."

She hastily pulled her hand away and offered him an apology. "I am sorry. I do not—"

He stopped her. "Do not apologize for desiring me. I love when you kiss me and when you touch me."

"Truly?" She sounded stunned.

"Aye, truly," he assured her.

She leaned to her side, her face scrunching in discomfort.

"Your back troubles you?"

"Aye, it pains me."

"Back to bed," he said firmly and stood to scoop her up into his arms and place her in bed, pulling the blankets up around her and arranging the pillows comfortably beneath her head.

She reached for his hand before he could move away. "I do not understand my feelings."

"You will in time."

"But is there enough time?" She sounded anxious, concerned, and almost fearful that they would not have enough time together.

He leaned down close and rubbed his cheek to hers. "Trust me, I will make certain we have enough time."

"My brother will find me soon enough."

"Aye, he will, but by then this will be settled between you and me." He rubbed his cheek to hers once again. "Now rest, you have had a busy time." He left her side, though he did not want to. He would have preferred to remain beside her, snuggled against her, holding her and loving her. But at the moment that would not be a wise choice.

He kept himself busy cleaning up the bowls and cloths and preparing the evening meal for them. She dozed as he knew she would; though she insisted she was fine, her body continued to heal and often sought rest.

His mind stayed busy along with his hands. There was much they needed to discuss, though he doubted words would settle anything at the moment. Their emotions seemed to have the upper hand, and that was unusual for him. Sound reason, diligent thought, and right action always made for wise choices.

Presently, he lacked sound reason, his thoughts were chaotic, and right action was the farthest thing from his mind. So then, would his choice be unwise? He had to smile to himself, recalling that a wide grin would not help his lip.

Everything he felt for Brianna was right, good, and wise. She was meant for him and he for her. He thought not how others would react, for their feelings did not concern him. He would deal with her brother when the time came, though he doubted he would meet resistance. Her brother sounded as though he loved his sister very much and wished only for her happiness. And by the time her brother found them or he returned her to him, it would be obvious how they felt for each other.

It would all work out given time. He was positive, therefore he ignored the nagging little voice that reminded him that he should tell her more about himself. The fact that she accepted him now as he was surely meant that she would accept all of who he was.

"Royce."

He looked over at her. She pushed her dark hair away from her face and rubbed the sleep from her eyes. She looked beautiful, innocent, and sensual as she roused herself from her slumber, and he felt an overwhelming urge to protect her and make love to her.

He contained his emotion, difficult as it was.

"I am so thirsty; could I trouble you for a drink?"

"You never trouble me, Brianna," he said, moving about to fix a favorite herbal brew she had taught him to prepare.

"I know and that continues to surprise me. You are not like other men who think only of themselves. You have a deeply caring heart. I find it difficult to believe you are a warrior."

"I fight when I must."

"Aye, like many other men. They fight when they are told to fight and follow their leaders without thought or reason. All for more land and more power."

He brought her the drink. "You do not respect warriors."

"I respect those who fight for a solid cause or reason, but those who hunger to expand their purse or holdings I find greedy and selfish."

"A clan's land needs defending."

"Aye, but one clan swallows another when they war, and the battles seem endless. And the land and people often suffer."

"The land and people need protection."

"Then why do the people suffer if they are protected?" she asked earnestly, searching for a reasonable answer.

"It is the way of war and cannot be helped."

She disagreed. "It is the way of greedy men."

"Your brother, does he not war?"

"Only when necessary."

"Sometimes what may seem necessary to one is not to another."

She nodded. "A reason to war, two factions that cannot agree, so brute force determines the winner."

"It is the way of things."

After placing the cup on the chest, she tugged at his hand so that he would sit beside her. "Do you like to war?"

He gave her question serious thought, for he had asked himself the very same question many times over. It was the very reason that brought him to the solitude of this cottage. He wanted answers, but feared he would find no definitive one; or did he fear he would find an answer not to his liking?

"You give my question thought." She hugged his hand with hers. "It is not new to you."

"Nay, I sought solitude in search of answers."

"I interrupted your search, I am sorry."

"I am not." He was adamant. "Your interruption gave me more to think about."

She laughed. "Is that a nice way of saying I confuse you?"

He squeezed her hand lightly. "You gave me new places to search in."

"Places you have not thought of?"

"Places I hid from."

Her curiosity had her asking, "Why?"

He shrugged. "It is easier to hide than to face our doubts and fears."

She understood perfectly. "I hid from the truth of my marriage out of doubt and fear."

"What finally made you face the truth?"

"My sister-in-law and her friend Anne. They are both very strong women and were very kind to me. They helped me to see the truth of my marriage, and they helped me to discover my own strength. Had you any time alone before my unexpected arrival?"

"A brief time."

"Not enough for you to make any discoveries that would lead you to answers?"

"Answers elude me."

"Perhaps you are not ready for them," she said.

"I have thought that myself."

"Then talk with me of what troubles you, and perhaps we can discover the answers together." She seemed excited that she might be able to help him.

"I cannot talk of it with you."

"Why?" She sounded disappointed.

"I will not talk of battle with you."

"I talked with you of my battle."

"It is not the same," he insisted.

Her voice grew quiet. "My scars are as deep as yours; they are just not visible."

He admired her courage and tenacity.

"I heal as you do; why not let us heal together?" She threaded her fingers with his as if showing him that they could be one in this battle.

"Give me time."

She remembered how difficult it had been for her to face her own battle. She understood that it was not easy for him, and only when he was willing to face his doubts and fears truthfully could he emerge from the darkness to which he had retreated.

"When you are ready."

The thought that she did not insist but would wait until he was ready and be there for him filled him with a sense of peace.

"I appreciate your concern." He more than appreciated it, but those simple words would do for now.

"I care," she said with a hasty smile as though she surprised herself.

"Do you now?" he teased, leaning in closer as if he was about to capture a kiss.

She raised a quick hand to his chest. "You must not. Your lip."

"I have the urge to kiss you and cannot resist. What am I to do?"

She grinned and giggled softly. "Let me kiss you?"

She did not wait for an answer. She wrapped her arms around his neck and drew his face slowly down to her lips. She started with his cheek and made certain to cover every area of his face. She had never known the joy of kissing a man when and how she chose, and it simply thrilled her.

She stopped to tell him. "I love kissing you."

"I love you kissing me."

"Truly you do?"

He had to laugh. "Truly, and I will tell you it often so that you will not need to question it again."

"Tell me as often as you like."

"That I will. Now are you hungry?"

"Starving, but I would like to help with the meal."

"Nay, you will rest."

She protested. "I have rested. I am tired of resting."

"Your back continues to pain you."

"Because I spend too much time in this bed. I need to move around more."

Since he looked to digest her remark, she continued to attempt to convince him.

"I could sit on the chair by the table if I tire."

"Your word on that?" he asked.

A warrior's word was his honor. He looked to her for the same. She had no trouble giving it to him. "Aye, you have my word."

He reached for her leather slippers that sat beside the chest at the end of the bed.

She hastily slipped from beneath the covers to the edge of the bed. She swung her feet in eager anticipation.

She reminded him of a young innocent girl. Her skin was smooth and touched with a faint blush. Her eyes were rounded in excitement, her lips softly puffed from kissing him. She adjusted the comb in her hair, capturing the strands that refused confinement, though one or two managed to escape. Her simple beauty grabbed at his heart and twisted until he thought he had not a breath left in him.

He quickly kneeled on the floor to place her soft

leather slippers on her feet and restrain his pounding heart. His position only worsened his condition. He had to take hold of each of her ankles when slipping on the leather slippers. They were trim and so soft that his fingers itched to explore farther up her leg.

He had touched her often when caring for her, but his thoughts had always been for her well-being. Now, however, his thoughts were those of passion.

"Are you finished?" she asked with a hand to his shoulder.

The innocent gesture completely unnerved him. It sent a rush of heat racing through his body and settling in places that had him thinking that she was right where he wanted her.

She had a different thought and urged him along. "Help me to stand."

"Take my arm," he said, knowing that in a moment she would be flying off the bed of her own accord if he did not oblige her.

She was about to slip her arm with his when he stopped her.

"Nay, place your hands on my arm and let my strength help you stand. Then, if you require my assistance to walk, I will help you."

She was overjoyed at the thought of being independent once again and determined to remain so. She did as he directed, her hands grabbing hold of his hard, muscled arms. The strength of him startled her. She was not certain why since she had felt his strong arms many times before, yet somehow this time was different. Very different. Her body reacted like a woman who desired a man.

"Ready?"

She nodded, trying hard to ignore the tingle in her fingers from the heat of his skin. She focused her attention on the task at hand while the tingle crawled up her arm.

He stood close by her side, his body nearly touching hers.

She stood with deliberate slowness, wanting to make certain not to harm her back and not wanting to let go of his arm. When she was certain she could stand on her own, she removed her hands from him and looked up with pride into his face.

What she saw excited and frightened her.

Passion brewed in his eyes.

He wanted her.

13

〜

BRIANNA STARED AT HIM AS IF SHE WERE SEEING HIM for the first time. She did not scream or turn her eyes away in fright. She did not see his horrendous wounds. Instead she saw the depth of him. He possessed a loving heart and caring soul.

She placed her hand to his cheek. "I am not afraid."

"Good, for I would never harm you."

"I know that now and do not doubt it."

"Then tell me where we take this, Brianna," he said softly with a kiss to her palm, "for I want nothing more at this moment than to make love to you."

He left it for her to decide; he always left her with a choice. She had made a mistake the last time she had thought she loved a man, but then her husband had hid behind his charm. Royce hid nothing from her. He was who he was, a wounded warrior with a gentle heart.

Her choice was easy. "I would like the same."

He went to kiss her, but she stopped him with a gentle finger to his lip. "You will disturb your wound."

"I do not care."

She faintly touched her lips to his. "I do."

Her caring words heightened his passion. He had had many women over the years, and a few had expressed their feelings for him, but he never felt that any of them truly cared for him. The thought that Brianna did made him realize how very special she was to him and how very much he loved her.

He gently scooped her up into his arms. "In time you will come to know my lips on you. For now I will show you what my hands can do."

Gooseflesh ran over her warm skin. He had touched her so often when he tended her, now he would touch her differently. The thought excited her and she was as eager as he to return to bed.

He removed her slippers and then eased her out of her night shift. He did not take long to shed his own garments and lay beside her on the bed. They had seen each other naked, they had slept side by side, and they had touched. There was no unease between them, only an eager anticipation for what was to come.

She stroked his chest, loving the feel of his warm skin and the strength of his muscles. "I can kiss you," she offered with a smile.

"Aye, you can, and I would like that, but first I wish to touch you as only a man in love can do."

She heard him correctly, did she not? He spoke of love, loving her. She could not believe what she had heard. She had thought that he cared for her, but love? They had known each other for such a short time. Was it possible to fall in love so easily?

He tapped playfully at her nose and understood and

voiced her concern. "Why question that I love you? When you know you love me as well."

"You are certain?"

"Aye, I am certain that we love each other."

She laughed softly. "Not a doubt?"

He was serious. "Nay, not one."

She grew serious. "Why? Why do you love me?"

With the tips of his fingers he lightly stroked her face. "Because you are you."

She looked at him strangely, as if his words made no sense, but then his touch was doing maddening things to her senses. And she sighed with the pleasure of his fingers lightly traveling down along her neck and over her shoulders.

He attempted to answer her unasked question. "I love you for who you are, a gift that I will cherish forever."

She felt the same of him, but she could not speak the words, for he touched her in a way she had never been touched before. His fingers drifted with a lingering slowness along her chest and over her breast. With two fingers he teased her nipple, and when it grew taut, he brought his mouth down to lovingly stroke it with his tongue. Her sighs grew to moans when his tongue began to flicker at the tight pink bud.

Ripple after ripple of pure passion spread over her entire body, and she moaned from the pleasure he gave her. He treated her other nipple to the same pleasure.

He stopped after giving each nipple one last lingering lick, and she released a long sigh.

He rubbed his cheek next to hers. "I love the feel of you and—the taste of you."

She struggled to calm her heavy breathing so that she could tell him, "I have never known—"

His finger silenced her. "From this day on you will know what it truly means to be loved."

Her mind and body rejoiced at his words.

Love.

She had truly found love.

He pressed his cheek to hers. "Now feel the magic."

His fingers moved over her body, touching her ever so lightly, a faint brush of flesh against flesh. Her skin felt alive and sensitive to every stroke of his fingers. Her body warmed, her breathing grew heavy, and she grew moist between her legs. He was exciting her beyond reason.

He lingered over her flat stomach, purposely prolonging his descent, adding to the anticipation, the passion, the need to be touched. She moved almost to a rhythmic beat beneath his hand. Her body seemed to understand what he asked of her, and she responded accordingly. She herself did not understand the ache that throbbed deep inside her, but she did not fear it nor fight it, she simply savored it.

When she thought he would settle his touch between her legs, he surprised her by sitting up and running his feather touch down over her thighs, along her calves and her feet. He did the same to her other leg, but this time when his fingers drifted to between her legs, he gently and slowly parted them.

Then he touched.

A whispered touch that sent a wave of pleasure so potent that her moan echoed throughout the small cottage.

"You like that?" he asked, though he sounded like he knew the answer.

Her moan faded faintly in the room. "Very much."

"Then you will like this even more." He moved down between her legs and began to stroke her with his tongue.

She was lost. The world no longer existed. Nothing mattered but this moment, his touch, and his love. She had not known that making love could be so beautiful, so satisfying, and so unselfish.

His finger found her wet flesh and slowly stroked her

before slipping gently deep inside her. With each penetrating stroke her moans grew louder and louder, and she was certain that in no time she would climax and the exquisite beauty they shared would end.

"You must stop," she pleaded, "or I will proceed you."

"I want to taste your climax."

His words excited her, but memories invaded her passion, and she remembered how her husband's temper would flare if she should receive pleasure before him.

"And besides, I will make you come again and again before we finish."

"Nay, that is not possible."

He laughed. "I am going to show you just how possible that is."

His tongue licked, his finger worked magic, and she screamed with the pleasure of her first true climax.

She could not believe the sensation that faded with a ripple that refused to die, and it was on that ripple that he stirred her passion once again. And she could not believe that she responded eagerly.

When she thought she had experienced all the pleasure that was possible, he entered her. His strong arms wrapped around her, bringing her up against his chest, her own arms going around his broad back, and they moved together like a perfectly matched pair, exploding together in a powerful climax.

She called out his name, he moaned, resting his face to hers, and a tear slipped from the corner of her eye, for she realized that she had finally found a love that was real.

"Are you all right?" he asked anxiously as he moved off her and saw the single tear. "I have not hurt you, have I?"

"Nay, nay, you have made me feel like—" She was at a loss for words. "I never imagined it to be so wonderful."

"It is wonderful when two people love and share in the lovemaking."

"Aye," she agreed with a smile. "It makes all the difference."

Her stomach rumbled in hunger and she blushed.

He laughed and hugged her to him. "I am as hungry as you, only my stomach does not protest loudly."

She sat up with excitement. "Let us make a grand meal to celebrate."

"Aye," he said, running his hand up her arm. "Our love is something that should be celebrated."

She felt no shyness with him. How could she when he had touched her in all ways possible? She leaned down and kissed his cheek, then tenderly kissed his lips.

In a soft yet strong voice she said, "I love you."

BRIANNA GREW STRONGER EVERY DAY AND FOUND JOY in every moment she spent with Royce. They laughed often and loved just as often. She sometimes wondered if perhaps it was all a dream and that she would wake to find herself recovering from her accident.

She would pinch herself time and again to make certain she was awake and then laugh at her own foolishness. Then she would worry that she foolishly fell in love and then admonish herself for being foolhardy with her own worrisome thoughts.

Royce was the complete opposite of her. He simply accepted how he felt and insisted that she felt the same way, so, therefore, there was no problem.

"Your brother will clearly see how much we love each other and consent to our union," he said to her one morning when they had taken but a few steps outside the cottage.

The weather had calmed, her pain had subsided, and he

had taken her outside once before since she had complained about needing fresh air. It was now a daily occurrence for them to walk near the cottage each day, weather permitting.

Today the sun was strong, white clouds floated in a brilliant blue sky, the air was crisp, and she stood beside him, stunned.

"Our union?" she repeated.

He seemed to think nothing of his remark and adjusted his fur around her. "Aye, we will wed soon after our return."

"You have decided this?" she asked with a hint of annoyance.

He grinned, shook his head, then leaned down and placed a gentle kiss on her forehead. "I have handled this poorly and without thought. My love for you blinds me to proper manners, though if I was to do this properly, then it is your brother I should approach and request permission to take you as my wife."

Brianna had to smile. "I will be the one who decides whom I wed, and how can I decide that when I have not been asked?"

He laughed and the strong sound echoed in the stillness of the surrounding woods. "We will wed, of that I am certain, but I will appease your romantic side and properly request your hand in marriage."

If she had not been aware of his tender side, she would have taken affront to his arrogant proposal that they would wed merely because he was certain of it. But she could not be angry with him, for she understood that he spoke from his heart and in his own way.

She waited patiently for him to ask.

After he made certain his fur was secure around her, he took her hand and made ready to walk with her.

She stood firm where she was and asked, "Do you not intend to ask me?"

"Aye, in time."

"In time? Why not at this moment?"

"It will not do."

Her eyes rounded. "Will not do? And why not?"

"You expect it."

If her eyes could have widened further, they would have. "You confuse me. You tell me we will wed, you tell me you will ask me, and now you tell me I expect it." She shook her head.

He took her in his arms. "I am not your common man. I am strong in my thought and opinion, and when I make a decision, there is no changing it. I am used to following my own way of things and having my own way."

"I have become accustomed to the same luxury."

He smiled. "Then we will match wits often."

"You do not mind defeat, then?" she asked with a serious tone, though there was a twinkle in her eyes.

His grin portrayed his confidence. "I have known only victory."

"Then prepare for your first defeat," she challenged with her own confidence.

His laugh was hardy and he threw his arms wide. "Do I look as though you can defeat me?"

She looked him over and with an arrogant confidence wiggled her pinky in front of his face.

He smiled and shook his head in disbelief. "Are you brave or foolish?"

"Foolishly brave."

He gave her a quick kiss. "I love you."

Her heart skipped several beats and she sighed. "I still cannot believe that I have fallen so very much in love with you."

"It was my good looks that won you."

She laughed this time. "Aye, your looks certainly captured me when first we met."

He leaned his forehead to hers. "And now do my looks capture you?"

She brushed his lips with hers and cupped his cheek with her hand. "Aye, you are my handsome hero."

"Hero? I am your hero?" He looked startled.

She seemed as surprised as he. "Why would you not be my hero? You rescued me from death and tended me back to health with a tender hand and heart. You are a true hero."

He appeared to drift off in thought as he spoke. "Heroes often spill blood."

She knew his thoughts were elsewhere in a place that brought him pain. She wished to ease his suffering. "Come walk with me."

He did so, taking her hand in his as they strolled slowly away from the cottage.

Silence followed their trail, their leather boots leaving imprints in the snow that remained on the ground. It had been a week since the last snow, which had been but a sprinkling, and the ground had remained untouched except for their recent footprints.

They walked on the carpet of white hand in hand.

"I have spilled much blood, Brianna," Royce said, feeling she was owed some truth about him.

"You are a warrior; like most it could not be helped."

"I will spill more. The Highlands are in turmoil and the fighting will continue until we are left in peace."

She feared the fighting would never end, for those who led would always be hungry for more power and wealth. "I wonder if peace will ever be found for the Highlands."

"We will not know if we do not try, and if I do not try, my children will also bear arms, and I would prefer them to live in peace."

She stopped abruptly and looked up at him with round sad eyes. "I cannot give you children. You know this."

It seemed not to bother him. He simply said, "We will see."

She remained insistent. "Nay, Royce, I can bear you no sons or daughters."

His badly bruised and battered eye was healing nicely, and she could now see the vibrant darkness in both his eyes. And she could understand how the intense dark color could intimidate.

"My seed is potent."

"Aye, I am sure it is." Reluctantly she added, "But I am not fertile, so your seed falls on barren soil."

He smiled with his next remark. "I repeat, I have known no defeat."

She did not smile. "And I do not wish for your first defeat to be so disappointing." She waited a moment before she expressed a concern that tore at her heart. "If it is children you hope for, perhaps you should think twice before wedding me."

His tongue was sharp and quick. "Perhaps you should think twice before speaking foolishly."

She took an abrupt step away from him. "You are being foolish to think I can give you something I cannot."

"You are being foolish if you think that it matters."

She grew annoyed. "Your own words tell me this."

"I want children and I feel we will have children, but if I am wrong—and I know that I am not—it makes not a difference. I love you and I will wed you."

Sadness filled her eyes along with a glistening of tears. "You say this now, but what happens if no children come along? Will you not be disappointed with me? Will your love for me fade? Will you—"

"Stop!" His powerful shout echoed through the woods.

She stood as still and straight as the trees that surrounded them.

He grabbed hold of her shoulders and fixed his eyes on hers. "Listen well to me. I am twenty and eight, long past the age most men take a wife. I have waited to wed, for I wished to find a special woman to love. I swore when I found her that I would make her mine forever and that I would love her forever. The love I have for her and she for me will be the most important thing in my life, and with the passing years it will deepen and grow. Nothing matters but that love."

He took a breath and his dark eyes softened along with his voice. "I have found that love in you, Brianna. I want nothing more but for us to love. What follows I will accept as long as you remain by my side and love me forever."

Tears trickled down her face. Words failed her. Actions did not. She wrapped her arms around him and laid her head on his chest. She listened to the hard, steady beating of his heart, felt his warmth seep into her, and knew then what to say.

She looked up at him. "I will take your seed often and pray for a miracle."

He smiled and cupped her face in his large hands. "This you promise me?"

"Aye, I promise you." Her own smile was wide.

"And if I suggest that we return to the cottage and start on that promise?"

A teasing twinkle replaced her tears. "I would suggest that you carry me, for it would make for a quicker return to the cottage."

He roared with laughter and swung her up into his arms, his hasty retreat leaving heavy footprints in the snow.

14

〜

Brianna lay beside Royce, her head resting on his shoulder. It was near dawn and she woke with a strange feeling. Royce slept quietly, no worrisome thoughts disturbing him. She could not do the same. She felt uneasy, as though something was about to happen. What it was she did not know, but it disturbed her.

She had healed nicely over the last few weeks. Most of her bruises had faded away or at least faded to a pale yellowish hue, reminding her that they soon would be gone. Surprisingly the bruise on her lower back had faded faster than she had expected, that area having given her the most discomfort. Otherwise she could not say that she suffered much from her ordeal. Royce had been a kind and gentle healer, and it was because of him she had healed and felt so well.

He, however, was still healing from his wounds. The scar on his face had crusted and looked as though it would leave him with a heavy reminder of battle. His lip was near to healed and barely troubled him, and the swelling around his eye had all but gone. He appeared more human now, though the extent of damage his facial scar had caused made it difficult for her to picture him as he once was.

It mattered not to her, for she knew his heart and soul and they were beautiful. His facial features were no concern to her. How he treated her was of the utmost concern to her.

She cuddled closer to his warmth. She was comfortable lying naked beside him, which is how she now slept. She had learned soon enough that her night shift would not remain on her when they climbed into bed together, so after several times she did not bother to put it on. And she had to admit she liked waking in the middle of the night or in the morning and cuddling against his warm body. He would slip his arms around her and hold her close. She felt safe and protected and very much loved.

He had also taught her the joy and bliss of making love. There was not a day that went by that they did not make love and that she did not learn something new. He was gentle and understanding with her and encouraged her to explore.

She smiled, remembering how she had told him she wished to explore with her tongue. He quickly encouraged her, and that night was one that would live long in her memory, for she had not thought a woman could be in such control of a man.

They talked of getting wed, though he had yet to ask her. He was confident they would, and she was confident that he would ask her in time. She worried not about her brother's response to their union, for her brother wished her to be happy. Once he saw how very happy she was with Royce, she was certain Ian would agree to their union.

Ian would surely ask Royce to join their clan since he seemed more on his own. If he had been a part of a large clan, he would not be alone in this cottage healing his wounds. There would be clansmen and women to help him.

Now he would be alone no more. He would become part of the clan Cameron, Ian would probably give them a keep nearby, and life would be good for all.

Why, then, this thought of impending disruption?

What could possibly happen?

She knew her brother would greet Royce well, and she knew Royce would respond in kind. Whatever was disturbing her?

"What is wrong?" His arm slipped around her to draw her closer so that her head could rest on his chest, and he draped his leg over hers.

"I woke you."

"Nay, the thought of another day with you beside me woke me." He kissed her forehead.

"The days do seem more exciting and full since I began sharing them with you."

"And they will remain so. We will share much together."

"You sound so very certain," she said, her strange unease continuing to disturb her.

"What troubles you?" he asked, his arm wrapping more tightly around her, assuring her that she was well protected.

She stroked his chest, needing to touch him. "I do not know. I woke feeling . . ."

Her words trailed off, for she found it difficult to explain how she felt.

He encouraged her to speak. "Tell me and we will sort this out together."

Together.

They did much together, for there was only the two of them here and now. Is that what troubled her? Did she fear returning to a world outside this cottage? What did she think would happen?

"Talk with me," he said with a gentle squeeze.

She did not wish to spoil their day. "It is nothing, I worry needlessly."

"Let me worry with you," he encouraged, giving her bottom a loving pat.

She was reluctant to discuss her concerns. They were, after all, her own fears, and she should deal with them accordingly. She moved restlessly in his arms.

"You will tell me."

That he demanded was obvious. That he demanded out of concern was also obvious. She could not be angry with him for caring. His concern touched her heart and made her realize his love for her. It constantly amazed her that she had found such a strong, enduring love with him. They were strangers, yet they were not.

She settled in his arms and she could feel his tension ease with her calmness.

"I have thought too much over our return."

"All will go well," he assured her with a confidence that startled her.

"You really have not a shed of doubt?"

"There is no reason for doubt. From what you have told me of your brother, he cares only for your happiness. He would be the only one who could prevent our union, and he will not do that; therefore, there is no cause to worry."

"I tell myself the very same thing, but . . ."

Her words trailed off again as if she did not believe herself.

"Brianna." He called to her softly.

She looked up at him in question.

"Do you love me?"

She thought to tell him that he asked a foolish question, but she felt compelled to answer from her heart. "With all my heart and soul."

"As do I love you, and with a love as strong as ours, do you think there is anything that can keep us apart? Do you think that I would not fight for you? Do you think that I would not die for you?"

"Hush," she said with a finger to his lips. "My heart aches at such a thought. I do not know what I would do without you. I even find that I have grown accustomed to sharing a bed with you." She poked him playfully in the ribs. "Though your size takes up much of the bed."

"It is not my size that makes the bed small; it is the fact that you attach yourself to me and will give me no room to move," he teased in return.

"I will not argue the truth, for I do find it pleasant to nestle against you while I sleep. You are warm and comfortable and I cannot resist your body."

He poked playfully at her. "You certainly cannot resist my body; your thirst for me is insatiable."

She buried her blushing face against his bare chest. "I had not known—" She stopped herself from admitting how much joy she had discovered in making love and how much she desired him. She did what she was accustomed to doing, apologizing. "I am sorry—"

He stopped her this time. He grabbed her and hoisted her on top of him. "Never apologize for wanting me. I had not known the beauty of making love until I experienced it with you. I had not known love until I found you. You are mine and I am yours forever. We will love forever and beyond, and no one, not a soul, will come between us."

She kissed him as she often did, soft and gentle.

He, however, was feeling possessive, a need to demonstrate how strongly he cared for her, how much he wanted her, and how much that need pulsated within him.

He grabbed her about the waist and turned her onto her back, covering her body with his. He normally asked if she was all right, if anything pained her, if she was comfortable. He asked her nothing. He looked at her with a fire in his eyes that could not be denied.

His mouth descended on hers with a heated passion, and his body moved against hers with a determined purpose.

They had loved many times and many ways, but this time there was a need in him she had never felt before, and it fired her own passion. And though his kiss demanded and his touch was forceful, she knew he would never hurt her and that thought excited her all the more.

His mouth moved to her nipples and feasted there like a starving man. She tried to touch him, stroke him, kiss him, but he rebelled. He would have the upper hand, he would control, direct, take charge.

She could do nothing but surrender to his will, enjoying every touch, stroke, and kiss he rained upon her. He was like a man with an insatiable need and she the only sustenance that could satisfy him.

Time stood still; nothing existed but the two of them and their relentless need to love. He brought her to climax more times than she thought possible, and when she thought she was spent, unable to respond, he took her with such a loving force that she climaxed with him, his name an echoing cry on her lips.

He braced his damp body over hers, pressed his cheek

to hers, and whispered in an uneven voice, "I will not live life without you. You are mine. I will love you forever."

WITH THE MORNING MEAL DONE AND THE SUN BRIGHT in the blue sky, Brianna and Royce made ready for their daily walk in the woods. Brianna was anxious to be on their way. She had been collecting twigs and small branches so that she could fashion a basket, a task she had learned from her sister-in-law's friend Anne. It kept her mind and hands busy and she loved seeing the end results, a creation of beauty and patience, her creation.

"Hurry," she urged him. "I have much to collect."

"And I have much to carry," he teased her with an arm around her waist.

She stared at him a moment before asking, "This will not stop between us, walks in the woods, loving as we do, sharing our meals together?"

"Nay," he said softly with a kiss to her cheek. "We will share more walks and more loving and more meals."

To her own surprise she agreed with him. "Aye, we will."

His head shot up and he was suddenly alert to all that surrounded him. His hand instantly went to the sword that hung at his side, and with a firm hand he pushed Brianna behind him.

She grew alarmed, for she knew he sensed danger. She wisely moved as he directed, remained silent, and kept herself close to his back. He was a warrior; she would leave him to do what he did best.

She suddenly heard what his sharp warrior instincts had alerted him to. Horses and men approached, though at no great speed, and she sensed then that their time together was at an end.

Brianna recognized Blair in the distance. He always sat

his horse with ease and confidence as though he had not a care in the world. He fooled many an opponent that way, making them think him an easy target. They found out soon enough he was a formidable adversary.

She also watched Royce. He was a warrior who remained alert and prepared and ready to fight in an instant. His muscles were taut, his stance firm, and his attention focused. He would strike like a snake and do damage before anyone realized what had happened.

She understood this and did not wish to wait until it was too late to prevent an altercation. She stepped around Royce, keeping out of his reach, and ran toward the approaching men, waving.

"Blair!"

Brianna could see the relief in Blair's eyes when he spotted her, and he urged his horse toward her. Royce was at her side before Blair could dismount, and to Brianna's surprise Blair hesitated, glaring at Royce, before he carefully dismounted his horse, all the time keeping his eyes on Royce.

She ran up to Blair and threw her arms around him. He hugged her to him, but she sensed that he kept his focus on Royce.

"It is good to see you," she said, stepping back, though keeping hold of his arms.

"It is a relief to know you are well. Ian has been going crazy searching for you. He would let none rest, though none wanted to, until you were found." Blair gave her another hug, needing to feel that she was real and the ordeal was over.

When Brianna stepped back away from him, she noticed that the men with Blair kept a steady eye on Royce almost as if they feared he would assault them—though it was probably his scars that caught such an intense interest. Still, it unnerved her the blatant way they all stared at him.

She thought it best to introduce the two men, for Blair looked extremely uneasy with Royce. She could not say the same of Royce. He stood with an arrogant confidence that could intimidate the bravest of men.

"Blair," Brianna said with a smile that she hoped would be contagious, "I want you to meet the man who helped heal me after the accident." She held her hand out to Royce and he took it. "Blair, this is Royce. And, Royce, this is Blair, a good friend to me and my brother."

Both men understood the significance of her introduction. She was telling both men how much each of them meant to her, and without words she was expressing the hope that the two would be friends.

Blair extended his hand at the same moment Royce did, and they shook.

"Ian Cameron will be pleased to know that you gave his sister shelter and aid in her time of need. We had come across the battered carriage and the remains of the two men. We worried over Brianna's fate."

"I am sorry that I had no time to see to a proper burial. Brianna needed immediate attention," Royce said, slowly drawing Brianna back into his arms.

Blair watched his every move and noted the fact that his one hand remained on the hilt of his sword. "The Camerons are grateful."

Royce acknowledged his remark with a curt nod.

Brianna attempted to understand both men's reactions, though she puzzled over the tension in the air and the way the men on the horses whispered and watched the exchange.

She was surprised at Blair's next remark and the way he stared at Royce as he spoke. "Gather what things you have, Brianna, and we will be on our way."

Royce's arm went around her waist and pulled her tight against his side. "I leave with Brianna and we will leave in the morning. I wish to speak with Ian Cameron concerning his sister."

Blair attempted to stand his ground. "You are welcome to speak with him, but he has directed me to return his sister home safely and as soon as possible. She leaves with us now."

Royce responded before Brianna could voice her own objections. "Brianna continues to heal, and it would be best that she rest one more night in a soft bed instead of the hard ground. And I will see that Ian Cameron's sister is returned safely to him."

Brianna looked from one man to another. What was this contest of wills? Why did each feel the need to decide what she would do and when? And why did Blair seem prepared to fight? He had strength in numbers, ten men in all flanking him, and yet Blair himself, not to mention the men, seemed prepared to battle this one man.

She grew annoyed at such nonsense, broke loose from Royce, and stepped between them. "I will take my leave when I am ready, and presently I intend to go into the woods and collect the makings for my basket. You both can battle if you wish, but spill a drop of blood, and I will not return with either of you."

She stomped off without a glance to either. She wanted neither of them to follow. She was much too annoyed at their ridiculous behavior. Each wanted his own way, each wanted to be in command of the situation, each wanted to protect.

She could not very well fault them for caring, but their behavior was simply not acceptable. Blair could very well see that Royce had treated her well, and Royce could very well see that Blair was a good friend relieved at finding her.

Why, then, the strange looks, the hushed whispers, and the on-guard stance each man took? None of it made sense to her. Royce was one lone man against many. He could cause them little harm, and yet they acted as if he could harm them all.

Royce was large and his scarred features probably made him appear all the more dangerous, but it was preposterous to think that one man could put fear in many men.

She marched forward into the woods, a recently fallen slim branch catching her eye.

Both men watched her walk away, and both kept a steady eye on her until she stooped down to examine the fallen branch.

Blair then looked to Royce. "You care for her?"

"I care for her, but that is for me to discuss with her brother." Royce was firm in his response.

"Aye, it is for you to discuss with Ian, but answer me this." Blair glared at him. "Brianna does not know who you are, does she?"

15

"BRIANNA KNOWS NOTHING," ROYCE CONFIRMED. "And she will know nothing until I am ready to tell her."

"Her brother Ian may disagree with you," Blair advised, casting a glance toward Brianna. "He wishes his sister to find happiness."

"She has found it with me." Royce moved his hand off his sword, and all around him eased their rigid stances.

"Brianna knows not who you are," Blair said. "When she discovers the truth, what then?"

Royce had no answer. He had thought often on the consequences of keeping his identity from her, but it was more important that she discover who he truly was and not who many thought him to be. He had revealed much about himself to her, much that he had kept hidden even from himself.

"Brianna once trusted a man and suffered for it. Her brother will not see her hurt again."

Royce respected Blair for defending Brianna. "I would never hurt Brianna. I care too deeply for her. I will protect her with my life."

"Yet you keep the truth from her."

"She was ill and frightened when she first cast eyes on me. My thought was for her to heal—not worry over who tended her."

"Your clan knows where you are?" Blair asked.

"Aye, and there is no need for concern. I have no grievance with the clan Cameron." Royce glanced to Brianna and saw that she wandered farther into the woods. "We can speak of this later, though not in Brianna's presence."

"Ian will be grateful that you have seen to his sister's care—"

Royce finished for him. "But he will not be grateful that I care for his sister."

"He loves his sister."

"So do I," Royce said and walked off to join Brianna.

He caught up with her as she was carefully breaking smaller branches off the large, fallen branch. He came up behind her and waited, thinking she would have her say. Instead he faced silence as she continued her task, completely ignoring him.

Several snapping branches tested his patience until finally he said, "You are upset."

She turned then, her eyes blazing. "I will not be ordered about by you, Blair, or my brother. And I will not stand by and watch as a lifelong friend and the man I intend to wed act ridiculously."

He tried to temper her anger, but she did not give him the chance.

"I cannot understand how it seems that you two took an instant dislike to each other. Unless I am wrong—tell me I am wrong."

He tried, but she rushed on.

"You both wish me safely returned home, and yet you both are at odds over how to accomplish the same task. It makes little sense, yet I tried to remember that you are both men and men often make little sense."

"Brianna," he said quickly, but she was set on speaking her mind.

"Blair is a good man and my brother's closest friend. If he sees how much we care for each other and how kind and caring you are to me, he will speak well of you to my brother."

Her words reared his temper. "I need no one to speak for me."

"Well, you certainly do not seem to make friends easily. You looked all but ready to attack Blair and his men."

His stance had been guarded but for a reason, a reason he could not explain to her. "Your safety is my concern. I knew nothing of Blair or his men."

"You learned quick enough and still you were on guard."

"As was he," Royce reminded.

She dropped the branches she held, and her hands went to her hips. "Then tell me why. Why did you two treat each other as opponents?"

"Men are territorial. They protect their own."

Her eyes rounded. "You cannot be serious."

"Most serious." His voice was firm and his stance rigid. "What is mine no one harms. And you are mine."

Her hands slipped off her hips and her eyes softened. She walked up to him and placed her hand to his cheek.

He slipped his arms around her waist. "I am glad you understand what I say. You are not an object to me. I claim no ownership over you. It is my love for you that makes you *mine*."

"Then if it is your love for me that makes me yours, then my love for you makes you *mine*."

Her smile forced him to smile. "And are you territorial?"

She squeezed his cheek with her one hand. "No one *touches* what is mine."

He leaned down and swept his lips across hers. "I want no one touching me but you."

"I like touching you," she whispered near his ear and faintly brushed her lips over his scarred cheek.

Their kiss lingered in gentleness, both enjoying the taste of each other and both not wanting it to end. When it finally did with great reluctance on both their parts, Brianna rested her head on his shoulder.

"If you do not get along with Blair, I fear you will not find my brother a friend. Then I worry that we will not be together."

"Worry not. Your brother and I will understand each other."

"Understanding and getting along is not the same," she said. She slipped her arms around his waist and hugged him to her. "I do not wish to lose you."

He hugged her in return. "You will not lose me. You are mine and will remain so. I will allow nothing to come between us."

A chill raced over her and the feeling did not bode well with her. "Promise?"

"I give you my word, Brianna, and I do not give my word lightly."

"I trust you and your word."

"Always trust me and never doubt my word, Brianna, for I shall always keep it no matter what happens."

"I sometimes wonder if my accident was not the hands of fate. Otherwise we would have never met."

"We were destined to meet and now we live our destiny."

BRIANNA SAT AT THE TABLE WORKING ON THE TWIG basket, her thoughts her own, when Blair entered the cottage. Royce had gone off to hunt for the evening meal and Blair's men were camped outside.

"Come in, sit and talk with me," she encouraged as he hesitated at the door.

He made his way cautiously to the table.

Her husband had taught her to hold her tongue, but once he was no longer around, she soon returned to speaking her mind. She did so now. "You are judging Royce without even knowing him."

"You barely know him yourself," Blair said calmly, and sat across from her.

"Nay, I know him better than others, and perhaps I know him better than he does himself."

Blair knew it was senseless arguing with a woman who thought herself in love. But Brianna had suffered a terrible hurt, and he did not wish to see her suffer again.

"Could it be that you are grateful to him for saving your life?"

Brianna took no offense to his suggestion. "I gave that thought much consideration, and while I am grateful for his rescue and care, I have found in him a gentle heart and soul that I could love."

Blair held his tongue and Brianna saw his reluctance to speak.

She reached out and placed her hand on his fisted one. "I do not understand your response to Royce. I realize that when first you came upon us, your instincts were to protect me. But once you discovered that Royce was kind to me and that we care for each other, I thought you would be happy for me. He is a warrior and will serve the clan Cameron well. What is wrong with that?"

"You do not know him." Blair could say no more, for it was not his place.

"I know him well enough, and I know that no one has treated me the way Royce has treated me. He is kind and caring and I think he grows weary of warring." A soft smile touched her lips. "I thought that Ian might consider letting him train the men or even farm, anything but fight."

Blair dug his fingers into his palms. "And if he wishes to fight?"

Brianna's fingers returned to fashioning the softened twigs into a basket. "Look at his scars. Do you think any sane man would want to fight after having faced such a horrendous battle?"

"Only a true warrior."

"Warriors can grow weary of war."

"Not the ones born to become legends," Blair said.

"Royce was not meant to be a legend, and besides his heart and soul are too tender."

Blair frowned. "He intends to ask Ian for permission to wed you?"

Brianna's fingers slowed. "He will ask me first, for it is my decision, and Ian will agree if he knows that I am happy."

Blair cleared his throat as though reluctant to speak his mind.

"I will save you your unease," Brianna said, looking directly at Blair, "since my brother will ask you the question you find difficult to ask me. I chose to be intimate with Royce because I love him."

"A man can be tempted if alone in a cottage with a woman."

"Do you try to tell me that Royce but needed a woman

to appease his basic needs and that he feels nothing for me?"

Blair heard the annoyance in her voice but knew it was better she faced these possibilities now, for what she was about to face would be much more challenging. "You have not thought this yourself?"

She smiled again. "You know me well, Blair."

"I know you have suffered dearly and that you do not wish to suffer again. Therefore—"

"I would be careful in what I choose," Brianna finished.

Blair remained silent out of necessity.

"I know you want the best for me, Blair. Royce is the best for me. I not only love him, I trust him, and after what Arran did to me, I had thought I would never trust again."

Blair bit back the warning that wanted to rush from his lips. "This is for your brother to decide."

"Nay," she said with a firm shake of her head. "This is for me to decide."

The door opened and Royce entered the cottage. The two men exchanged a heated look.

"Brianna and I were just discussing trust," Blair said.

Royce dropped his fur on the bed and walked over to the table. He rested his hand on Brianna's shoulder after giving her cheek a kiss.

"Do you trust, Royce?" Blair asked.

"None of what I hear and little of what I see."

Blair laughed, though it was forced. "A wise choice."

"More necessary than wise," Royce said and changed the subject. "I killed enough game to feed all. Your men are preparing it now. You are welcome to join Brianna and me for the evening meal."

"You must join us, Blair," Brianna said eagerly. "We

can entertain Royce with stories of how you and Ian would tease and torment me as a young child."

"If it is the truth he wants to hear, then I will be telling him how you followed us about and caused more disturbances than the both of us."

Royce smiled and leaned down beside Brianna, though he looked to Blair. "I would like to hear of her antics when young."

"Me?" she said, as if affronted by his remark, then smiled. "I was a perfect young lady."

"A perfect terror," Blair said with a hardy laugh.

"I want to hear it all," Royce said and received a poke in the ribs from Brianna.

"You will hear it all from me," Brianna insisted.

Blair would not be denied. "I will add my share of things."

Brianna was relieved that the tension between the two men dissipated. She had worried that they would fail to get along and that failure would weigh heavily with Ian.

It did not sit well with her that the two men were at odds upon meeting. She had not expected such a reaction, and now she worried over her brother's reaction to Royce.

After Ian had found out how poorly Arran had treated her, he had become extremely protective of her and encouraged her to seek her own strength. When she had informed him that she did not wish to ever marry again, he did not seem to mind. He did not even attempt to change her mind, nor did her sister-in-law.

What would he say now when she told him she wished to wed?

Would he honor her request or worry that she was making a foolish mistake yet again? And would he seek to protect her from herself?

Royce was confident of the outcome. Why could she not be as confident? What troubled her? Why did she think she would face difficulty? Perhaps she was conditioned to expect it as she had been in her marriage. It was as if she always waited for something to happen. Even though all appeared at peace, her husband would suddenly find fault with her and berate her until she felt little worth for herself.

She had to remember that Royce was nothing like Arran. He was truthful with her, and she need not worry about sudden surprises.

She turned and kissed his cheek and right in front of Blair said, "I love you."

He kissed her back. "As I do you."

She looked to Blair. "You will tell Ian how happy I am?"

Blair hesitated and then Brianna gave him that pleading look she had always given him as a child. The one that he always surrendered to and that always got him into trouble. He threw his hands up into the air.

"Whatever you want, Brianna."

She smiled, pleased at his response.

Royce shook his head. "Is that how she managed you to do her biding? With a simple look?"

Blair nodded. "A fact I am not proud of. So I advise you to be careful, my friend, or she will soon have you doing the same."

Royce grinned. "She already has."

16

⟡

THEY LEFT AT DAWN. BLAIR HAD ADVISED THAT THE journey would take but a day. She had not realized she had been that close to home. When she had left on her journey, her mind had been too occupied with the news of her husband's death to give attention to how far they had traveled. She had not thought herself that close to home, but all the while she was but a day's journey away.

She rode with Royce comfortably settled in front of him and cuddled close to his warmth. The day was cloudy, the air crisp, and the silence heavy around them.

"The men are quiet," she said, wondering over their silence. While there was rarely constant conversation on a journey, a word here or there was often heard along with laughter. But today there was nothing, only the stillness of the surrounding land and the sounds of the winter woods. And she noticed that the men's eyes strayed often to Royce.

"They pay attention to their surroundings, as they should," Royce said, sounding like a leader of men.

"But they have not spoken a word since we left early this morning. That seems unusual to me."

"They do their duty," Royce insisted.

"My brother's men are well trained to observe and to fight when necessary. They are good men, but it troubles me that they stare at you so blatantly. They know the horrors of battle. They know that they could suffer as you have, so why then do they so rudely keep their eyes on you?"

He offered a reason that she would find acceptable. "They care for you and do not know me. They wish to make certain that nothing happens to you."

His response did not appease her. "That is no excuse for rudeness. They see me happy with you. They see you treat me with respect. Your scars tell them you fought bravely and victoriously. What else need they know?"

"How do you know I fought victoriously?"

She shrugged. "You would have it no other way."

He laughed and all around him turned their heads to look. "You have come to know me well."

She rested her head on his shoulder. "Aye, that I have and I like what I have found."

"What have you found?" He hugged her close to him, the scent of her filling his nostrils. She smelled of the sweet-scented herbs she worked with and the earthy smell of the twigs that she fashioned into baskets.

Her response was quick. "A man I can trust and love."

"You can always trust me, Brianna, you must remember that. Promise me that you will."

He seemed anxious that she agree and his body tensed. She wished for him not to worry and offered him assurance. "Do not concern yourself, for my trust in you is unconditional."

He kissed her forehead. "Good. This pleases me, but I must admit that part of me is upset."

"Why?" She raised her head off his shoulder, concerned that he was feeling troubled.

He sighed, shook his head, and admitted, "I thought it was my looks that won your heart."

She smiled and poked him in the chest. "Your looks captured my immediate attention."

He ran a tender finger down her cheek. "I had not meant to frighten you."

She tugged at his braid. "I frightened myself, and besides, I have told you I care not for looks."

She focused on his face for the first time in days and noticed that his wounds were healing nicely. She could also see that beyond his scars there appeared good-looking features, and the thought that he might be more handsome than she had considered made her tense.

"What is wrong?" he was quick to ask when her body grew taut against him.

She would not admit her fears; she could not, for she would sound foolish. Why would any woman turn down a handsome man? She had a hundred reasons and yet not many that would sound sane to others; therefore, she would keep her thoughts to herself.

"Tell me," he said firmly.

"Nothing is wrong." She returned her head to rest on his shoulder, thinking it would bring his questioning to a close.

He would not be denied. "You tell me you trust me, and then you will not tell me what troubles you when obviously something does." He gave her waist a gentle squeeze. "This is trusting me?"

He was right, but she remained reluctant. "My thought was silly and unimportant."

"Your thoughts are important to me. Tell me."

She raised her head and smiled. "You are relentless."

He grinned. "Determined."

She hesitated.

"Would you not tell me the same? Would you not wish to know what troubled me so that you could help ease my concern? Is that not what two people in love do for each other?"

She placed a hand to his chest. "You continue to teach me much about love that I did not know."

"You knew," he insisted. "You were denied what you deserved, but no more. You will have all you deserve, for I will make certain of it."

"You are good to me." She sounded as though she could not believe her own words.

"And you are good to me. Another trait of two people in love."

She whispered as if revealing a secret. "We must be very much in love, then."

He leaned down closer to her face. "Very much."

She giggled with delight when he brushed several kisses across her face.

"Now tell me what troubled you."

"I thought you had forgotten."

He playfully poked her in the side. "Trying to divert my attention, were you?"

She grabbed for his playful hand and took a firm hold of it. "I thought I had been successful."

"I do not wish to see you troubled and will do anything in my power to prevent it or help you through it." He eased his hand from her grasp and laced his fingers with hers.

She held on to him and he to her. "I am so very glad the heavens sent you to me."

"Fate works in strange ways. To question it would be

foolish; to accept it would be wise. I accept us without question."

"You forever say things to me that make me realize how truly blessed I am that you love me."

"Remember that." His words were firm.

"You say that often to me, but how can I forget it?"

"Just remember—promise me you will remember how deeply I love you."

She gripped his hand as tightly as her meager strength would allow. "I have told you I would and I give you my word that I will."

"Good." He seemed satisfied. "Now again, what troubled you?"

"It is no longer of importance."

"It is to me. Tell me."

To argue the issue was futile, so she surrendered. "Looking upon you I realized that beneath your scars that heal lies a handsome man."

"The one scar is deep and will remain with me forever. I will never be handsome again."

Brianna suddenly felt selfish. She had not given thought to how his facial scars would make him feel. He would never look as he once did; he was changed forever and yet he was whom he had always been. A good and kind man.

"But then you care not for handsome men, so perhaps I should be grateful for my scars."

"Nay." She was quick to argue, her hand going to cup his face. "I am foolish. I think because I had a handsome husband who was deceitful that all handsome men deceive. You have taught me different, I must remember it."

Royce kissed the palm of her hand. "I do not deceive nor will I ever deceive you. You have my word on that."

She smiled. "Then I have no worries."

"Good, then we can concentrate on planning a wedding."

"You have yet to ask my permission."

He laughed and the men once again cautiously glanced his way.

"It is your brother's permission I must seek."

She placed her hand in her lap and, sounding like a petulant child, said, "He will ask me if I wish to wed you."

"What will you tell him?" He kept a smile on his face, for he enjoyed teasing her.

"That you have yet to ask me."

"He will allow you this decision?"

"I will not wed unless *I wish* to wed," she said adamantly.

His hand was quick to grab her chin and gently squeeze her cheeks so that she looked to make funny faces at him. "Do you wish to wed me?"

"Is that how you intend to ask me?"

He ran gentle fingers over her lips and down her neck. "Nay, it is not, and besides, I already know your answer."

"So then you think it unnecessary to ask me?"

His hand trailed down to her breast, which he gave a slow squeeze, and he tenderly pinched her nipple, which instantly hardened between his fingers.

She was grateful that her fur wrap kept his intimate touch private, and she lingered in the exquisite pleasure of the moment.

He whispered near her ear. "Wed me, Brianna, for life would not be worth living without you."

She felt tears well in her eyes. She had not thought to hear those words ever, and she most definitely did not expect to hear them spoken with such love. Tears slipped down her cheeks as she answered, "Aye, I will wed you,

Royce, for I cannot bear to think of a day spent without you."

He kissed her tears away and then kissed her with a hungry gentleness. "We will wed immediately."

She nodded enthusiastically, knowing full well that they would not be sharing a bed until vows were exchanged. "Immediately."

They took their time, knowing by day's end they would reach her home. The weather remained cloudy and Brianna was grateful it did not rain. She was already beginning to feel the effects of riding for several hours. Her lower back began to pain her. It was the one lingering result of the accident.

She did not wish to complain; she was as eager as the men to return home. She missed her brother, sister-in-law, her friend Anne, and her nephew Duncan, and she was eager for them all to meet Royce. It would be a good reunion.

First, however, she would need to recover from the pain she would certainly suffer if she continued on in this fashion. She attempted to adjust her bottom in front of Royce without making it too obvious that she was uncomfortable.

It did not work.

"Something pains you?"

She was truthful. "Aye, my back."

She need say no more; none could ignore his demanding voice. "We stop now!"

To her surprise, Blair and the men did as he commanded, though Blair approached them as Royce helped her to dismount.

"Brianna needs to rest," Royce said before Blair could speak. "Her back has yet to fully heal from the accident."

She intended to inform them both that a short rest would be sufficient, but when she took all her weight herself, Royce having let go of her waist, the pain shot through her lower back and she almost collapsed.

Blair slid off his horse, but Royce already had his arms around her.

Blair appeared concerned. "I had not realized she was not sufficiently recovered."

"I am fine," Brianna insisted, keeping her hand firmly on Royce's arm.

"You are having difficulty standing on your own—that is not fine," Blair all but snapped at her. "You should have told me. We could have waited at least a few days." He turned to Royce. "My apologies for not listening to you. I should have remembered how stubborn she is."

"I am not stubborn," she insisted emphatically.

"She is determined," Royce said with a smile.

Blair had to laugh. "You know her well. Then you know that she will tell you when she has rested enough for the journey to continue."

"That decision will be mine," Royce informed him in a tone that advised he would not have it any other way.

Blair laughed again and walked away.

"I can decide for myself," Brianna said, the pain beginning to ease and feeling a bit of her hard-won freedom vanish before her eyes.

"I have no doubt that you can. Do you wish to sit?"

"Nay," she said with a shake of her head. "The hard ground will only serve to aggravate the pain. I wish to walk some."

"It will not pain you to do so?"

She was honest. "At first, but the walking will eventually ease it."

He supported much of her weight as they walked slowly along the worn path the horses traveled.

"If you have no doubt that I can decide for myself, why, then, would you decide for me?"

"Because I wish to protect you."

"From whom?"

He eased his hold on her as her steps became stronger. "Yourself."

She stopped and glared at him, ready to battle, when suddenly she changed her mind. "You truly cannot bear to see me suffer, can you?"

"I would suffer all your pain if I could."

She stepped forward to slip her arms around his waist and lay her head to his chest. "I am so blessed to have you love me."

His arms circled her, making certain most of her weight rested against him. "You may not feel that way in a few years. You may grow tired of me."

"Never," she said with conviction. "I will take joy in you waking by my side each morning and great pleasure in falling asleep in your arms every night."

"I will remind you of these words one day."

"You will not need to. I will cherish our time together and look forward to every moment I spend with you."

He lifted her chin with a gentle finger so that their eyes could meet. "It is I who am blessed to have you."

She smiled. "We will do well together. I am sure of it."

"Aye, we will, for I am sure as well."

They kissed, lingering for several moments, then walked down the path and off into the woods, where they kissed and touched and wished they were back at the cottage. After Royce was certain that she was feeling better, they returned to the horses.

Blair suggested that they could camp for the night if Brianna did not feel up to continuing the journey.

Brianna insisted that she wished to arrive home this evening, that she was anxious to see her family and have them meet Royce.

Blair nodded, looked to Royce, and ordered his men to mount their horses.

Several hours later, as dusk covered the land, they arrived at the clan Cameron keep.

As the horses approached the village surrounding the keep, Royce whispered in her ear, "Remember."

17

THE VILLAGERS CALLED OUT GREETINGS AS THE MEN
entered, but they grew silent when their eyes fell on
Royce. He was a stranger scarred by battle and owed respect. She had thought they would understand and be
more accepting of him. They were not. Their stares were
blatant and their whispers hushed. She felt a sad disappointment for him and herself.

Her brother would be different, Brianna was certain of
that. He would greet Royce with the respect due a battle-
scarred warrior.

The keep was of impressive size, though not overly
large. It was well crafted and situated wisely for battle and
protection. It loomed dark in the gathering gloom of
night, though two huge torches mounted on either side of
the large wooden doors lit the entrance.

Blair had ordered the men to return to their families
before they reached the keep. Brianna was grateful, for

then she would have the privacy of reuniting with her family and introducing Royce without anyone about. There would be time for all to learn of her impending marriage soon enough.

Royce helped her to dismount and assisted her up the few stone steps, Blair at her other side. The two men exchanged knowing glances before entering, but Brianna was too excited to notice.

"Ian!" she shouted upon entering the great hall and seeing her brother standing near the dais. She ran right into his arms.

He was a handsome man of formidable size and possessed a charm that empowered him. His reddish brown hair fell past his shoulders and his eyes were sometimes blue and sometimes green depending on his emotions. He stood several inches over six feet and was a skillful warrior and leader, and Brianna was proud of him.

He hugged her fiercely to him. "Thank the good Lord, I thought you were dead."

She hugged him back, tears glistening in her eyes. There was only the two of them, their mother and father having passed on.

"I am too stubborn," she announced, kissing his cheek.

"Determined," a familiar voice corrected.

Brianna turned to see her sister-in-law, Moira, entering the great hall with her six-month-old son, Duncan, in her arms. Her friend Anne came up from behind her, hurrying past Moira to hug Brianna.

Anne was barely a few inches over five feet with beautiful blond hair, a pretty face, and an independent nature. She was also Blair's wife.

"It is good to see you safe," Anne said after the hug. "And good that my husband was successful in finding you."

Anne walked toward her husband. He in turn hurried to

her side to greet her with a hug that swept her off her feet. "I said that I would find her and I did. Now I deserve that reward you promised me."

Anne playfully swatted at him and turned bright red. "You are no gentleman."

Moira handed her son to his father and threw her arms around Brianna. "I have prayed for your safe return."

Brianna welcomed her embrace. Moira was five years older than her brother's twenty and five years, and plain in features, though her wide intelligent eyes produced a different kind of beauty that many found appealing, especially her brother Ian.

He loved her with all his heart, as she did him. They made a good pair, and Brianna had envied them their love. Now, however, she had found her very own.

She turned to give her nephew a quick hug and kiss, promising him that she would spend time with him later, and then hurried over to Royce, grabbing his hand and pulling him toward Ian, though he went willingly.

Brianna could not hide her excitement. "Ian, I want you to meet someone special."

Sudden silence descended over the great hall. Even the few servants who mulled about froze where they stood and stared with wide eyes at Royce.

Brianna grew alarmed when Ian's eyes fired with heat and he sent a quick glance to Blair. Blair in turn gently urged his wife aside and moved to stand beside Ian. Anne hastily joined Moira, and they quietly moved away from the men.

Blair spoke. "He saved your sister's life."

Brianna did not understand. No introductions had been made and yet Ian seemed to know Royce.

"I am grateful," Ian said with a guarded stance.

Royce barely nodded in return.

Brianna felt the need to explain. "Royce took exceptional care of me."

Ian kept his eyes on Royce. "Again I am grateful."

Brianna was beginning to grow annoyed and she spoke bluntly. "I was severely injured and could do nothing for myself. Royce saw to my every need."

Ian spoke calmly, though it was obvious he measured his words carefully. "I am indebted to you."

Royce finally spoke and shocked all. "Then I request permission to wed your sister."

Brianna's eyes widened in surprise, though it took only a moment for her to smile, slip her arm through his, and look to her brother. "I love him. I do not know how it happened nor do I care. He is a good man with a tender heart and soul, and I wish to be his wife."

Royce smiled, kissed her cheek, and focused on Ian. "What say you?"

Ian stepped forward. "I want my sister to be happy."

Brianna smiled, relieved that things finally looked as if they would work out all right.

"As do I," Royce said and waited. He knew what would follow, and he placed his hand over Brianna's, where it rested on his arm.

Ian kept his eyes on Royce when he asked, "Brianna, do you know who this man is?"

Brianna spoke with pride. "He is a warrior. I thought he would serve the clan Cameron well."

Blair moved up behind Ian, and Brianna noticed that several of her brother's fiercest men had entered the great hall and were lined up along the sides.

"He serves his own clan well," Ian said.

"You know Royce? He is not a stranger to you?" she asked, puzzled.

"I had the opportunity to see him fight."

"He is a skilled warrior." Once again she spoke with pride.

Ian turned his attention to his sister. "He is a legendary warrior."

Her puzzlement grew. "Legendary?"

"His reputation precedes him."

A sense of foreboding swept over her, and she attempted to ease her arm off his. Royce held firmly to her hand.

"What is this my brother speaks of?" She could not keep the tremble out of her voice. "Who are you?"

Royce found it difficult to tell her. He knew her well and knew her reaction would not be to his liking. He simply said, "Remember."

Brianna looked to her brother for an answer since she realized that she was the only one present who did not know Royce was a legend.

"He is chieftain of the clan Campbell. He is the infamous Royce Campbell."

Brianna's legs grew weak and her heart fluttered until she thought she would pass out, but she let no one know of her reaction. She stood straight and proud and spoke calmly, turning her attention to Royce.

"I have heard many stories of your exploits. You are known as a fearless leader who leads a fearsome clan. It is said you know no fear and yet men fear your presence, and women—women want nothing more than to please the mighty warrior. I have heard told that you have no tenderness or compassion in your heart. And it is whispered that you were born without a soul."

A tear threatened to spill and she fought with all the courage she possessed to hold it back. She would show no weakness. "You were not truthful with me."

"I told you no lies," Royce said, making certain all heard him. "You asked few questions of me."

"I thought—" She paused, thinking how foolish she had been yet again and shook her head slowly. "I thought the time would come when you would confide in me. I did not wish to intrude on what I thought were painful memories."

She looked to Ian. "I am forever foolish."

She moved to step away from Royce, but he kept a firm hand on her. "You know *me*."

"I thought I did." Sadness welled up inside her, and she could not stop the tear from falling.

Royce wiped it away with a gentle finger. "I love you, Brianna."

"You kept the truth from me. How can I ever trust what you tell me is true?"

He wiped at the tears that followed. "Remember—that is all I ask of you. Please remember."

"At this moment I cannot. I am confused and hurt and can think of nothing else. I thought you a gentle man who cared." She shook her head. "Your reputation speaks otherwise."

At that moment his heart ached more for her than it did for himself. He had not wanted to hurt her, and he had thought it best she did not know his identity. He had not wished to frighten her any further than she was already frightened when he first found her. He was well aware of his reputation. He had forged it with his own blood and sweat and created a mighty clan whom all feared. He fought for kings and peasants alike, and he had fought victoriously and with honor. And many times he had fought with a cold heart—and, he often thought, an empty soul.

Those reasons had driven him to seek solitude after the last battle. He had not intended to completely keep his identity from her, but she had seemed so vulnerable, and when she began to speak of her past and her husband, he felt it was best that she did not know the darker side of him. So he had purposely remained silent.

While the legendary warrior Royce Campbell knew no fear in battle, he now feared losing the woman he loved, and battle was the only way in which he remained victorious, so he spoke as a man who commanded.

"Once we wed you will come—"

She stopped him, yanking her hand forcefully from his grasp and stepping away from him. "Wed? I can never wed you."

"I understand you are upset—"

She stopped him again. "Upset? Nay, you understand nothing. But understand this—I will not wed you." She looked to her brother. "I do not wish to wed him."

Ian walked over to her and placed a comforting arm around her waist. "It is your choice."

"It is not her choice," Royce said with a strength in his voice that caused many in the hall to shiver.

Ian stepped in front of his sister, and Blair moved in beside him.

Royce showed not an ounce of fear, though he stood alone in the hall. "My clan has no quarrel with you."

He was letting Ian know that if they harmed him in any way, his clan would retaliate with force.

Ian would not be intimidated. "Nor do I want one."

"Then hear me out."

Ian nodded, always more ready to talk through problems than raise a weapon to settle them.

"I love your sister and will see to her care and protection. She is upset now, but in time—"

Brianna stopped him. "Nay, in time I will not change my mind. I will not wed you and that is final. I ask that my brother give you the same courtesy that you did me. Food and shelter until you return to your clan."

"My clan is aware that I am here and will join me

shortly, but I will not take my leave until you agree to wed me."

Ian spoke before his sister could. "How does your clan know your whereabouts?"

"They knew where I sought solitude and kept a watchful eye over me. As soon as your men arrived, my men gathered and followed. They are not far from this keep at this moment, and if I do not speak with them before it grows late, they will attack."

"I saw no one following us," Blair said, annoyed that he and his men might not have been as alert as they should have been.

"I command a well-trained and highly skilled group of men. You would not see them if they did not want to be seen."

"I have heard of their skills," Ian said, impressed. "I do not doubt your word, and you are welcome to contact your men whenever you wish. As I have told you, I have no quarrel with you."

"And I have no quarrel with you." Royce paused, then raised his voice for all to hear. "But I will wed your sister."

"The decision is hers," Ian said. "I will not force her to wed."

"Even if she is with child?" Royce asked, looking to Brianna.

Brianna did not wish to announce to the entire hall that she was unable to conceive a child. Her failure as a woman concerned no one but her.

Her brother sensed her unease. "We will discuss this in private."

Moira handed her son to Anne and walked over to Brianna. She slipped her arm around her shoulder. "We will continue this in the solar."

Brianna was grateful for Moira's support. She had

wondered if her shaking legs would carry her or if she would collapse like a foolish woman. She grasped hold of Moira's offered hand as they walked.

"All will be fine," Moira assured her. "Ian will see to it."

"I will not marry him," she insisted, wondering who she was attempting to convince—Moira or herself.

"It will be as you wish."

Brianna nodded, agreeing with her sister-in-law. It would be her decision and hers alone. There was no worry that there would be a child. She could not give Royce one, not ever. Why did that thought make her feel so sad? He was not what she thought him to be.

Remember.

She felt too numb to remember anything. At the moment she felt only the hurt and pain of being deceived and being so very foolish.

Ian followed Royce into the room after Brianna and Moira had entered. Moira directed her to a chair by the hearth, but Brianna preferred to remain standing. She felt more in control, more determined.

"You should sit or your back will begin to pain you," Royce said with concern.

Ian and Moira exchanged glances, both aware that Royce was sincere in his concern for Brianna.

"Your back troubles you?" Moira asked.

"It is fine," Brianna said, though Royce had been right—the pain in her back had grown worse since dismounting the horse and standing as long as she had. She should seek her bed, but she had no thought to do that, for she would surely spend all her time there crying.

"She is being stubborn," Royce said with an annoyed wave of his hand. "Her back troubled her on the journey here. We stopped once for her to rest, but she needs rest now. She should not be standing; bed is where she should be."

"Brianna," Ian said firmly, "do not be stubborn. We can discuss this matter tomorrow."

"This matter will be settled now," she demanded. "And in little time, for *I will not wed him.*"

"And if there is a child?" Royce asked, walking up to her.

Brianna did not back away from him, but raised her chin. "There is no child and you know it."

"You are so certain that you cannot conceive a child?"

"Aye, I am."

Ian and Moira let the two argue, taking each other's hand as they listened with interest to the battle of wills.

"Then you should have no objection to agreeing to wed me if you are with child," Royce said, his challenge issued.

Brianna did not hesitate; there was no reason. This was one battle he would lose. She suddenly wondered if he did wish to lose it. He knew that she could give him no children; perhaps this was his way of being rid of her. The thought brought a heavy weight to her heart, but she kept her chin high. "I will wed you if I am with child."

"You give me your word on it?" Royce asked.

"Aye, you have my word and—"

Royce did not allow her to finish. He turned to Ian. "You have heard her give me her word. You will honor this arrangement?"

"I will not object to it," Ian said. "My sister has made her choice."

Tears threatened Brianna's eyes, and she wanted desperately to run from the room and never set eyes on Royce again, but her pride would not allow her to leave. She would stand firm and be courageous even though her heart was breaking.

Royce turned back to Brianna and leaned in close to her, his words meant only for her ears. "I never lose."

18

Royce stood in silence, facing Ian. Brianna and Moira had taken their leave, Moira finally having insisted that Brianna should rest, and he could not have agreed more, though he kept his opinion silent. He worried that Brianna was being stubborn and ignoring the ache that he knew she suffered, for it had plagued her much on the journey.

He had spent much time considering the consequences of his decision not to inform her of his identity. At first the decision had been a practical one, since she had reacted with fright to his appearance. There had been no point in adding to her fear, so he had kept his infamous identity from her. After fate had seemed to step in, he found himself unwilling to admit to his legendary exploits. He had wanted her to come to know him, not the legend. He wanted her to know that he had a heart and soul that ached to be loved as much as he wanted to love someone. He had found all his heart's desires in her, and he had not wanted to lose them.

That had made the choice easy for him, though he understood there would be consequences to his decision. He now faced those consequences and would deal with them as a warrior who had just begun the fiercest and most necessary battle of his life.

"A drink?" Ian offered, the silence having grown too heavy in the confined room.

"Aye, a drink I could use right now," Royce admitted, his voice filled with the confident arrogance of a warrior who demonstrated no fear.

Ian was a victorious warrior in his own right but often preferred to war with words. He walked to the narrow table, poured them each an ale, and returned to where Royce stood near the hearth. "It is only the two of us now," he said, handing him a full tankard. "Say what you will."

Royce grinned. "You remind me much of your sister. Brave even when faced with difficult odds."

"I am not foolish enough to think that my clan can match your clan's strength, but know I am not foolish in regard to my sister."

"I counted on that," Royce said, raising his tankard as if in a toast before taking a hefty swallow.

"Sit," Ian offered as he took one of the chairs near the hearth.

Royce understood it was time for them to talk, and this was what he had waited for. He knew her brother by reputation and knew that he was a sensible man. He would understand when he explained to him how it was best that Brianna and he wed, child or not. He intended to take his time so that there would be no doubt in Ian's mind that he agreed it was best for them to wed.

He took another swallow of ale, saw that Ian waited

patiently for him to speak, and understood the importance of how he relayed his intentions. He would be practical and firm and, above all, sensible about this whole matter.

He took another gulp of ale, then said, "I love your sister and cannot live without her."

Ian smiled and nodded. "This is what I have waited to hear."

Royce leaned back in the chair and sighed like a man relieved of a heavy burden. "I do not know how it happened. I cannot even tell you when it happened, it just did. One day I realized that I loved her beyond reason. It made no sense to me and at times still does not. I only know that it is real, and I thrill at the thought of our love. I miss her right this very moment. We have spent every hour of every day together for the last several weeks, and I do not like when she is not by my side. I ache for her presence." He shook his head, feeling completely confused by it all.

Ian laughed, a good hardy laugh. "I know exactly what you are feeling, for I experienced the same myself. It was like a punch to the body, but never physically feeling the punch, only being affected by it."

"Aye, that is it." Royce rubbed his jaw. "I prefer the punch."

Ian laughed again. "I agree. It is easier to deal with and the pain fades. The emotion that follows this undetectable punch is devastating to the senses. You sometimes feel a fool."

"Or behave foolishly."

Ian nodded in agreement and his face softened in a smile. "But then there are those moments together that linger in your memory and heart and you thank the Lord every day for all the foolishness."

Royce nodded with him. "I feel that Brianna is a cherished gift sent from the heavens, and I swear I will do everything in my power to see her happy and content."

"This I also wished to hear."

"I have no quarrel with you or your clan and have no intentions of warring with you regardless of your decision, and yet I thought to war with you if you did not grant me permission to wed your sister. A foolish thought." Royce shook his head at his own foolishness.

"An understandable thought of a man in love," Ian said.

"Madly in love, insanely in love, ridiculously in love, and loving every moment of it."

Ian stood, patted his shoulder, and took his empty tankard from him to refill along with his own. "I noticed that my sister feels the same for you."

"I know she loves me as much as I love her. She is being stubborn." He folded his arms across his massive chest.

"*Determined,* we say around here," Ian said, returning to his seat and handing the full tankard to Royce.

"Your wife's doing, from what I hear."

Ian smiled. "You will find Moira's hand in many things around here, and I warn you she is extremely intelligent, so be careful in your dealings with her."

He cringed. "Must I deal with her? I deal much better with men."

"She is protective of Brianna. She was a great help to her in her time of need."

"Brianna spoke of her husband."

Ian looked surprised. "She confided in you about Arran?"

"We talked much during our confinement, and I must say that I hope he suffered in death for his sins."

"I was told that his body was burned beyond recognition. They identified him from the ring that he wore."

"How can you be certain it was he who burned?" Royce asked.

"I sent men to view the remains. It was one of them who discovered the ring amongst the charred flesh and pocketed it as proof. The man fit Arran's height and size, and the cloth he wore was of the Cameron clan. I saw no reason to doubt the body his."

"Brianna knows nothing of this?"

"Nay, she did not ask and I saw no reason to tell her. I think she was relieved that her ordeal had finally come to an end and she was free to travel about without several men to protect her."

"I will protect her now." Royce was insistent.

Ian was just as insistent. "She is my sister and my responsibility until she weds you, then she is yours to protect."

Royce smiled. "I have permission to wed her regardless of whether she carries my child or not?"

"I had not known that she thought herself barren," Ian said with concern.

"She is not."

"You are so sure?"

Royce nodded. "A spineless coward has not the balls to father a child."

Ian roared with laughter. "So you think, then, I will be an uncle soon?"

"Aye, you will, and I a father," Royce said with pride.

"And if not?"

"I will find another way to convince your sister to wed me."

"I will not force her to wed you," Ian said.

"I understand and respect you for that, but I know. How do I know?" He shrugged. "I do not understand, I only know that Brianna will bear me children."

"Then we will soon celebrate a wedding," Ian said and raised his tankard in a toast.

Royce raised his. "I am grateful to you and I promise

you this. I will protect Brianna with my life and not even death will keep me from seeing her safe, I love her that much."

"This pleases me to hear and it pleases me to call you brother," Ian said and extended his hand to him.

Royce gave his hand a hardy shake. "I must take my leave in a few days and see to clan matters. I will leave some of my men behind—" Royce raised his hand to stop Ian from interrupting. "I leave the men as a show of strength that our clans will soon unite."

Ian nodded in acceptance.

Royce continued. "It should be time enough upon my return to know if Brianna is with child. But I advise that you plan a wedding regardless of her objections."

"We shall have a large celebration."

"I will return with many men to help in the celebration."

"They are welcome," Ian said.

"All will go well," Royce said confidently.

"Aye, it will," Ian agreed.

Royce grew quiet and silence filled the room.

"You miss my sister."

Royce sighed. "Like a lovesick lad."

Ian leaned close to him and whispered, "I will tell you where her bedchamber is."

Royce grinned and listened.

BRIANNA STOOD BY THE HEARTH IN HER BEDCHAM-ber. The roaring fire cast a much-needed heat over her chilled body. She wore her white linen night shift and was barefoot. She had been snug beneath the wool blankets on her bed but found that she could not get warm. Finally in a need to chase her chill, she climbed out of bed and came to stand in front of the fire's warmth.

She could not stop thinking of Royce. He had sounded so confident that she carried his child. She placed a hand to her flat stomach. She would have loved to have given him a child—many children, if it was possible. But it was not and he knew that. Why, then, did he persist in this ridiculous pursuit? Nothing would come of it except that he would be free of her.

Did he want to be free of her?

Was there no truth to his words to her?

Had he ever really loved her?

And why with all these endless questions did she still love him?

She shook her head. Love made fools of people. Or was it the need to love and be loved that made people foolish? She had actually believed that Royce truly loved her. He had been kind and caring.

But then, what else could he have been to her? She had been injured and needed care. But it was a kind and caring soul that tended the injured. He could have left her to her own fate, not given a thought to her well-being. But he had not; he had carried her back to his cottage and had tenderly cared for her in every way.

She shook her head again. None of this made sense, and the more she attempted to make sense of it, the more confused she became.

Remember.

That word echoed in her head and forced her to remember how gentle and loving he had been with her. Could all of that have been lies?

A heavy sigh escaped her. She did not want to think that he did not truly love her. She wanted him to love her as much as she loved him. They had been so happy together alone in the cottage. But then, she had not known the truth about him.

Would it have made a difference?

And had she not learned about him during that time?

Had she not come to truly know him and not the legend? If she had known him to be the legendary warrior Royce Campbell, how, then, would she have reacted to him?

She grew tired of the confusion and the endless questions, and she hurt desperately from the thought that she would never feel his arms around her again. She had found a comfort and safety in his arms that she had never felt before, and she longed for his arms at this moment.

"You should be in bed," Royce whispered from behind her before his arms circled her waist.

"You should not be here." She tried to sound annoyed that he intruded on her privacy, but she was not. She was glad for his presence.

"Aye, you are right," he agreed with a slow and lazy kiss to her neck. "You should be with me in my bed."

She silently reprimanded herself for smiling at his suggestion.

"You do not deny that you want to be there as much as I want you there?"

Her body was beginning to respond to his kisses, and if she were not careful, she would surrender without a thought or a care. "I cannot deny the truth, can you?"

His lips traveled up her neck to rest near her ear. "I cannot and I have spoken it to you."

She feared the answer she might hear but asked her question. "Have you always spoken the truth to me?"

He was quick to respond. "I have not lied to you, Brianna. I love you, and as crazy as I may sound, I feel as if I grow to love you more each day. Believe me, Brianna, please."

She wanted to believe him. The aching plea in his voice told her to believe him, and her body trembled with the need for her to believe him.

He felt her slight tremble and tightened his hold on her waist, forcing her body to relax against his. "Does your back pain you?"

She was honest in her answer. "A little."

"You should be in bed."

"I could not sleep and I grew cold beneath the covers."

"Because I was not there to warm you." He nibbled at her ear.

She tried to ignore the rush of heat that raced over her, but it felt entirely too good to disregard. "You did keep me warm."

"Let me keep you warm again."

She attempted to be annoyed with him. "You have no right to be here."

"I have every right. You are mine."

"I belong to no one," she argued.

"Nay, we belong to each other, and that you cannot deny, for you know it in your heart—and soul."

It was difficult to fight the truth, and that was what she wanted from him—the truth. "Why did you not tell me?"

"It would have served no purpose. You would have been frightened of me."

"I was frightened of you when I first laid eyes on you."

He kissed her cheek. "You were frightened of my scarred face and learned soon enough you need not fear the man. I am that man."

She shook her head, disagreeing. "I know not who you are."

"Aye, you do know who I am, but you stubbornly wish to ignore it."

"You are not who I thought."

"I am who you thought me to be—only there is more to me."

"More that makes me question," she said softly. "You seek battle more than you seek peace."

"Not by choice."

"I thought you a warrior who could finally find peace with me and that we could live a simple life." She sounded as if her dreams had been destroyed.

"I have found peace with you."

"How long will that peace last before you go off to fight and conquer?"

"As long as I have you, that peace will always be in my heart."

She winced at the sharp pain that stabbed at her back and allowed all her weight to fall against him.

He asked no permission and gave his action no thought—he simply scooped her up into his strong arms and carried her to bed. He gently placed her down and tucked the covers around her.

She thought he would take his leave but instead he hastily disrobed, and she was about to object when she stopped herself. She did not want him to leave. She wanted his warm body next to hers, though she did not seek to make love with him. She simply wanted him there beside her.

He slipped beneath the blankets and moved up against her. "This night shift is not necessary. I will keep you warm." He had it off her in seconds and had her against him, the heat of his body seeping into her cool flesh and toasting her body to a gentle and satisfying warmth.

She closed her eyes and thought of them alone in the cottage and so very much in love. There was just the two of them. The outside world did not exist.

Royce held her close and stroked her back, her head resting on his chest.

"Rest," he whispered.

Her eyes fluttered closed.

He whispered once more as she drifted to sleep, "Remember."

19

❧

BRIANNA FOUND HERSELF AT A LOSS THE NEXT DAY. She did not want to speak with anyone; she wanted nothing more than to be left alone. Everyone seemed to have an opinion about her situation. Moira and Anne had naturally taken her side, both women having an independent nature and having taught Brianna to reclaim her own.

Ian and Blair seemed sympathetic to Royce, since they both had dealt with the perils and joys of falling in love.

She had grown impatient as they offered their words of wisdom, and while she understood that they only wished to help, she wished for them all to leave her alone. She ached for the solitude of the cottage, and if she were able, she would ride off on her own to the simple small dwelling and reside there for as long as it took to settle her problem.

Finally having felt she could take no more, and desperately seeking solitude, she wrapped herself in her warm wool cloak, pulled up the hood, and took off for a much needed walk alone.

She was only a few feet from the keep when she noticed a man following her. He did not hide his intentions but kept firm and steady on her trail. He was large with bright red hair and a nose that had been broken more than once. He looked to be of a pleasant nature, nodding a greeting to those who dared look his way, his size being a little intimidating. There was no doubt that he was one of Royce's men, and the thought irritated her.

Brianna paused once or twice to see what he would do, and he stopped and waited patiently for her to continue walking. By the time she neared the outskirts of the village, she had had enough. She turned and confronted him.

"Why do you follow me?" she snapped, turning on him in such a flurry that the large man actually backed away from her.

"I mean you no harm," he said apologetically. "Royce ordered me to guard you well, and so I shall."

He had a gentle voice for one so large and Brianna felt guilty at the harsh way she addressed him. She softened her tone when she said, "I need no one to guard me."

"I must obey Royce." Again he sounded apologetic.

She attempted to keep her patience. "Tell him what I tell you. I need no guard."

"I cannot leave your side, for then I will disobey his orders."

Her patience was growing short. "You mean to follow me, then, wherever I go."

He was hesitant to answer. "Aye, that I do."

"I wish to be alone." She kept a tight rein on her temper; after all, he was not the one she was angry with.

"I will keep my distance and give you time to yourself."

"I want to be by myself, completely alone, no one about, just me, me, me!" Her voice rose with every word.

He seemed not to know what to do with her. He simply shrugged.

"Where is Royce?" she demanded.

He seemed relieved by her query and answered with haste. "He sees to the men."

"Take me to him," she ordered firmly.

He nodded once, again looking relieved.

She followed beside him as he led her to a large clearing not far outside the village. Men tended horses, others cooked over an open fire, while others polished their swords or tended to their bows and arrows. Royce stood in the middle of a band of men that maybe numbered twenty. They all paid heed to his words.

The man she followed stepped to the side as they approached the circle of men. She continued marching forward, the men moving out of her path.

She entered the circle and stopped. "I will have a word with you."

"When I am finished, we will talk," he said pleasantly, though his words were measured well.

"Nay, we will talk now."

Hushed whispers raced around the circle of men, and Royce cast a quick eye around. Silence fell instantly.

"When I am done." It was a demand he issued her, and she intended no part of it.

"Then hear me well now. I will have none of your men guard me. I wish to be alone and alone I shall be." She turned to go.

"You shall have a guard."

Her temper flared. "You cannot dictate to me."

"Aye, I can and I will. You are mine and what is mine I keep safe."

Her temper snapped. "You are not my husband and have no right."

"I will be your husband and have the right."

By now most of the camp had gathered nearby, and from the corner of her eye she caught her brother and Blair approaching. She was tired of being dictated to, she was tired of always having her brother come to her defense, and she would not have it any longer.

"Keep your men from me," she said with a controlled anger and turned and walked away.

"Brianna," Royce called out.

She would not pay heed to him; she continued walking.

"Brianna!" He grew louder.

Her brother and Blair remained on the side, watching, and she grew annoyed when she saw that they were smiling. She grew more annoyed when she heard heavy footsteps behind her and knew that Royce was fast approaching.

She decided she had had enough. She wanted solitude and she would have it. All she needed to do was reach the woods nearby. Once amongst the dense woods, she would lose him, for she had played there as a child and knew every inch of the forest.

She picked up her pace, testing her legs and finding that they were strong and even seemed eager for a run. She took off with a laugh and a sense of freedom that thrilled her.

Her hood dropped away from her head, her cloak flew out around her, and her dark hair burst free of the combs that confined the heavy strands. With the crisp winter air stinging her cheeks and feeling so very much alive, she was overwhelmed by the sensation that she was flying as free as a bird.

She heard Royce call out to her again, though his footsteps sounded at a distance, and she was pleased that she could run faster than him. She was not far from the edge of the woods, and soon the dense trees would conceal her and she would be free to do as she pleased.

The pain struck her suddenly, and she went down to the ground hard and fast, her head hitting the hard earth and dazing her so that she could do naught but lay helpless.

She heard the rushed footsteps, the raised voices, but could not make sense of them. She knew only that until the pain subsided and her head stopped spinning, she could not move.

Royce reached her first, though Ian and Blair came up behind him in mere moments.

"Brianna, are you all right?" Royce asked, dropping to his knees beside her. His hands instantly moved beneath her to lift her.

She screamed louder than she intended, for the slightest movement aggravated the pain. "Do not touch me."

"Did she break a bone?" Ian asked with concern.

"I do not know," Royce answered, fearful of touching her and causing her further suffering.

"Nay," she assured them, her voice lower, though filled with discomfort.

"What happened?" Royce asked, feeling much too helpless.

"A sharp pain—" She could say no more, for the pain ran down her leg once again when she made the slightest effort to move. A tear trickled from her eye, this pain being more intense than the first.

"She needs to be off this cold ground," Ian said, upset at seeing his sister's tears.

"I will not be"—she had to pause for a breath as the pain continued to radiate down her leg—"touched until I am ready."

Ian looked to Royce. "She cannot continue to lie here. The ground is cold and damp and will do her no good."

"Ian is right," Moira said, joining her husband at his side. "She will suffer a chill, and that often brings on the fever."

Royce needed to hear no more. He leaned down close so that Brianna could only hear his words. "Show me your determination."

She realized his intention and agreed with a bare nod.

He spared her no time to consider the wisdom of his actions; he scooped her up in one solid swing into his arms.

She bit back her cry and fought to hold firm to her tears, and she immediately buried her face against his chest.

"Cry if you wish," he whispered, pressing his face to hers. "Even the mightiest warrior sheds tears when he feels pain."

"Have you cried?" she asked, her arms tight around his neck.

He did not answer, and she patiently allowed him his silence.

His answer came slowly. "Everyone cries sometime in his life."

The pain became suddenly unimportant. The fact that the legendary Royce Campbell had cried one time in his life was important. You had to have feelings to cry, and to have feelings you had to have a heart.

They neared the keep and she lifted her head, her eyes glistening with tears yet to be shed. "You have cried."

He had thought her a beauty, but at that moment, with the tears sparkling in her brilliant blue eyes, her flushed and damp cheeks, her dark hair out of control from her ordeal, and the tender understanding in her voice, he never thought her more beautiful. And his heart raced at the fact that she belonged to him and he to her. He loved her so much that it hurt him to think of ever being without her.

They entered the keep.

"Will you tell me?" She did not demand, she simply requested, and she wished that all who followed behind them would go away and leave them alone. This was a private moment.

"Will you tell me why you ran?" He carried her up the steps to her bedchamber.

Soon they would not be alone, and neither of them would have their answers.

"Freedom," she whispered and laid her head on his shoulder.

He nodded. "I understand."

And with those words he entered her bedchamber and with a solid jolt of his boot-clad foot sent the door slamming behind them.

"Can we be free together?"

She stared at him for a moment, his scar bright red and frightening the way it consumed the one side of his face. It made one wonder how he lived through such a horrific ordeal or made one think how skilled a warrior he must be to have survived. And yet what she truly saw was a man with a tender heart who wanted to be free with her and only her.

She smiled and placed her cheek against his scarred one. "I would like that."

Brianna heard her brother protest right outside the door, but a gentler tone calmed him and she knew that Moira had things in hand.

"Please ease me to my feet?" Brianna asked of him. "The pain has eased and I wish to see if I can walk without discomfort."

Royce seemed reluctant to comply with her request. "Are you certain that is wise?"

"Nay," she answered honestly, "but it is what I feel I need to do."

Royce understood. Sometimes you had to tempt fate. "I will be right beside you."

She placed a hand to his cheek and wished with all her heart to ask, *Always will you be beside me?* Instead she simply nodded.

He saw the wounded look in her brilliant blue eyes, and his heart ached. How did he convince her that he loved her, that every word he had spoken to her had been from his heart?

She had no difficulty standing, though a dull ache reminded her that she had foolishly run when she was not yet fully healed. In time the pain would be gone for good, but the ache in her heart? That she did not think would ever go away.

Royce slipped her cloak off her shoulders. "You should rest."

Brianna looked to the bed and recalled how he had held her in his arms last night, and whenever she turned or fussed, his hands were there to soothe her. She wanted him, but she also wanted to trust him without doubt. She needed that from him, she needed it for herself.

She walked to the chair by the hearth and slowly eased herself down to sit.

Royce did not offer his help; she would only refuse it. She needed a sense of freedom, and he would give it to her for he himself felt the same.

"I answered your question; will you now answer mine?" she asked and leaned back in the chair.

He walked to the bed and snatched the folded wool blanket from the end. He placed it over Brianna's lap, tucking it in around her. He sat down on the floor in front of her and began to remove her leather boots.

He seemed to concentrate on every movement he

made, his touch firm yet gentle, and she did not disturb him. She waited for him to speak, for she was certain he would.

His strong fingers rubbed her cold feet; his thumbs massaged her insteps and soles until she felt completely relaxed and rested her head back against the chair.

"My grandmother was a wise woman and taught me about strength and fairness. She understood things many did not and saw much more than most. She talked to me endlessly about life and its constant joys and disappointments, and she talked of people and how easy it was to know if one was friend or foe."

"I would have loved to meet her," she said, knowing his grandmother had passed on.

He smiled, glancing up at her, and his fingers stilled for just a moment. "She would have loved you, and she would have been happy that you were to be my wife."

She did not argue with him; now was not the time.

"I was a grown man when she died, but her death tore at my heart, and it was the one and only time I have ever cried, and I did so alone, where no one would see me or judge me as weak."

"It is not weak to shed tears for someone you love."

"When you lead men, you show no fear and spill no tears."

"When you love, there are no rules, you simply follow your heart."

He laughed softly. "You sound as wise as my grandmother."

Brianna wished to hear more about her. "She raised you?"

He nodded. "My parents passed within a short time of each other, and I have no siblings. I was young and eager to lead the clan, but my grandmother had other ideas. She told me that I had lessons to learn before I could be a strong and effective leader. She made it known to the clan that peace would prevail, no battles would be fought, until I gained in knowledge and strength."

"No one objected?"

He grinned. "No one argued with my grandmother."

Brianna grew excited, sitting up in the chair to hear more. "She was a leader herself."

"Aye, that she was, and a good and fair one. She understood the way of things and people. She taught me what it meant to lead a clan wisely."

He paused in thought, and she knew he was recalling memories.

"And she loved me with all her heart."

Brianna spilled the tears that Royce would not now allow himself to spill. She sympathized for him, for she understood the pain of losing parents, especially ones who were so good and loving.

Royce looked up at Brianna. "She would tell me every day that she loved me, for she warned me that one never knows what the day may bring."

Her heart suddenly ached for him and for her and for the love that she was not certain they would ever get to share.

He raised himself on bended knees in front of her. "I love you, Brianna, you must always remember that, always keep it in your heart. I love you and I will never stop loving you."

Her reply was an eager whisper of his name. "Royce."

He came to her as he always did when she called to him with urgency, and it took only moments for him to gather her up into his arms and walk to the bed.

"Stop me now if this is not what you want."

He gave her a choice. He always gave her a choice, and she made the choice easily. "I want this."

20

ROYCE HAD THEM BOTH UNDRESSED IN MERE MIN-
utes, and it was with tender hands that he caressed her
body. It was a soft and lazy touch that titillated and
thrilled and caused her to completely lose her senses.

There was not a spot of flesh he did not touch. He ran
the pads of his fingers over every inch of her with a delicate touch that drove her wild. Her body responded,
moving against him like a woman hungry to quench her
thirst.

She did not think and she did not care for anything except the two of them and what they shared. He touched
her with an intimacy she had not known existed and now
that she did, she wondered how she could ever function
normally again.

His hands heated her flesh until she thought she would
go mad for the want of him. She hugged his muscled arms
and then pushed at them as if denying her own desires,

though it did little good for it only made him respond more ardently.

"What are you doing to me?" she asked with labored breath.

He whispered his response with a nibble to her neck. "I am making love to you."

She wanted to rejoice, for she had not thought she would ever know the joys of love.

He suckled at her breasts until she thought she would lose her wits, and when his hands moved to intimately caress her, she cried out with the want of him. It was a fast and furious coupling, as though they could not get enough of each other, as though this was their last time together, as though they were saying good-bye, and Brianna climaxed with tears.

"It is not over between you and me," Royce said, kissing her tears away.

"I cannot give you a child." Her voice was full of regret.

He lay beside her, his hand moving to splay over her flat stomach. "I have no doubt that my child nestles within you."

Her tears spilled freely and she did not care, for she hoped with all her heart that he spoke the truth. Unfortunately, she knew otherwise, and therefore the tears refused to stop.

He kissed them away as he had done before. "We will wed upon my return."

He was so sure, but then here she was, lying in his arms after having made love with him. What did she expect him to think?

"We will wed," he reaffirmed adamantly.

"If it were that easy."

"It is. Accept it so that we may begin our life together." He brushed her cheek with his. "A very long life."

She thought to protest, but it would do little good. He thought himself right, and there would be no changing his mind. Time would tell, and then she would have a decision to make. Wed him or let him go.

She continued to struggle with the fact that he had not told her the truth. But if truth were told, he had simply avoided the truth. He had not lied to her. She had assumed him a simple warrior with no particular clan ties. She had been the foolish one, though he had not treated her like a fool. He had encouraged her and had given her choices.

"You are silent. What troubles you?" he asked, hugging her against him.

"Too many things to speak of."

"Too many things you are unwilling to speak of."

"Can I not have a private thought from you?" she asked.

"There is no need for private thoughts between us. We are one, you and I, and can discuss whatever is on our minds."

"Good," she said with a challenge. "Tell me of the battle that left you scarred."

Her question was one more of trust. Would he share with her his pain as she had done?

His hesitation was brief and he took a deep breath as though he needed confidence to relate the tale. "It was a battle that should not have been fought. The deaths were senseless, the suffering just as senseless, and all because of greed and power."

He sounded tired to her, not physically but emotionally, and she listened, knowing he needed to heal within, as she had once needed to do.

"My father had given his word many years ago, and I was compelled to honor it. I had no choice, though I attempted to convince the laird of this clan otherwise. He was a man full of rage and would not listen to reason." He stroked her arm, needing to feel her soft flesh as he spoke. "I knew many would die, but I also knew that more would die if I did not fight alongside him. It was horrendous."

He grew silent and she knew he was reliving the battle.

"Time stops on the battlefield. Pain is not felt and the smell of blood is a stimulant that keeps you going. With weapon in hand you fight until you die or remain standing until there is no more left to kill."

Her heart grew heavy listening to him.

"In the thick of battle you fight without thought or reason."

He turned silent and she could sense that his thoughts troubled him, that the pain of this battle went much deeper than he would admit to himself. She waited, knowing he would continue. He needed to continue.

"I fight alongside my men. I do not expect from them what I would not expect from myself. Too much was expected of my men and for what? I could no longer watch my men die senseless deaths. I challenged the laird of the opposing clan so that the bloody battle could end."

Her breath caught in her throat. "You could have died."

"Death waits for us all. It is life that matters. If we do not live it truthfully and with honor to ourselves and to others, then we never truly live. In truth I did not wish to see any more of my men die."

"You would have given your life for them?" The thought of him dying rushed tears to her eyes.

"My life was not in question; my honor and actions were."

She did not know if she wished to hear more and yet part of her wished to hear it all. "And this challenge is what caused your scars?"

"Aye, every one of them."

"This man you fought left you with these scars?"

He waited as if weighing his response. "Nay, he did not."

She looked at him, confused. "Then who? Who did this to you?"

"His men attacked me before I was to meet with him."

"You were alone? Was there no one to help you?" Her heart beat wildly at the thought that he was one against many.

"Not one. I stood alone."

She understood now why he was a legend. He was fearless and relentless in battle, and he stood standing no matter how many fell around him. "You were victorious."

"Aye, though I suffered many blows."

"But you remained standing."

His pride surfaced. "Always."

"And the man you were to fight?"

"I fought him."

"Wounded as you were?" she asked, thinking that he could not have been able to see out of his injured eye and must have bled profusely from his lip and the wound to his face. How did he ever fight?

"It was necessary."

"The battle ended," she said, knowing full well he had taken the man's life.

"Aye, it ended and we buried our dead and returned home."

"You did not."

"This battle left more than the scars on my face."

"It scarred your soul," she said with a gentle hand to his face.

He kissed her palm. "That is why I sought solitude—to make sense of it all."

She felt guilty. "And my presence did not allow you that."

He placed her hand to his cheek. "Your presence healed my soul."

His words touched her heart and her tears spilled freely.

"I thank God for the day you entered my life."

Words failed her; actions did not. She moved to cover his body with hers, stretching out along the length of him.

"Do you know what you do?"

"Nay," she said with a smile, "but I will learn."

His smile was wide. "I will help you."

She shook her head. "Nay, this is for me to do." She pushed at his arms so he was forced to rest them above his head, and then she kissed him starting on his forehead.

He shivered, for he knew full well her intentions, and he did not think himself capable of letting her completely have her way with him, but he would try. Try hard, for it was her wish to do so.

She kissed almost every inch of his face and moved slowly to his neck, where she licked and nibbled, enjoying the delicious taste of him. She took her time exploring his flesh, for every inch of him tempted her tongue, and she could not pass up a single morsel.

She was branding him for sure, for he felt on fire. The heat ran through him, rushing his blood, causing his heart to beat wildly, firing his loins until he wanted nothing more than to grab her, shove her beneath him, and drive into her with an urgency that frightened him. And if she continued feeding on him with a lazy slowness, he would surely lose control.

"Brianna." His heavy breath whispered her name in warning.

She paid no heed to him, lost in the pleasure of her passion. She moved down to his chest, her mouth instantly seeking his nipples, and she feasted, her soft mewling sounds driving him to the edge of insanity.

He grew hard—so hard that he hurt with a relentless ache, and he attempted to warn her once again. "Brianna."

She heard nothing but her own soft moans, and they heated her own passion. She continued her pursuit of pleasure, moving farther down him.

It was a slow descent with her hot mouth scorching his flesh. His moans surprised him, for it was he who had always caused his partner to moan in pleasure. And she did bring him pleasure, intense pleasure.

She purred and moaned and slipped slowly down along him, her mouth following, and when she descended over him for that first taste, he knew he would be lost if he did not take control.

He reached down, grabbed her around her waist, and turned her so that she lay solidly beneath him. "I can stand it no more, I must be inside you."

He gave her no time to respond, but entered her with an urgency that had her crying out in pleasure, and he rode her hard and fast, she responding with her own urgent need.

She cried out in pleasure and clung firmly to his muscled arms. It seemed that neither of them wished it to end. They held firm to their control, fighting the sensation that continued to rush at them, that continued to beg for release.

Brianna surrendered first, his name an urgent cry on her lips. "Royce."

He needed to hear no more. He surrendered along with her, and they climaxed as they had coupled, fast and furious.

They slept soon after, tired and content, a silent prayer on Brianna's lips asking for a miracle.

21

It was time for Royce to leave. His men were ready and waiting, as was he—waiting for Brianna. He had thought she would come and bid him good-bye. After last night he had assumed they had settled their differences. Obviously they had not. She continued to deny the truth, the truth of her love for him.

"She can be stubborn," Ian said, standing beside Royce. Ian noticed the tight grasp Royce had on the reins of his horse and knew he was annoyed.

"Too stubborn," Royce snapped. "She knew full well that I intended to leave this morning. She is purposely ignoring my departure."

"Women, who can understand them?" Blair offered, walking up to join the two men.

"Let Anne hear you say that and you will get an earful," Ian said with a laugh.

"Aye"—Blair grinned—"but I calm her soon enough with my charming tongue."

"I do not know how to charm; it is not my way." Royce glanced toward the village a short distance away. He hoped he would see her hurrying past the many villagers who were busy going about their daily chores, but there was no sign of her. His disappointment turned to annoyance and his anger rapidly took over.

Could she not put her stubbornness aside and bid him farewell? Would she not miss him? His own heart felt as if it were being ripped in two at the thought of not seeing her for several weeks. He wanted to hold her tightly one more time, kiss her softly, and tell her how much he loved her. Tell her that he did not want to leave her ever.

He mounted his horse swiftly and turned to his men. "Stay as you are. I will return shortly." He turned to Ian. "Do you know where she is?"

"The last time I saw her she was walking with Moira and Anne north of the keep."

Royce galloped away with a firm hand on the reins and a heated look in his dark eyes.

"He is angry," Blair said to Ian. "You do not worry for Brianna?"

"He will not hurt her, he loves her. And my sister is being foolishly stubborn and will regret her actions later on when it is too late to do anything about it."

"A common error we all make one time or another," Blair said.

"True enough," Ian agreed, "but Brianna has suffered enough. It is time for her to be happy, and she is happy with Royce."

"You do not fault him for not speaking the truth to her?"

"I was guilty of the same myself with Moira. Sometimes it is necessary."

"I do not think Moira or Brianna would agree with that remark," Blair said with a wide smile.

Ian grinned. "Aye, but it is Royce who must deal with his woman. We have already dealt with ours."

Blair slapped him on the back. "Then let us go watch the fun."

BRIANNA WALKED IN SILENCE WHILE MOIRA AND Anne chatted. She nodded now and again when they addressed her, though she could not say what they asked her. Her thoughts were in turmoil and her heart ached.

She had argued with herself this morning as to whether she should bid Royce farewell or not. This was not to be a final farewell, for he was to return; yet in her heart and mind she feared this would be a final farewell. They would never again love as they did last night, and the thought brought tears to her eyes.

"You are teary much of late," Moira said, stopping when she heard her sister-in-law sniffle. "Why not go to him?"

Brianna cried and grew annoyed with herself. "I am confused."

"You are confused because you are emotional," Moira corrected. "Your heart rules, not your head."

"I can make sense of nothing." Brianna threw her hands up in the air as though she completely surrendered—to what, she did not know.

"Love often does that."

"It hurts to love." Her tears refused to stop falling, and with an impatient swipe she wiped them away, though more followed.

Moira laid a gentle hand on her arm. "What hurts is that which we refuse to admit. Do you love him?"

"Aye, I love him. I do not refuse to admit that."

"You do if you refuse to bid him farewell."

Her tears flowed strongly and sobs broke her words. "He will never be mine."

"Does he love you?"

"Aye, he does," Brianna answered without hesitation.

"Then why do you believe that he will never be yours?"

She had no clear answer, and doubt and fear haunted her. She had thought Arran had loved her and she him. Now she could see how wrong their marriage had been and how foolish she had been to believe his many lies. Royce had not been completely truthful to her, as Arran had not been. Would she repeat the same mistake?

Moira was perceptive and questioned, "Do you fear Royce is as deceptive as Arran was?"

Brianna sniffled back her tears. "I do not believe him to be, but then, I did not believe Arran could be deceiving. I fear that I am a poor judge of character."

"Women love deeply and not always wisely, but then, we love with our hearts, not our minds. If we would listen to reason, we might not make the mistakes we often do."

"Reason tells me to be cautious with my heart while my heart tells me to surrender, thus the confusion."

Moira gave her arm a comforting pat. "Then this time apart from him will be beneficial."

"Then why do I not look forward to this separation? My heart already aches for him and he has only left."

"He has not left yet." Moira pointed past Brianna's shoulder and she turned.

Royce was riding straight for them, and his look was one of a man ready for battle. A chill ran through her and she braced herself for their encounter. But as she watched him approach, her defenses began to melt.

He looked magnificent on his stallion; he rode with pride and confidence. All he passed quickly scurried out of his path, and she could understand why men trembled with fear in his presence and women surrendered to him. He was a portrait of power even with the scars. Yet she knew a different man, a tenderhearted man who had dealt with her with patience and understanding.

She did not fear the man she saw; she loved him and she paid heed to her heart.

Royce slowed his horse as he reached Brianna. His anger had mounted and he was ready to confront her. He dismounted with ease and took quick strides toward her.

Moira and Anne had walked off a distance to give the couple privacy.

He bore down on her and Brianna saw the anger in his eyes. She also saw his disappointment. She had hurt him and in hurting him she had hurt herself. Her heart ached for him and for her.

She did what she always did when she needed him. She called his name and it trembled on her lips, and tears once again threatened to spill. "Royce!"

"Damn," he mumbled, catching sight of her tears and hearing the desperation in her voice. He opened his arms to her and she ran to him.

He hugged her tightly, her cries muffled against his chest.

Ian and Blair joined their wives, each receiving a poke to their ribs for grinning so widely.

"I will miss you," he said, his hand stroking her back.

"And I you," she said, raising her head to look at him.

Her bright blue eyes sparkled from her tears, her creamy cheeks were flushed a soft pink, and her lips begged to be kissed.

She did not wait for him, she kissed him like a woman too long denied. They held tight to each other, and their kiss ignited their passion.

He grabbed her face with a gentle firmness. "I do not want to leave you."

Her own tears annoyed her, for she did not seem to have control of them, and his words worried her, for once again the thought that they would not be together haunted her.

"I will not be gone long," he said, his hand moving to circle her waist. "And we will marry upon my return."

She did not argue with him; the choice would be hers. She rested her head to his chest.

"You will rest and take care of yourself while I am gone." He was firm in his edict.

That brought her head up with a snap. "I will do as I please."

He laughed. "Aye, I know you will, but you will answer to me if there are consequences to your actions."

She was about to object when she decided that if she were answerable, then so was he. "And you will answer to me."

She heard her brother and Blair laugh along with Royce.

Brianna stepped away from him, or at least she attempted to. He was too quick and too strong. She was locked in his arms before she took one step.

He kissed her soundly, hugged her close, and whispered, "I will answer to you anytime."

"You promise?"

"Aye, I promise. Now kiss me good-bye."

She hesitated, for once she kissed him, he would be gone.

He rubbed his cheek to hers. "I will return soon."

She brushed her lips over his before kissing him as though she never wanted him to leave her. They hugged each other tightly before they parted, and he mounted his horse.

Royce looked to Ian. "Take care of her."

Ian nodded. "She will be safe."

He looked to Brianna one last time and then turned and rode off.

She stood staring at him until he was out of sight, and then she began to cry again.

Ian started walking toward her but Moira stopped him. "Let her be."

Brianna walked off on her own, letting her tears fall and her heart ache.

SEVERAL DAYS PASSED WITH BRIANNA KEEPING TO herself. She spent the time alone in thought, deep in thought, until she could stand her solitary time no longer.

She climbed the winding stairs to Moira's workshop. Moira had been raised in a convent since the time she was twelve. She had always been inquisitive, and when a monk arrived seeking shelter and care at the convent, she soon found an eager teacher. When she had arrived at the keep, she had found an empty tower room and had converted it to her workshop, where she did her studies and experiments.

Brianna had been an eager student herself when she learned of Moira's unique skills. She now needed to immerse herself in something other than her confused and indecisive thoughts.

"Do you need help?" Brianna asked of Moira, peeking her head around the door.

Moira waved her in. "Help is always appreciated."

Brianna hurried in, quietly eager to talk with her, seeing that Duncan was fast asleep in a fur near the hearth. "I have been sulking."

"Understandable."

"Do you understand everything?" Brianna joined her on one of the stools that sat at the worktable.

"When a situation is examined, it can be understood, though not always accepted."

"As with you and my brother when you first met?" Brianna asked, her curiosity caught by the bubbling potions in front of her.

Moira made a notation in her journal, then laid the quill aside. "Aye, I did not understand your brother's intentions until I paid close heed to his words and actions and realized that his decision was meant for the good of many. I could not fault him for being unselfish."

"It took you time to realize this?"

"Of course. I was angry at being used and understandably so, and yet your brother was an honorable man with good intentions, and then . . ." She smiled with delight. "He fell helplessly in love with me."

"And you with him." Brianna smiled.

"I had never thought to love." Moira was serious. "I had thought the remainder of my days would be spent in the convent, and I was content with that. I learned much and continued to learn. I had not known a man's touch, a lover's kiss, or the depths of love, so I did not know what I missed. Your brother changed all that for me, and I am grateful, for my knowledge would never have reached its full potential locked away in a convent."

"You have no regrets?"

"Not one."

Brianna thought on this and wondered over her own regrets.

"We cannot change our past. It is the present that should concern us. What do you wish of your life now?"

Brianna considered Moira's words. "I wish to feel free to love."

"Why do you not feel free to love?"

"I worry that I make the same mistake—that I trust too easily and too foolishly."

"You compare Royce to Arran."

Brianna nodded. "At times I cannot help it. I know it is foolish of me, but then, I think it is foolish if I do not look for similar traits. If I go blindly into this marriage, what then? Do I suffer the same fate?"

"You thought Arran was honest and honorable, and you gave your heart without question."

She almost laughed, but the sound was anything but humorous. "Arran charmed me and won my heart easily, but then I believed every word he told me."

"Now you wonder if you should believe Royce."

"He is not who I thought," she said sadly.

"Who did you think he was?"

"A warrior with a tender, caring nature. A man who simply wanted to love and be loved."

"Has your opinion of him changed?" Moira asked.

Brianna remained silent in thought.

"Does he not wish to love and be loved?"

"He was not honest with me."

"He spoke not of his exploits, the battles he fought; he spoke as a man, a man who simply wished to love. Was that wrong of him?"

Brianna had no answer.

"What if he had confided the truth to you? Would you have feared him? Would you have judged him differently? Would you have wanted to remain alone with him in that cottage?"

"When I first looked upon his injured face, I screamed. I thought him a demon. He spoke softly to me and assured me that he meant me no harm. His touch was gentle and now . . ." Her words drifted off and she grew silent.

Moira finished for her. "And now you wonder how a legendary warrior could touch with such gentleness when his hand wields a mighty sword."

"I sometimes think him two men."

"Sometimes men must be two men. Your brother must harden his heart at times when decisions must be made, and that is not easy for him, for he is a caring man and loves deeply."

"Then do I accept the two sides of Royce?"

"I cannot answer for you. I can tell you that it is not easy for them carrying such a heavy responsibility. I would not want to make some of the choices presented to them. I would not want to know that I sent men to die."

Brianna recalled the story of Royce's wounds and how he chose to chance death so that his men could live. She sighed heavily. "I do not know why this troubles me so. Royce is courageous, honorable, truthful in his intentions."

"Then what prevents you from wedding him? You were insistent that you would never again wed a handsome man, and his scars have seen to altering his fine features."

Brianna immediately defended Royce. "He is a fine-looking man even with his scars."

Moira smiled. "Then what is the problem?"

Brianna did not need time to think. She knew the answer—had known it—but had refused to admit it. She whispered, "Me."

Moira simply nodded.

"I am stubborn."

"It is not always easy to admit our own faults, and besides, you are not stubborn, you are—"

"Determined," Brianna finished with a soft laugh.

"Why are you determined not to wed Royce?"

"It is not that I do not wish to wed him."

"Then again, what is the problem? You say you love him and you do wish to wed him, so why do you hesitate?"

Brianna understood that Moira questioned her so that

she would question herself, but the answers did not come easily. "I have repeatedly asked myself that."

"And have found no answer?"

"None that makes sense," Brianna admitted.

"Then there is no sound reason for you not to wed Royce, and I remind you again that you do love him—a good reason *to* wed him."

"I had always thought to wed for love, and I had thought that I had when I wed Arran."

"Royce is not like Arran, and I think you know that."

"Aye, they are completely different; Arran was a coward, Royce has courage," Brianna said. "I found that I could not trust Arran. . . ."

Moira questioned her reluctance to continue. "Do you refuse to trust Royce? Has he given you any reason besides not completely divulging his identity to you for you not to trust him?"

She shrugged. "He has been good to me, but I wonder why he waited until I stood before my brother to speak the truth."

"Fear," Moira answered.

Brianna looked at her strangely. "He is a legendary warrior who has faced death in countless battles."

"It was merely his life in question then, now it is his heart. What if he had told you before leaving the cottage? Would you have wanted him to return here with you? Or would your anger have spoken before your heart had time to warn you?"

"Stubborn," she whispered, knowing full well she would have reacted emotionally and probably with regret.

"The choice is yours, Brianna, but then, is that not what Royce told you? Are you angry because he allowed you a choice? For that is what he did."

Brianna had not considered that. She had told Royce that she could bear him no children. He had insisted she could, but he had given her the choice to wed him on that very condition. If she did carry his child they would wed, if she did not the choice was hers. Was he actually saying the choice was hers all along?

Brianna sighed with frustration. "I am more confused than ever."

Moira laughed. "I feel the same myself at times."

"Even with all the knowledge you have gained?"

"Knowledge does not guarantee clarity of life."

"Then I am doomed," Brianna said on a laugh. "I thought that once I gained your knowledge, my life would be easy."

Moira spoke as a teacher to a student. "The key is understanding; it opens many doors. You have time before his return. Use it wisely."

"I do not know where to begin, confusion clutters my mind. I think one way and then I think another way. I ask endless questions of which I can find no answers."

"Then do not look at the answers, study the questions."

Duncan stirred and began to fuss.

Brianna was about to hurry over to him when she looked to Moira.

"Go take care of him; he has missed you."

Brianna hurried to the baby's side. She scooped him up and cuddled him to her, kissing his soft cheek. "I have missed you."

Duncan gave her a huge smile, then rested his cheek to hers.

She wanted to cry; she felt the tears well in her eyes and silently scolded herself for crying so much. Where was her strength and courage? Where was her determination?

"The questions," Moira advised, seeing her near to tears, "study the questions."

22

⤜⤛

THE DAYS PASSED MORE SWIFTLY THAN BRIANNA HAD
expected. She kept herself busy with endless tasks and
spent much time with Duncan. Her only solitary time was
when she climbed into bed at night, and as of late she had
been so tired, she fell asleep as soon as her head rested on
the pillow. The early mornings when she woke were the
times she spent in thought.

The dawn rose on gray skies, for winter had set in with
a flourish. The cold wind would whistle through the keep,
and the fires would roar with heat, and she would snuggle
beneath the wool blankets and think about Royce.

She thought often of their time together in the cottage,
of his actions, his words and of his love. And she thought
of all the choices he had given her and continued to give
her.

She placed her hand to her stomach, a hint of a smile
surfacing. She had counted the days over and over, think-

ing perhaps she was wrong, but in her heart she knew she was not. She attempted to deny the obvious at first, and when that was not possible, she began to accept and began to pray that it be true, that Royce's child did nestle in her womb.

Arran had convinced her that she was barren, and after some time passed, she began to believe him. After all, why was she not conceiving? He repeatedly told her that she was a failure as a wife and as a woman. It was all her fault and he had to suffer because of her ineptness.

A grin surfaced slowly, growing wide. Arran had been wrong. She was not a failure as a woman. He was a failure as a man. Royce was not; he was truly a man, for it mattered not to him if she could give him a child. He loved her regardless and made love to her regardless. Royce knew how to love. Arran knew nothing of love.

And now because of love, a child nestled within her.

She intended to tell no one. This was her secret and she would share it with no one but Royce and only when she chose to do so.

He would be returning soon, and she had decided on one important issue. It would be her choice to wed and not because she carried his child, but because they both wished it and wished it because of love.

Royce's scars were visible; hers were not. Arran had left her with many fears, and if she were not careful, those fears would prevent her from loving and being loved. Moira had been right when she suggested that she examine the questions instead of looking for answers. In her questions she learned about her fears and where they originated. Now that she was armed with that information, she could better understand her circumstances and make wiser decisions.

Feeling better than she had of late, she climbed out of bed to dress. The sudden movement caused her to feel faint and she grew nauseated. She hurried to the bucket of water near the hearth and drenched her face, hoping it would alleviate her unease. Her nausea grew worse, and she grabbed for a nearby bowl. Having not eaten since last evening, there was nothing to rid in her stomach, and when she was done she made her way back to bed and collapsed.

She smiled, laughed, and hugged herself, though she felt wretched. She carried Royce's babe, and the thought made her so happy that it did not matter how terrible she felt. She was happy, happier than she had ever been.

An hour later she rose, feeling much better and looking forward to the day. She dressed in a deep purple tunic and pale blue underdress. She pinned up her hair with polished bone combs, allowing several stubborn strands to fall along her neck and frame her face. A soft blush painted her cheeks and her blue eyes sparkled. She felt and looked radiant, and there was not a person in or out of the keep who did not comment.

The day was busy helping Moira in her workshop, playing with Duncan, and foraging in the woods with Anne for a strange array of things that Moira requested. She had barely grabbed a cup of hot cider from the kitchen and was just about to retire to her room for a rest when a villager burst through the great hall doors admitting a gust of winter wind along with his excitement.

"He returns!"

Brianna froze, knowing full well whom he spoke of and feeling her own excitement at Royce's return.

Ian entered the great hall, tossing his fur to a bench and walking toward her. His cheeks were red from the wind, his dark hair in disarray, and his strides determined.

"You are ready for his return?"

Moira appeared and answered for her, slipping her arm

through her husband's. "She is ready." She looked to Brianna with a smile.

Brianna returned her smile and nodded. "Aye, I am ready."

"Is there anything you wish of me, Brianna?" Ian asked, wanting his sister to know that whatever her decision, he would abide by it.

She laughed softly. "For you to continue to be the loving brother you have always been."

"You make it easy," he said and kissed her cheek.

A commotion outside the double doors caught their attention, and the three walked to stand in front of the dais, waiting to greet Royce and his men.

Brianna's heart pounded in anticipation. It had been several weeks since his departure, and there was not a day she had not thought about him, not a day she had not missed him, not a day she had not loved him.

The doors burst open and several men marched in wearing the blue and green tartan of the clan Campbell. They preceded their leader out of respect and protection, though immediately moved to the side, leaving room for his entrance.

Brianna waited, her breath caught in her throat, her heart beating wildly, and then she saw him and the sight of him made her gasp and step closer to her brother.

His scars had healed; even the deep one on his face was nothing more than a thin pale red line. His lip was normal, his eye no longer swollen and red. His eyes were stunning, a dark wintergreen color and intense in their boldness as though he saw all and knew all. His long dark hair was a rich mahogany and the two braids that hung on either side were entwined with pale leather strips. She was familiar with his body, but he seemed bigger and stronger to her somehow. Perhaps it was the pride in the way he wore his tartan or the glimmer of the gold brooch at his shoulder. Whatever the reason, he looked more handsome than Brianna ever thought possible.

He was in essence a stranger to her, and she moved even closer to her brother.

Ian placed a comforting arm around his sister, offering his protection and support.

Royce walked forward with an arrogant confidence and an eagerness that could not be denied. He was happy and eager to see her, and he made no pretense of his feelings. He tempered his stride when he saw the hesitancy in her eyes and the way she remained near to her brother.

He remained confident when he addressed Ian. "It is good to be back."

Ian extended his hand. "It is good to have you back."

Their hands fell away, and Royce looked to Brianna. "I have missed you."

She spoke truthfully. "You look different."

"I have healed, but I am who I have always been." He should have patience. He had warned himself of its necessity, but standing here in front of her after having thought about her endlessly for the last several weeks made patience near impossible. "We need to talk."

"You and your men must be hungry and tired," Brianna said, hoping to delay speaking with him privately.

"My men will eat and rest in time. Right now I wish for us to speak."

Brianna sounded as adamant as he did. "Eat and rest first—we can talk later."

Royce had not waited these many weeks to return to her only to have her ignore him. He had expected a different welcome, a much warmer and loving welcome, and he found his patience dwindling rapidly.

Ian stepped forward, actually stepping between them. "A brief rest might prove beneficial to all."

Royce would not disrespect Ian, and feeling as though

he were ready to force the issue, he thought it best to agree. "As you wish."

Brianna made haste to leave. "I will see to the food."

Ian allowed his sister her way, though Royce made certain he was heard. "We will speak later, Brianna."

She did not acknowledge him but simply hurried from the room, with Moira close behind.

Royce was blunt. "Does Brianna carry my child?"

"I do not know," Ian said. "She has not spoken of it to me or my wife."

Royce rubbed his chin hard. "She is stubborn beyond reason. I had thought this time apart might make her miss me."

"She has missed you."

"She avoids me." He pointed to where Brianna had disappeared beyond a door.

"Give her time," Ian advised.

"I have given her enough time," Royce said, and without a glance to Ian, went in search of Brianna.

She had barely stopped in the kitchen to announce that they had guests when she hurried out and circled around the great hall so that she could retreat to her bedchamber. She could feign an illness for the evening and put off speaking to Royce until tomorrow or perhaps the next day. She only knew that she did not wish to speak with him right now.

He looked so different to her, as though he were a complete stranger. She had thought he would heal and had hoped he would heal well. He had, his fine features returning in force and leaving him as handsome as ever. She had not thought to deal with that, and it had upset her.

She told herself he was not a different man. Looking at him, however, she could not easily convince herself of that. All she knew was that he was completely different from the man who so lovingly tended her in the cottage.

She slipped quietly into her bedchamber, closed the door behind her, and there she waited.

Moira came to her some time later. "He searched for you and grows impatient."

Brianna sat on the bed, her legs crossed, hugging a pillow and remaining silent.

"He has healed well."

She was quick to answer. "Aye, so much so that he appears a different man to me."

"He remains who he is," Moira said, "except that he has lost his heart to you."

She grew defensive, though she did not know why. "He gave me a choice."

"A conditional choice, but then, you cannot bear a child, can you?" Moira asked with a smile.

Brianna sighed, half in frustration and half in relief. "How did you know?"

"It was obvious. You cry all the time, your appetite has increased, and you rest more than usual."

"Does Ian know?"

Moira shook her head. "He suspects nothing, though he has asked me."

"And?" Brianna asked anxiously.

"I could not tell him what I did not know."

"I do not wish to deceive anyone—I only wish to make my own choice."

Moira patted her arm. "I understand, I felt the same myself, but you cannot avoid Royce for long."

"I know and I will talk with him when I am ready."

Moira nodded. "Then I will tell him that you do not feel well, that your head aches and you wish to rest. But there is tomorrow."

"At least I have tonight."

"I will see that you have food."

"Oh, please do, I am so hungry," Brianna said anxiously.

Moira laughed. "All Royce needs to do is watch you and he will know."

"Then I will stay away from him until I am ready to talk with him."

Moira walked to the door. "That will not be easy. He is as determined as you."

It did not prove easy at all, though Brianna avoided him for the remainder of the night and most of the next day. When she would catch a glimpse of him, she would quickly vanish, which was her present intention. She had seen him a short time ago speaking with Ian in the great hall, and she made a hasty stop in the kitchen for bread and cheese and intended to once again spend the evening in her bedchamber.

Quietly she climbed the stairs, and yawning, she slipped into her room, locking the door behind her.

"Tired?"

She dropped the bread and cheese in fright and turned to face Royce, who was stretched out on her bed.

He immediately stood and walked toward her. "Do not bother to ask me what I am doing here, for you know full well why."

She scooped up the bread and cheese and walked to the small table near the hearth to set it down.

He was tired of being avoided and followed her. "Why?"

She attempted ignorance. "Whatever do you mean?"

"Do not treat me like a fool."

He stood close, much too close. She could smell on him the scent of the rich earth and the freshness of a winter's day. How could he smell so delicious? And how could she be so hungry for him? She retreated a step, a short distance since the hearth was directly behind her.

"There is nowhere for you to go, Brianna. You have no choice but to talk with me."

She spoke softly. "You have always given me a choice; will you not do so now?"

"If that is what you wish, though first you will answer one question for me."

She knew what he would ask and attempted to avoid it. "Tomorrow we shall talk."

"You will answer my question first."

He was adamant; she could tell there would be no changing his mind.

"I have been as patient as I can be."

It was a warning and she heeded it. She turned her chin up, stuck her chest out, planted her hands on her hips, and waited.

He took a deep breath, his chest expanding, and asked on a hushed whisper, "Will you wed me?"

She had been prepared for a different question, and his query startled her so much that her legs grew weak and she reached out for support. He grabbed her by the shoulders, steadying her.

"Listen well, Brianna." He stepped closer, his touch turning gentle and his words firm. "I love you and it matters not if you can bear children. I have missed you terribly, and I do not wish to live life without you. I want you as my wife now and always. So again I ask, will you wed me?"

She stared at him wide-eyed, unable to speak, for words failed her. She had expected him to ask her if she carried his child, and instead he asked her to wed him. Had he planned this all along? The thought helped her to respond.

"Had you always intended for the decision to be mine?"

His hands moved to her waist. "I could have it no other

way. I could never force you to wed me. The choice has always been yours."

"Then why have me agree to wed you if I carry your child if the choice has always been mine?" She brought her hands to rest on his arms. She could feel the warmth of his skin through his linen shirt, and she ached to touch him. She had missed him so very much.

He grinned. "A good warrior always has a second plan of attack."

A smile escaped her; she could not contain it. "You planned on being victorious?"

"I never lose."

"You think I will wed you?"

"I prayed that you would," he said with a hushed reverence, as though his words were a prayer in themselves.

She stared at him, attempting to understand this legendary warrior, this man who fearlessly entered battles, this man who solemnly prayed that she would wed him, this man who gave her choices.

"You look different," she said, offering what explanation she could for her behavior. "I thought you different."

"Close your eyes."

"Why?" she asked, confused at his request.

"Trust me and close your eyes."

He asked for her trust and she gave it. She closed her eyes.

"Listen to my voice. Do I not sound as I always have to you? Do you remember when we first met and you screamed in fear, then when you woke again and I introduced myself?"

She nodded, recalling the moment well and remembering how caring his voice had sounded, just like now.

"I will introduce myself again if you wish me to."

She smiled as she nodded, interested in what he would say.

He placed his face near hers and whispered, "I am a warrior who has recently seen battle. I was left with many scars. Many I did not think would heal, many that were deep and painful. I thought I could heal on my own; I was *determined* to heal on my own. Then I met you, who needed to heal from an accident and from her own battle. We healed each other. We are alike, you and I, warriors— determined warriors. And I lost my heart to you, and I know you lost your heart to me."

Tears welled behind her closed eyes.

"You know me well, Brianna, like no other has known me. My looks matter not; do not see me with your eyes, see me with your heart."

He kissed her cheek, and with his finger to her chin he turned her face so her lips would meet his. His kiss caressed and sent shivers racing through her.

"I love you," he murmured. "Wed me because you love me—*me*, Brianna, not the warrior or the legend, but *me*."

She could not deny her love for him, and she could not deny that with her eyes closed she heard and envisioned the man she had fallen in love with—the scarred warrior who had captured her heart.

She did as he had suggested: she saw with her heart and chose with her heart. She opened her eyes, a teardrop rolling down her cheek. With her hand to his cheek she said softly, "I love you so very much that it frightens me."

He kissed her fingers. "There is nothing to fear between you and me."

"I think that is what frightens me: this love of ours is so powerful, so different, so beautiful that I wonder if it is real."

"Never doubt that it is, Brianna, for there is nothing that can prevent us from loving, not even death. This I promise you. Now say you will wed me, for our love demands it."

She laughed softly and whispered in his ear, "I will wed you, Royce Campbell."

He caught her around the waist and scooped her up into his strong arms and spun around yelling, "She agrees to wed me!"

"Stop! Stop!" she cried out on a laugh, though it sounded more like a whimper.

The door burst open and Moira and Anne rushed into the room, Ian and Blair entering close behind them.

"Put her down, you fool—she is with child!" Moira shouted.

23

Moira cringed at her outburst, recalling how the same was done to her. Anne had then been the culprit, and now it was she.

Ian laughed, slipping his arm around his wife. "A memory recalled," he teased and kissed her cheek.

Anne sympathized with Moira, knowing how she felt, though her concern at the time was for Moira, and she understood that Moira felt the same protectiveness toward Brianna.

Blair found delight in it all and grinned.

Royce and Brianna remained silent, their eyes fixed on each other.

Royce spoke first. "You are sure?"

"Aye, I am sure your babe nestles comfortably inside me."

"When?" Royce asked anxiously.

"When the summer is near to ending."

Ian attempted to usher everyone out of the room so that his sister and Royce could have privacy.

But before he could, Royce turned to him. "We wed tomorrow."

It was Moira and Anne who objected.

"Not enough time to prepare," Moira insisted.

"Her dress is not complete," Anne added.

"What dress?" Brianna asked, surprised.

"It was to be a surprise," Anne said.

Brianna laughed. "It is."

"Tomorrow," Royce repeated.

Ian took charge. "I think three days' time would give sufficient preparation time and be suitable for all." He waited for objections. Most important, he waited for his sister to object; if she did not wish this, he would not grant permission.

Brianna smiled at her brother and rested her head on Royce's shoulder with a yawn.

Ian knew that his sister was satisfied, and it was obvious she was tired and wished time alone with her future husband.

Moira realized the same. "There is much to be done; we'd better get started now."

They hurried to the door, Moira and Anne already making plans.

Ian stopped and looked back to Royce. "We will talk tomorrow."

"As you wish," he said, giving him due respect.

"I am happy for you, little sister, and pleased that I will be an uncle," Ian offered with a smile.

"I am pleased you are my brother and have such patience with me. Thank you, Ian."

Ian nodded and looked to Royce. "Protect her well."

"You have my word on it."

"Then I have no need for worry." Ian closed the door behind him, giving them their privacy.

Royce carried her to the bed and placed her down carefully, then sat down beside her. His hand went to rest on her stomach. "You feel well?"

"Aye, though I eat much too much, grow tired too often, and cry much too easily."

"Eat as much as you want, rest as much as you want, and cry as much as you want, it matters not to me. What matters is that you are well and happy."

"I could not believe it at first," she confided in him. "It took me time and being sick in the morning to completely accept the fact that I was with child. I had so wanted a child but had convinced myself that it would never be."

"Your husband is the one who had you convinced, and as you see, he was wrong." His hand rubbed her stomach. "Our child rests comfortably, and there will be more to follow."

She laughed. "I have yet to give you one and you ask for more?"

"We are in love and enjoy loving. How can there not be more children?"

She sighed, reaching out to rest a hand on his. "You are right. We love often and I do not want that to end, I want us to always love as we do."

He caught her hand in his and brought it to his lips, placing a kiss on her palm. "We shall. That is why I have no doubt other children will follow this one."

She yawned again.

"You should rest," he said with concern.

She shook her head. "I am hungry."

Royce looked at the table where the bread and cheese lay. "Is that all you wish, bread and cheese? Or shall I get you more?"

She slipped her hand from his and began to rub his chest. "It is not food I hunger for."

He attempted to control his desire—after all, she was tired—but it did not help with the way her hand drifted down lower and lower along his body. "You need rest."

Her laughter was soft and teasing. "I need you."

He liked her aggressiveness. "You have grown bold."

"I have grown wise." Her hand settled over him, and she lightly squeezed the hard length of him.

He could not prevent the moan that escaped his lips. He had been too long without her, and he desired her as much as she did him, and that thought ignited his passion even more.

"I have learned that to deny myself what I truly desire is foolish. I have denied for too long my desire for you, and now that we will be husband and wife, there is no reason for me to deny myself or you any longer. I have the right to want you."

"Aye, you have that right and you should enjoy that right." He moaned again, for she squeezed him just a little harder and it felt good, very good.

"It has been too long and I feel much too needy, but somehow it does not matter. All that matters is that we make love."

"Much too long," he said. "And if you continue to touch me that way, it will be much too short a time we spend together."

She giggled. "I enjoy touching you."

"And I enjoy touching you."

"Then can we not touch together?"

His actions were his response. He reluctantly eased her hand off him and began to disrobe. She joined him, shedding her garments as quickly as possible.

They stretched out beside each other on the bed and they began to touch.

His hands took pleasure in her breasts and she in his chest. Their touches were gentle caresses that left them wanting more. Their kisses were a blend of softness and eagerness, and when their hands drifted down to more intimate places, their kisses took on more passion.

Brianna felt free to feel as she wished and speak as she wished for the first time in her life. They had loved before, but now knowing they would be wed and spend the rest of their lives together because they both wished it gave her a sense of freedom she had never known.

And she loved the thought that she could be so free and safe with him.

"I want to taste you."

He moaned at the image her remark produced. "And I you."

"Is it possible we can do so at the same time?" she asked eagerly.

"Anything is possible if it is desired enough."

"I desire you." She kissed him like a lover in need.

When their lips parted, he moved down over her and positioned them so that they both could enjoy each other, but at first taste he knew they could not last long. And it was with her pitiful moan and the rush of his name to her lips that he moved over her and entered her with a swiftness that surprised but satisfied them both.

He slipped his arm behind her back and brought her chest to his as he drove into her with strong, hard thrusts.

She clung to him, the feel of him sending her tumbling over the edge of sanity. She did not want him to stop; she wanted him to go on and on and on until he was left completely breathless.

And he did.

She cried out to him in the end, wave after wave of pleasure washing over them both, and she realized without a doubt that life would be nothing without him. They belonged together, he and her.

He took her in his arms and held her until their breathing slowed.

"Hungry or tired?" he asked, his breath a bit labored.

"Both."

He heard the tiredness in her response. "Eat and then sleep?"

"Eat. I am famished." The thought of food restored her energy.

"More than bread and cheese?"

"Much more," she answered with a laugh.

"Then I will see to a feast."

"Then you will truly be my hero."

"You are an easy lass to impress," he said with a tender pat to her backside.

She yawned and stretched, moving away from him to roll on her stomach.

He leaned over her. "You are all right?"

"I feel wonderful. I had not thought that making love could be so grand. We must do it often."

"As often as you like," he assured her with several kisses to her shoulder. "Now I get you food."

"Please," she said, sounding as if she were starving.

He dressed and left the room, returning soon with a small feast.

She had slipped on a robe while he was gone and sat by the fire waiting. Her thoughts had been happy ones. She had made a choice, a good choice, and was pleased with her decision.

Life would go on and for the better. She would allow herself to love and live as she had not done before, and she felt relieved. Relieved that she had the strength not only to go on but to live a full and content life.

They talked and laughed as they ate and made plans for the future. They even discussed names for their child.

"If a boy I would like to name him after my father—Connor."

"A strong name, I like it, but what if a daughter?"

He thought, knowing the name he wished, but feeling if he chose a son's name, she had the right to choose a daughter's name.

"Your grandmother, what was she called?"

"Breda," he said softly.

"Then Breda it shall be," she said, reaching for another piece of cheese and bread, the meat pie not filling enough.

He was speechless for a moment. "There is no name you wish to give a daughter? Your mother's name?"

She shook her head, finishing the piece of cheese. "I think a daughter would do well with your grandmother's name. She meant much to you, as would a daughter."

He was about to kiss her in appreciation for her thoughtfulness and because he loved kissing her when she suddenly yawned.

"You should rest now," he insisted, clearing away the tray of food on the bed.

"You will stay with me?" she asked, snuggling beneath the blankets and yawning again.

"Always," he said, kissing her forehead, then depositing the tray on the small table before climbing into bed and cuddling up against her. "I will always be with you, and I will forever keep you safe."

"I am happy," she said on a yawn. "Finally all is settled and we will live happily together."

"For always and always," he whispered in her ear.

"Always does exist, does it not?" she asked anxiously. "Nothing can rob us of this happiness, can it?"

"Nothing, I will not allow it." He was adamant. "You and I are meant to be together. We will be husband and wife in a few short days. There is nothing that will stop us from wedding. *Nothing.*"

Brianna shivered. "I pray it is so."

"It is so, worry not," he said with a gentle squeeze. "Now sleep and rest, for there is much for you to do before our wedding day."

She moved as close as she could against him and attempted to still her fears. Rational or not, they haunted her and she could not ignore them. And she silently prayed that all would be well.

24

GRAY SKIES GREETED HER ON HER WEDDING DAY, BUT it seemed as if the sun shined brightly in and around the keep. Everyone was busy, each in their own way preparing for the wedding.

A grand feast was to be held in the great hall, and all were invited. There would be eating, drinking, and merriment, for everyone was happy for Brianna and Royce.

Moira and Anne were insisting that Brianna rest before the ceremony and celebration, but she was not tired. She felt full of life, and she felt happier than she had been in a very long time.

She did, however, feel that she needed time alone, and she had slipped on her fur-lined wool cloak, pulled up the hood, and sneaked out of the keep. She walked the narrow, barely detectable path to the stream that ran not far from the keep. It was a path she and her brother had traveled when either were troubled and in need of solitary time or time together, just the two of them. It was the place where Ian had informed her of their parents' passing and where he had told her that Arran's escape had been successful. She came here now to lay her past to rest.

A snap of a branch caught her attention, and she did not need to turn and see who followed her. "I expected you."

Ian walked up behind his sister and slipped his hand in hers. "I could always tell when you needed to come here."

They strolled along near the stream.

"This is what you want?" Ian asked.

She had expected the question from him. He wanted to make certain that she was certain. She laughed. "I must admit that a few days ago I probably would not have been able to answer you, for I simply had no answer. My heart knew what I wanted, but my emotions ruled and I could make sense of nothing."

"Not so now?"

She smiled. "Now I know for certain what my heart has attempted to convince me of. I love Royce and all my fears and doubts will not change my feelings for him. So my answer is aye, I wish very much to wed Royce."

"He is a good man and I feel he will treat you well."

"I feel the same."

"Then why did you come here?"

She squeezed his hand. "To let go of the past."

"Do you wish to be alone?"

She shook her head. "Nay, it is not necessary. We have shared much together, and it is good that you are here with me now."

The winter wind whispered a soft melody as they continued walking.

"Do you believe that love is blind?" Brianna asked.

Ian laughed. "It is we who are blind. Love seems to

know exactly what it is doing, and I believe it cautions us when necessary; we, however, do not listen."

"I think you are right. Looking back when I first met Arran, there were signs of his selfishness that I chose to ignore. I made an unwise choice."

"Now you make a wise choice."

"Very wise," Brianna said, hugging her brother's arm. "I must tell you, though, that sometimes I fear I will wake to find this has all been a dream."

Ian pinched her arm.

"That hurt," she said, retaliating with her elbow to his ribs.

"If it hurts you cannot be dreaming." Ian rubbed at his side. "It is good to see that once again you are fast to defend yourself."

"Your wife was a great help in helping me to regain my strengths, and I have no intention of ever giving them away so easily again."

The wind grew blustery and Brianna shivered from the sting at her cheeks.

"I think we are in for a storm, for I feel something brewing," Ian said, turning them so that they headed back to the keep.

Brianna was quick to agree. "I feel the same myself."

She recited a silent prayer in hopes that it would help ease her own unease. She could not quite say what caused the feeling, and it had only recently appeared, shadowing her excitement.

A yawn warned that she grew tired.

"There will be much merriment this evening. If you wish to enjoy it, I would suggest a rest."

"A short rest, for I wish to enjoy this entire day."

They returned to the keep, and Brianna retired to her bedchamber to rest. Sleep eluded her, her restless thoughts keeping her awake. She had not expected to love again, and she certainly had not expected to realize that she had not truly loved her husband the way she had thought she did. She wondered if perhaps she had loved the idea of love.

With Royce it was different, and she could, after stepping past her stubbornness, understand the depths of the love she had for him and he for her.

Finally life would be good again.

Her eyes had barely drifted closed when Moira and Anne rushed into the room.

"Time to get ready," Anne announced excitedly.

"You feel well?" Moira asked, concerned.

Brianna sat up with a yawn and a stretch. "I feel wonderful. How could I not? It is my wedding day."

Moira hugged her and smiled. "And it will be a wedding day you will long remember."

Anne fussed over the white wool dress that lay draped over the chair. "You should see all the food, and the great hall is decorated in its finest winter greenery. It will be a grand celebration."

The two women helped Brianna to dress, and when they were finished they stepped back to examine the bride. Tears welled in their eyes.

"You look beautiful," Moira said, and Anne agreed with a vigorous nod while wiping the tears from her eyes.

She felt beautiful, but it was not the dress that caused the feeling, it was Royce, for he forever commented on her beauty until she finally began to believe his words.

Anne scooped up the head wreath fashioned from winter greenery and dried herbs and hurried over to Brianna to place it on her head.

It was a snug fit and complimented her rich dark hair that fell past her shoulders in a mass of riotous curls. Her freshly scrubbed face glowed, her cheeks were tinged soft pink from her stroll in the crisp winter weather, and her lips glistened as though touched by the morning dew.

A pounding on the door caused the three women to jump.

"I am here to escort my sister," Ian said proudly.

Moira let him in, though not before she showered kisses on him and whispered, "I am so thrilled for your sister."

Guilt assaulted him and he grabbed his wife around the waist and hugged her tightly. "I wish our wedding could have been different."

She kissed his cheek. "We have each other, that is all that matters to me."

"I am a lucky man."

"That you are," she agreed, "and I will show you how lucky tonight."

He nuzzled her neck. "Promise?"

"Promise," she whispered softly and sealed it with a kiss.

Anne and Brianna grinned as the couple turned their attention to them.

Ian's eyes widened when he saw his sister. "You look radiant, Brianna."

"I feel radiant," she said, certain she would continue to smile the day away.

"All is ready in the hall, and Royce grows impatient," Ian said with a chuckle.

Brianna walked up to her brother and slipped her arm around his. "And I am just as impatient."

"Then let us go and celebrate this glorious occasion."

Moira and Anne preceded them through the door and hurried ahead of them into the great hall. A fire roared in the large hearth, the mantel draped with greenery, pines, and berries. The tables were prepared for a feast with a variety of foods and drinks. The hall was packed with villagers and Royce's men, all scrubbed clean and dressed in their best garments.

The cleric who was to perform the ceremony stood before the dais in his plain brown robe clutching a book and staring at Royce. The poor little man looked frightened to death, and she could not blame him. Royce looked intimidating, dressed in his finest garments with his shiny sword draped at his side, and the scar on his face reminding all of his courage and strength.

Royce smiled at her when their eyes met, and though they were only a few steps apart, she wanted to hurry to his side, grab hold of his hand, and never let go.

He seemed to feel the same, for he did not wait, he took the extra steps to her and eagerly took her from her brother.

"Keep her safe," Ian said to him before releasing his sister.

"You have my word," Royce said and took hold of Brianna's hand.

They took their places before the cleric, ready to exchange vows.

The little man began to speak, but his voice faltered and he had to take a moment to clear his throat. When he spoke again, his voice trembled, but this time he was persistent, and after several minutes his trembling subsided and he spoke the Lord's words with confidence.

Brianna barely heard his words, her attention focused on Royce and the way he looked at her. He loved her; she could see it in his eyes, it was written on his face, and she could feel it in her heart. She had never thought to find such a strong love, and a small part of her continued to fear that this was all a dream.

Royce seemed to understand and squeezed her hand, as if letting her know that he was there beside her and that this was all real and that soon, very soon they would be husband and wife.

It was, however, not soon enough for Brianna. She wanted the ceremony done and finished. She wanted to be his right now this very moment, and she could not say why it was so very important to her, but it was.

The words were slow in coming from the cleric, or perhaps it was Brianna's own impatience that made them seem so. When finally their vows were exchanged, she wanted to cry with joy, but there was more to the ceremony and she would need to be patient.

When it was done, the last word spoken, the cleric finally quiet, Brianna looked to Royce and her smile grew wide. He took her into his arms, shouts of joy and cheers filled the hall, and Royce whispered in her ear, "I love you from the depths of my soul."

Her arms wrapped around his neck, and she pressed close to him, needing to know he was real, this was real, and that they were husband and wife. "I thank God for you."

They kissed and the cheers grew louder.

They were briefly lost in their own world, and then family and friends crowded them, offering congratulations and demanding that it was time to celebrate.

Royce whispered in her ear so none could hear, "Later it will be just you and I, and we will love."

She squeezed his hand in response and smiled, already impatient for the celebration to be over and yet looking forward to sharing this joyous time with family and friends.

A sudden chill descended over her. A strange chill, for the hall was warm and comfortable, and she could not understand where the chill came from.

"Are you all right?" Royce asked, drawing her close to him.

She nodded, feeling foolish. She had nothing to fear—Royce was now her husband and would protect her. He was, after all, a legendary warrior, and few would dare go up against him.

Ale started flowing, music playing, and people singing—the celebration had begun. The last of well-wishers drifted off to join in the fun, leaving the newly-wed couple to finally have a moment alone with family.

Ian and Moira and Anne and Blair stood by the couple talking, their voices raised so they could be heard over the merriment.

Then suddenly the joyous voices faded until only murmurs were heard, and all eyes centered on a lone figure who entered the great hall. A dark hooded cloak covered his features, and he appeared a shadow in the bright hall. He moved with steady strides and confidence.

A chill raced over Brianna, and she moved close to Royce as though seeking his protection and not understanding why she needed it until the figure came to a stop before them and threw back the hood.

Brianna's eyes widened in shock and her body began to tremble.

"Hello, dear wife, I have missed you."

25

"ARRAN," BRIANNA SAID, ADDRESSING HER HUSBAND
she had believed dead.

Her husband.

With Arran alive that meant her marriage to Royce was not binding. She remained Arran's wife though she carried another man's child. She instinctively covered her stomach with her hand as if protecting her unborn babe.

Royce wrapped a protective arm around his wife's waist and drew her tightly against his side. His actions made his intentions clear. Brianna belonged to him and no one would take her from him.

"I missed the ceremony," Arran said and his voice turned stern. "I am sorry, I could have saved you time since you already belong to me."

Ian stepped forward before anyone could respond, and Blair moved up alongside him. Ian held his temper, though his tone warned that his anger sat close to the surface. "Why have you returned when you know you will be made to pay for your crimes?"

Arran threw his hands wide in a gesture of surrender. "I was blinded by greed and power and had foolishly ignored what was most important, my wife and the clan."

Brianna grew nauseated, for she knew her husband well, and he was being deceptively charming, the first step in convincing everyone of his innocence.

"I ask forgiveness for my ignorance. I did not think wisely, I thought selfishly. I know I should not be given another chance. I know that my crimes deserve imprisonment or death, but I ask for mercy from you, Ian, and I ask for a chance to make amends. If you cannot grant me this, then I ask that I may be imprisoned here within the keep so that I may at least make amends to *my wife*."

The hall was silent and all waited. Waited for Ian's response and waited to see what the legendary warrior would do.

"You do not deserve my sister," Ian said, folding his arms across his chest and tucking his fists out of sight, fearing he would raise his hand to Arran.

"True, I have been cruel to her in the past, I will not deny that," Arran said, sighing as if regretful. "But this time away from her and the clan made me realize my own selfishness and the consequences of being so selfish. A day has not gone by that I have not regretted my actions. If only I could go back and change the past, I would, but I cannot. I can only repent and tell you that whatever fate you decide for me, I will accept, for I know I deserve punishment."

Moira spoke up, to no one's surprise. "You have lied before, you lie again."

A chorus of ayes filled the room, but the unanimous opinion did not dissuade Arran. "I understand your doubt, especially you, Moira, for I had thought you in the way, and I foolishly attempted to remove you."

Ian stepped toward him. "For that alone I should kill you."

"And I would feel the same if I were you," Arran said, sounding sympathetic. "But I beg you to consider your sister. I love her and wish to do right by her. I want to make her happy. I want her to forgive me and see that I am the loving man she once thought I was."

Royce could remain silent no longer. "Brianna no longer belongs to you. She is mine."

Arran spoke with patience. "I understand how you must feel, and it is good to know that someone of your strength and power would look after my wife. But she is my wife and will remain my wife; therefore she cannot belong to you."

Royce was adamant, his powerful voice causing many to cringe. "She is *my wife,* she *belongs to me,* and—*she carries my child.*"

Arran's face grew bright red and his eyes settled on Brianna with a fury that sent a chill through her.

Her old fears surfaced, though she allowed no one to know. She remained standing beside Royce with her head high, for she was proud that she carried Royce's child and she wished everyone to know.

Arran tempered his emotions and hung his head as though saddened by the news. Then he raised his head and looked to Royce. "I will raise your child as if he were my own."

Silence fell in the great hall, and many who stood nearby stepped back in fear of Royce's reaction.

Royce was calm and confident when he spoke. "If Ian does not kill you, I will."

Arran actually paled and moved back several steps. "I wish you no harm."

Royce released Brianna, nudging her to Moira's side. She went reluctantly. He moved forward toward Arran.

"You are a coward."

Arran's face turned scarlet at the obvious challenge. "I have behaved cowardly, but I am not a coward. I wish only to love my wife even if she carries your child."

"You will not have *my wife or my child*."

"Brianna is legally mine." Arran's patience was beginning to wane. "Therefore, the child is legally mine if I so choose."

Royce almost reached out to choke him, but he stopped himself, his fists tightening at his sides. He would not allow himself to think that this coward would have any right to Brianna or his child. He would see him dead first.

"You can choose nothing. Ian will decide your fate."

Arran visibly cringed. "I know Ian to be a fair man." He spoke loudly for all to hear and for many to sympathize with his plight. "I pray that he will be fair in his judgment. That is why I returned to meet my fate and extend my regret for my foolish actions. I have suffered much while I was gone, and I will suffer more if necessary. I only ask for mercy and a chance to make amends."

Royce moved forward with such speed that Arran had no chance to move. They finally stood face to face.

Royce spoke for only Arran to hear. "No matter what Ian decides, you will eventually face me and me alone. I will have no mercy."

Arran shook with fear no matter how hard he attempted to control his tremble. "You have no right to *my wife*."

"I have every right, for she loves me."

Arran whispered harshly, "Brianna does not know how to love a man."

Royce did not stop himself. His hand flew to Arran's

neck, grabbed a hard hold, lifted him off the floor, and held him there, his feet dangling.

"Speak ill of my wife and I will snap your worthless neck," Royce threatened.

Arran choked and fought, grabbing at Royce's hand and attempting to break his hold. His strength was that of many men; there was no breaking free.

Ian stepped forward and Royce's men converged around him before Ian could gain on them. Blair moved to Ian's side and the hall looked about ready to fight, and all for the sake of a coward.

"Enough," Ian said, his voice thundering in the hall. "His fate is mine to decide."

Royce lowered Arran to the ground, but before releasing him he whispered, "You and I shall settle this."

Ian stepped past Royce's men, shoving those aside who would not move. When he reached Arran, he spoke loud enough for the entire hall to hear. "You will be held in the rooms beneath the keep until your fate is decided."

Arran appeared relieved. "As you wish, though I beg you to let me speak with my wife."

"Nay," Royce said. "She has nothing to say to you."

"I have things I must say to her," Arran said, looking to Ian.

"It is my sister's choice," Ian said.

"Nay, it is mine," Royce said forcefully. "*My wife* will not speak to him."

"I will speak with my wife!" Arran shouted for all to hear, especially Brianna.

Brianna shivered at the thought. She had no desire to speak with him or be near him. She wanted nothing to do with him and feared that as his wife she would have no choice. She remained close to Moira, grabbing hold of her hand for support.

"You need not speak to him," Moira assured her. "You heard your brother. It is your choice."

"Brianna, please talk with me. I am sorry," Arran begged.

Brianna wanted to cover her ears and drown his pleas, but she would appear a coward, and she wished to show strength.

Ian finally settled it. "You will not disturb my sister now. If she wishes she will speak to you; otherwise you will remain silent." Ian then looked to Royce. "Please see to Brianna while I finish dealing with him."

Royce understood that Ian felt that his sister had seen enough and that he and she required time alone to discuss this unexpected situation.

"I will speak with you later."

Royce nodded to Ian, knowing that it was necessary for them to talk alone. What would be decided, Royce did not know. He only knew that Brianna would remain his; he would not surrender her.

Royce took Brianna in his arms, and together they left the hall, the celebration at an end.

Brianna hurried out of Royce's arms when they entered her bedchamber and rushed to the fireplace, holding her hands out to warm them. The chill would not leave her; she felt the cold down to her bones and she could not get warm. She rubbed her hands together and then rubbed her arms.

Royce came up behind her, pressed his body against hers, and rubbed at her arms.

They spoke not a word, both attempting to understand their circumstances.

Royce made it known how he felt. "You are mine and I will not let you go."

Brianna shared her fear. "I am married to Arran. What choice do I really have?"

"The choice is yours," he assured her. "To me we are wed, and I will take you from here at this moment if you wish."

She pulled away from him, yanking the wreath from her head and tossing it on the table. "We are not wed, and how can I leave while my husband awaits his fate?"

"You owe him nothing."

"My vows say otherwise."

"His vows meant nothing to him," Royce said, attempting to make her see reason.

She shook her head. "He is my husband and I do not want to be his wife, but what do I do?"

"Come away with me," he urged, taking a step toward her.

She moved away from him. "I cannot continue to run from my fears. This must be settled between him and me."

"He lies and will continue to lie."

"I know," she admitted. "That is why this must be settled now."

"Your brother will settle it, and if not him, then I."

She feared what both men would do, and yet, had not Arran caused his own fate?

"I must speak to my brother about this."

Royce objected. "Nay, I will speak with him."

"Do what you must, but so must I."

"You are stubborn," he insisted.

"Determined," she reminded.

Royce took a slow step toward her, and she did not retreat from him. "I love you and will not let you go."

"I love you and do not wish to leave you, but I am another man's wife and that must be settled first."

"You carry my child," he reminded, his hand settling over her stomach.

She covered his hand with hers.

"Both of you are mine."

She did not know how to respond. What did she do when she carried the child of the man she loved and was married to a man she despised? And what if her brother imprisoned Arran for his crimes? She remained legally wed to him and was not a free woman. Did she go with Royce and live in sin?

"There is much to be discussed and decided," she said, hoping that with sound reason a satisfying conclusion could be reached.

"The only discussion necessary is when you will be ready for departure."

"I cannot run away."

"We have a right to be together." He sounded angry, but Brianna knew he suffered.

"Until this is settled you and I have no right. Please, Royce, be patient. I fear losing you."

He took her in his arms and held her close. "You will not lose me; this I promise you."

A knock on the door interrupted them. Moira peeked around the edge. "I do not wish to disturb you, but Ian wishes to speak with Royce."

"Not me?" Brianna asked.

Moira entered, shaking her head. "He feels you should rest tonight and that tomorrow is soon enough to speak with you."

"Your brother is right," Royce said, reluctantly releasing her. "This has been upsetting for you. You should rest. I will return when I am done."

Brianna voiced her irritation. "This is my life, my decision."

Royce disagreed. "You are my wife and my responsibility. I will see to this."

His command did not sit well with her. For too long decisions had been made for her and always in her best interest. Not until she was free of Arran and on her own did she realize how much she enjoyed her independence. She did not wish to lose that now, not after it had taken her so long to regain it.

"This is for me to decide." She was firm. No tremble or shiver threatened to weaken her.

Royce wisely chose patience over anger. "We love each other, Brianna; therefore, it requires a mutual decision between us and us alone."

He was right; this decision would affect them both and their child. She could not be selfish about it, but then, she should not be disregarded.

"All the more reason that I should be present when you and Ian speak."

A sensible retort but one Royce did not agree with, though he remained patient. "Allow me to speak with your brother, and then we both will speak with him together."

"If you speak with him alone, then I speak with him alone. We are either together or not."

His patience was beginning to thin. "There are some things men discuss that are not for women to hear."

"If it concerns me, I wish to hear it."

Moira had remained silent until now. "I agree with you, Brianna. If a woman does not speak and demand, her life will never be hers."

Royce knew when he was outnumbered. "Let me speak with Ian and—"

"Let us all join Ian," Moira said, walking over to Brianna and hooking her arm with hers.

He was wise enough to realize he had lost the skirmish and wondered if Ian would be more victorious, though having grown to know Moira, he doubted it.

Royce walked to the door and held it open. "After you, ladies."

Arm in arm and with satisfied smiles Moira and Brianna preceded Royce out the door.

Ian looked past his wife and sister as they entered his solar to Royce, who followed behind them.

Royce grinned, shrugged, and cast an eye toward Moira.

Ian shook his head, accepting defeat.

Brianna spoke up. "I have a right to be here, Ian."

"I suppose you do, so I will not argue with you, since it would be pointless, especially since my wife stands beside you."

"That I do," Moira said, if anyone should doubt it.

"Arran rests more comfortably than he deserves in the keep's dungeon," Ian said, knowing it was useless to disagree with the two women and wanting to settle this matter as quickly as possible. "He insists on speaking with you, Brianna."

Royce answered for her. "She will not speak with him."

"It is up to Brianna," Ian reminded.

Royce looked to Brianna, and she understood that what he had said was true, this was a matter that required consideration between them, and she could not do that standing beside Moira. She should be standing by the man she truly considered her husband.

She walked over to Royce and slipped her hand in his. "It is something that Royce and I must decide together."

Royce raised their joined hands to kiss hers. "I am proud you are mine."

His words stirred her heart. It had been many years since anyone had ever told her they were proud of her, and she thrilled at the thought that he took pride in her.

Ian was glad to see them unite over this. "Then you do not wish to speak with him?"

"I truly do not know what I would say to him. He stirs old memories and fears I thought I had laid to rest."

"You have nothing to fear," Royce said harshly, angry that another caused her fear. "I will always protect you."

"I know," Brianna said with a soft smile. "I have no doubt of that, but a small part of me wonders . . ."

Royce understood and it did not sit well with him. "You wonder if I truly can protect you?"

"Arran is my husband." Brianna's voice trembled. "He has rights with me that you do not. He is deceptive and he charms without most realizing it."

"Your brother is not ignorant," Royce insisted. "He will see that he is made to pay for his crimes. He will sentence him to death and be done with this matter."

"He cannot," Brianna said, turning to her brother. "If you order his execution, all will say that you did so only so that Royce and I could wed."

"You understand my dilemma," Ian said with a sense of relief.

Royce shook his head. "I do not understand. Ian leads the clan and his decision is law. Arran attempted to take Moira's life. That is a crime punishable by death. He should get what he deserves."

"I have shown mercy before and Arran knows this," Ian explained.

"You cannot think of letting him go without punishment?" Royce asked incredulously.

"Nay, I would not do that," Ian assured him. "He deserves imprisonment, but my sister does not, and there lies my dilemma. If I sentence him to imprisonment, my sister remains his wife and is not free to wed you. If I sentence him to death, Brianna is right, many will talk and doubt my fairness as a leader."

Royce understood all too well the difficulty of leading

a clan. "A leader cannot always be fair; he must do what is right and oftentimes difficult."

Ian agreed. "Aye, you are right and this is a difficult decision."

Royce lost all patience. "Do what you will with Arran, but Brianna leaves here tonight with me."

"That is not wise," Ian said firmly. "Until this is settled, Brianna should remain here."

"And be sentenced to imprisonment along with Arran? For she will never be free as long as he remains alive."

"I understand your concern," Ian said, remaining calm. "But Arran will not be able to tolerate imprisonment for long, and he will make an unwise move."

"Until then you expect Brianna and me to wait?"

"I ask for patience from you both."

There was no patience in Royce's response. "Your sister carries my child; time is limited."

Brianna could not prevent the strong yawn that attacked her, and she suddenly felt weary and wanted nothing more but to seek her bed. She rested her body against Royce.

He felt her weariness and grew concerned, scooping her up into his arms. "She has had enough for one day."

Ian nodded. "I agree. She should rest. We will talk tomorrow."

"Tomorrow," Royce said and left the room, hugging Brianna close to him.

He placed her on her bed, tucking a wool blanket around her. "I will return in a few moments and help settle you for the night."

She yawned again. "I do not wish to sleep alone, not tonight."

"I will return, I promise." He kissed her cheek.

Brianna fell into a troubled sleep, drifting in and out of

wakefulness. She wanted Royce to return; she missed his warmth and the comfort of his body beside her.

A sound alerted her to his presence, and she waited for him to join her.

"Brianna," he whispered in her ear.

She turned from her side to her back, and as soon as she did so, she was scooped up into his arms.

He held her close. "It is time for us to leave."

26

By the time Brianna roused herself enough to respond, Royce was carrying her out of the keep.

"What are you doing?"

A cloak was thrown around her just before they left the keep, muffled voices followed them, and the cold night air stung her cheeks.

Having received no answer, she asked again, "What are you doing?"

"We are leaving here."

"I cannot—"

"I can," Royce said with a strength that sent a chill through Brianna, though she preferred to think it was the cold night air that gave her the shivers.

"Royce—"

He gave her no time to object. "We leave here now. I will have it no other way."

How did she make him see reason? How could she convince him this was not a wise choice?

They approached the area where his men camped, and they were all mounted and ready to take their leave. Royce wasted no time, he handed Brianna to one of his men, mounted his mare, and she was handed up to him. He placed her securely across his lap, wrapping his fur-lined cloak around her and grabbing the reins.

"Sleep," he ordered. "We ride most of the night."

"You cannot do this." She attempted once more to convince him that this was not right.

"I can and I have," he said, directing his horse away from the village, his men following.

She suddenly realized the quiet that surrounded them: not a horse whined, not a man spoke, not a sound stirred except for the winter wind. She was astounded by the group's ability to remain silent when there were so many. They truly were remarkable warriors.

Her voice was soft and could be heard by none but Royce. "My brother will not like this."

"He will understand and possibly be relieved."

"Why? Why do you do this when you know it will solve nothing?"

"I will see you suffer no more. Now rest, we have a long journey."

How could she rest when this was not what she wanted? Running from the problem was no way to solve it.

"Why do you not give me a choice now when you have always given me one?"

He needed no time to answer. "Your choice would be made out of duty and would not be a wise one."

"Is it not for me to decide, wise or not?"

His hand moved to her stomach. "Not with my child

nestled inside you. I have a right to decide my child's fate."

"My brother would have handled this well—"

"In time," Royce said. "I do not wish to wait. We belong together. I wish to watch you grow round with my child, I wish to be there when our babe is born and know that you and he are well. And while I agree with your brother that it is only a matter of time before Arran does something stupid, I do not want to wait an hour, a day, a week, or a month."

The fur slipped from her shoulder, and the cold wind raced across her. She shivered and snuggled against his warmth. He adjusted the fur around her, tucking the end under his arm so that he could keep the cold away from her.

He favored the feel of her nestled against him. It was where she belonged and where she would remain. He would allow no one to take her away from him. He would kill for her, and he would die for her if necessary. His love for her was that strong, and he was that committed to a life with her.

Since she did not respond he asked, "Are you angry with me?"

"Truthfully, I cannot be, for I feel the same as you. I do not wish to be apart from you, and I wish you beside me when our babe breathes his first breath." She paused, reluctant to continue but knowing she must. "I have a duty whether you or I like it or not. And now my brother will be left to deal with the consequences of actions that were not of my choosing."

"Your brother is a brave and skillful leader."

"Where was my bravery in running away?"

"You did not run away; I abducted you."

Her yawn irritated her. She was tired and wished to continue this debate, but she felt sleep creep over her, and she knew that soon her eyes would close no matter how hard she tried to keep them open.

"We can talk of this later. You need to rest."

"This was not right, Royce." Her voice sounded as drowsy as she felt.

"Feel as you must, for I did what was necessary." He was not sorry; he was firm in his convictions, and no one would make him feel otherwise. He loved her and he would love her forever.

Brianna fell asleep with all intentions of continuing this discussion at a more appropriate time. That time was longer than she had imagined.

The journey was not an easy one, at least for Brianna. Royce and his men were accustomed to harsh conditions and cold weather. She was not and the babe appeared to feel the same way.

Her stomach protested in the morning and in the evening. She could barely keep food down even though the men did a fine job of hunting and preparing the game. She slept much when riding in Royce's arms and slept soundly at night cuddled next to him on the hard ground. But she longed for the comfort and warmth of a solid shelter.

It did not come until Brianna thought she could stand it no more. She had lost count of the days after two weeks, but she knew it had to be close to a month, for she could feel a faint flutter in her slightly rounded stomach.

She was more relieved than surprised when they first approached the village that surrounded Royce's keep. It was large and thrived with activity. They received a warm and hearty welcome. The clan was truly glad to see them and shouted good wishes to Royce and his new bride.

Brianna wondered what they would think when they learned the truth. She was a married woman, not free to wed, and certainly not free to bear another man's child.

The keep was twice the size of her clan's and well maintained. Everyone she met appeared friendly and accepting of her, but they did not know the truth.

Royce took her directly to his bedchamber. The room was immense to Brianna, with a fireplace that consumed an entire wall and a bed that could easily sleep four. Rich tapestries hung from the walls depicting battle scenes, and a table sat covered with a variety of foods, the delicious scents making her mouth salivate.

It was close to dusk, and while she was bone tired and hungry, she felt filthy from the journey. She had washed as best she could, but it was not enough compared to her usual routine. She wanted to bathe before she did anything. Of course there was also the need for clothes, since when Royce took her from the keep, he had not thought to take her clothes along.

She was about to ask him if a bath was possible when he spoke.

"I have ordered a bath to be readied for you."

"Bless you," she said with relief. She would have said more, for there was much for them to discuss, but a knock interrupted their privacy, and two men entered followed by several women carrying buckets of steaming water.

She sighed with the thought of soaking in the hot water.

A short, round woman entered last and issued orders that all obeyed. She wore her gray hair braided and pinned to the back of her head, and she had bright red full cheeks that showed a deep dimple when she smiled, which she did when she looked to Brianna.

"An honor to have you here, m'lady. I am Della and will see to any of your needs."

Brianna could see that she was a woman accustomed to being in charge, and Brianna was accustomed to doing for herself. She hoped there would not be a problem.

"Thank you, Della," she said, thinking the short reply would dismiss the woman.

It did not. Della took immediate charge.

"Let me get you out of those filthy garments." Della walked right up to her, her chubby fingers rapidly working on her garment, while directing the returning servants to hurry with more buckets so that the water would remain hot.

The smirk on Royce's face made Brianna realize that he was accustomed to Della's authoritative manner, though the smirk soon vanished when the woman announced, "A bath is being prepared for you, Royce, in your solar."

This time Brianna smirked while she watched him about to protest.

Della was quicker with her tongue. "Go and wash up while I see to the lady of the keep. She looks about to drop from exhaustion, and she looks about starved. Did you not feed her on the journey?"

Royce attempted to respond but never got a chance.

"Lord be praised you are with child," Della said, a smile spreading wide across her full face. Her glance went straight to Royce. "And you made this poor woman journey here in her condition and without a woman to tend to her needs. Shame on you! Now, go wash up so that I may give her the proper care she requires."

Brianna decided that she liked Della.

Royce thought to object, but Della gave him a look that warned against it.

He shook his head and looked to Brianna. "I will not be long."

She grinned and waved at him.

He left, still shaking his head.

"He is a good man, he will do well by you," Della said in a no-nonsense manner.

Brianna did not doubt that. "I know I am lucky to have him."

Della looked at her with wide dark eyes. "And he is lucky to have you. You will be good for him."

"I hope so," she said on a sigh, worried that all would not turn out as well as she hoped.

"He protects what is his."

She knew Della attempted to reassure her, but the woman did not know that she did not actually belong to Royce. She was another man's wife.

"And *you are his*," Della said firmly. "The clan understands this and will do what is necessary."

Brianna also understood then that Della was aware of the situation and wished her to know that she was accepted.

"Thank you," Brianna said, grateful for the support.

The bath proved heavenly, and Della gave her time alone to relax and soak in the heat of the hot water. The woman returned with several garments, including a dark green velvet robe that once worn Brianna did not think she would ever want to take off. It was warm and cozy, soft to the touch, and the fit was just about perfect.

"It belonged to his grandmother," Della said, her eyes misting. "She was a good woman. These other garments I will have fitted for you, and I will make certain one is done for tomorrow."

"I do not wish to make unnecessary work for anyone. I can see to it myself."

Della looked startled. "You are the lady of the keep and will do no such thing."

Royce entered the room. "She is ordering you about already. I thought she might wait until tomorrow."

"That would be wasting precious time, and the Lord knows there is never enough time," Della said, pulling out one of the chairs at the table. "Now, come eat, m'lady. You and the babe need nourishment."

Brianna did not argue; she hurried over to the table.

"What about me?" Royce asked with a thump to his chest.

"You are capable of taking care of yourself," Della informed him and made certain Brianna's plate was filled high.

Royce joined Brianna at the table, mumbling beneath his breath.

Della picked up Brianna's soiled garments and walked to the door, looking at Royce. "She needs her rest tonight."

Royce almost choked on the piece of cheese he had in his mouth.

Brianna covered her mouth, hiding her smile.

Royce pointed to the door and swallowed the cheese. "Out of my bedchamber, woman."

His order did not disturb her in the least. "Mind what I say."

He shook his head after the door closed. "I do not know why I tolerate her."

Brianna knew. "She was a dear friend of your grandmother's, and she loves you as much as your grandmother did."

"Aye, that is true," he said with a smile, "and that is why she rules this keep."

Brianna broke a piece of dark bread from a fresh loaf. "The people know we are not wed?"

"Our situation is known. It is necessary." He would say no more, but Brianna understood and did not like the thought.

"You will not battle over me."

"I will do what is necessary." He was adamant.

She was stubborn. "I will not allow it."

He laughed. "And how would you prevent it?"

"I will do what is necessary."

His temper surfaced. "You will not return to your husband. We belong together."

"I will not have men die because of me." Tears pooled in her eyes. "Especially you."

He moved from his chair to kneel beside her. "No one will die. We will settle this." He did not make it a promise, for he knew that if necessary he would take Arran's life.

She kissed his cheek. "Aye, we will settle this." She felt hopeful though concerned. "I hope my brother is not angry with me."

Royce returned to his seat, slicing chunks of cheese for them both. "He will not be angry and he probably would have done the same thing himself if he were in my situation."

Brianna grew somber, placing the piece of bread she had not even nibbled on aside. "We cannot live in sin forever, Royce."

"We love each other; that is not a sin."

"I thought him dead, and Lord forgive me, but I was glad when I was told he was dead. I felt relieved and free. Why could he not have remained dead?"

He understood that she needed to speak her feelings, and he wished her to confide in him, so he listened.

"He caused me so much pain and suffering, and now he returns to cause me more. I know he will attempt to deceive my brother with his charm. I watched him do it time and time again. Everyone thought him a loving husband." She laughed softly. "Everyone but Moira. She knew him for what he was when she first met him. She is very observant."

"She is observant," Royce agreed. "There is not much that gets by her at the keep."

"That is true, she—" Brianna stopped suddenly and gasped. "Moira knew that you intended to abduct me."

"She had an idea," he corrected, "and she insisted I tell her nothing, for she informed me that she would not lie to her husband if asked; therefore, she could not say what she did not know."

"Why would she want me away from the keep?"

"I would suspect for your protection."

"But—"

"If Arran proved able to attempt to take Moira's life in the keep, what would prevent him from attempting to take yours? Ian took measures to protect his wife, yet Arran found a way around those measures. Who knows what friends Arran has in the keep?"

"I had not thought of that."

"I did and evidently so did your sister-in-law."

"Is that why you think Ian will be relieved to learn that you took me away?"

He nodded. "It would not look good for him to send you away, but if I should take matters into my own hands, nothing could be said."

"Why, then, do I feel a duty to remain and face my fate?"

"Honor, courage, *stubbornness*," he said with a smile.

"I do not want Arran to think me afraid of him."

"I think he knew that when you refused to speak with him."

"But does not a coward refuse to face his foe?" she asked.

"He was aware that you made your choice freely and you stood beside me. A coward would not be that brave."

She leaned across to him, placing her hand to his cheek. "I was proud to stand beside you so that all knew how much I love you and—" She paused a moment. "Because I was fearful that Arran's return meant that we could never be together."

He took her hand and kissed her palm. "That is not going to happen. We will be together forever, we will love forever."

"I want to believe that."

"Then believe it, for it will be. This I promise you."

27

TIME FLEW BY, WITH DAYS TURNING QUICKLY INTO
weeks, followed by months. Brianna found herself content and happy in Royce's home. If she was not spending
time with him, which was unusual, she was busy with
Della and several of the other women who saw to the running of the keep.

Royce encouraged her to assume the duties of his
wife and see to the running of the keep, but she feared if
she did it would be harder if the day came she had to
leave. The thought upset her, and she tried not to dwell
on it. Royce appeared to have no doubts that she would
remain with him, as did the clan. They simply accepted
her as Royce's wife regardless that she was wed to another man.

She had rounded much in the last month, though her
time was still three months away. She was no longer
weepy or as tired as she had been; she actually felt more

vital. Royce constantly reminded her to rest even though she insisted she did not need to.

Life had been very good since her arrival here, and she wished it could remain so, but she had doubts, and those doubts haunted her now and again. When they did, she would seek the solace of the woods that bordered the keep.

She was never without a guard, and while it annoyed her that once again she was deprived of her freedom, she understood the necessity of it. The men did keep a distance, allowing her some privacy, though they never allowed her out of their sights.

She walked now in the early afternoon sunlight. The day was beautiful, the sky a brilliant blue, the air warm and rich with the heavy scents of spring. She had pinned her hair up with combs, though a few strands fell loose, and she wore a pale blue dress and tunic altered to accommodate her changing shape.

Several fallen branches caught her eye. It had been some time since last she fashioned a basket, and her idle hands itched to be busy. She quickly set to work gathering branches that would suit her needs.

"You are too busy for a woman who carries a child."

Brianna smiled and turned to watch her husband approach. He appeared to grow more handsome with each day. The scar on his face had healed to a thin, barely visible line, and his dark green eyes were alight with a vibrancy that could not be ignored. It was obvious that he was happy.

"I have sat idle all morning," she said and turned her cheek for a kiss.

Royce laughed, grabbed her chin, squeezed until her lips puckered, and then kissed her.

She laughed when he finished.

"You laugh at my kisses?" he asked teasingly.

"I can do better," she challenged.

"Of course you can; you had an excellent teacher."

"Perhaps it is time for the teacher to learn from the student."

Royce grinned. "I am always willing to learn."

"Then bring your lips to mine and let me teach you."

Before he could do as she directed, Brianna let out a yelp, dropped the sticks in her hand, and grabbed hold of her stomach.

Royce's arm went instantly around her. "What is wrong?"

She laughed, taking hold of his hand and placing it against her rounded stomach. "The babe kicked me. Can you feel?"

Not to disappoint the father, the babe kicked again.

They both laughed.

"He is a strong one."

"Aye, she is."

Royce kissed her cheek. "Lass or lad, it matters not to me, for we will have many sons and daughters together."

Brianna rested back against his hard body. "I wish I was as confident as you."

"I have enough confidence for us both."

"Then there is no need for me to worry."

He wrapped his arms around her, resting his hands over her belly. "I keep telling you that."

"Happiness eluded me, and now that I have it, I suppose I fear it will not last."

He whispered in her ear. "Do not tell anyone this, but our happiness will last a lifetime."

"I pray that is so."

"Know it is so." He nibbled at her ear and along her neck until she shivered.

"I forever want you," she said, amazed at the fact.

"Then return to the keep with me now so that I may give you what you want."

"The clan already talks about us. Whatever will they say if they see us sneak off to your bedchamber in daylight?"

He nuzzled her neck. "They will gossip of our love for each other and tell stories of the dark-haired beauty who captured and tamed their leader."

She giggled and added to the story. "And everyone lived in peace and happiness forever."

"Royce!"

They both raised their heads to see who called his name so anxiously.

It was John, the large man with the gentle voice who often guarded her. Beside him stood another man, shorter in height and stature and wearing the clan Cameron plaid.

Brianna shivered in her husband's arms.

"Worry not," he whispered before taking her hand and signaling the men to approach.

Brianna recognized the man. He was one of her brother's most competent warriors. His name was William. His mother had come upon the clan returning from a skirmish. She asked for shelter, she was heavy with child, and the men brought her back to live with the clan. His mother and he were fiercely loyal to the clan, and William himself was awaiting the birth of his first child in the autumn.

She greeted him with a smile, for Royce's dark eyes lingered harshly on the man. "It is good to see you, William. How is Margaret?"

"It is good to see you well and safe, Brianna. My Margaret is being fussed over by my mother, who cannot wait for her grandbabe to be born so she can fuss over him."

Brianna laughed. "I am glad to hear that all remains the same for the clan."

"Not all," William said reluctantly. "Your brother sent me with news."

Brianna held tightly to her husband's hand.

"Arran has escaped."

"When?" Royce asked and motioned to John, who immediately walked up behind Brianna.

Now it begins, she thought, just like before. She was once again a prisoner.

"I left the day of his escape. Ian was leaving a day or so after me, but he comes with many, so his journey is slower."

"Let us return to the safety of the keep. We can talk there." Royce kept a firm arm around Brianna as they walked, and John remained close at her back. William walked in front of her. With the three men surrounding her, she was safe.

Why, then, did she not feel safe?

Tongues began to wag as they walked through the village. It was obvious that the three men protected her, which meant she needed protection. Several of Royce's men took up their swords and followed the small group to the keep.

Brianna was shivering and sat down on the first bench upon entering the keep.

Brianna heard Della give orders for a hot drink to be prepared and hurried to her side.

"Take her up to our bedchamber so she may rest," Royce instructed at Della's approach.

"Nay," Brianna said with a firm shake of her head. "I will hear what William has to say."

Royce did not force her to leave; she had every right to be present.

"How did he escape?" Royce asked, directing William to sit.

John was already pouring tankards of ale for the men,

and a servant had placed a steaming cup of herbal brew in front of Brianna. She gratefully cupped her hands around it to still her shivers.

William took a hardy swallow before answering. "He had help."

"Who? Who would help him?" Brianna asked, thinking it impossible that anyone would be loyal to Arran.

"Ian discovered that Arran paid two men to take up residence within the clan a month or more ago when he obviously made plans to return. He wanted them in place in case he needed assistance and more than likely promised them more money after they helped him secure his freedom."

"Then there are three?" Royce questioned.

William swallowed another mouthful and his eyes widened when a large platter of food was set in front of him. "Ian does not believe the men he hired remained faithful. He recalls them being lazy and not willing to do their share. Their interest was filling their pockets with coins."

"This man must seek shelter somewhere," John said, refilling William's tankard and his own. Royce had yet to drink from his.

Brianna offered information that might prove helpful. "Arran's family had land but lost it in a skirmish. He had spoken often of the keep and how it was left to ruin since the clan who now owned it did not wish to take up residence there." She shook her head. "I do not know where it is, though he had mentioned it was north of Ian's land."

"Ian does not believe he is alone," William said. "He thinks his men wait for him somewhere."

Brianna was confused and could not understand why Arran returned. "Why would Arran take the chance and return when he knew he faced punishment?"

"Coins," Royce said and then took a drink of ale.

Brianna remained confused. "How would he get coins and from whom?"

Royce offered an explanation. "Arran would return, plead his plight, have the hired men free him, kidnap you, and demand ransom from your brother."

"Why not have the two men kidnap me?"

Royce hesitated and William and John remained silent. It was obvious they knew the answer, and she did not, and it was obvious that Royce did not wish to tell her.

She waited, sipped her tea, and the realization came to her like a striking blow to the face. "Arran intended to kill me."

"He blames you," Royce said, his hand going to rest over her trembling one. "In his deranged mind he believes that you thwarted his plans of ruling the clan. That you betrayed him when you befriended Moira, the enemy to him, so now you should suffer for your betrayal."

"Ian requested that I remain here until his arrival," William said and reached for a thick slice of brown bread.

"Of course you shall," Royce said. "And did he instruct you to guard his sister?"

William almost choked on the bread. He quickly took a swallow of ale and cleared his throat. "He ordered me to keep a watchful eye on Brianna, but he made it clear that she was in good and safe hands with you."

"An extra pair of watchful eyes always helps," Royce said and turned to John. "You know what to do. I will be my wife's constant companion. It will only be a matter of time before Arran attempts to take Brianna. Allow no strangers near the keep and make certain the whole village is watchful."

John nodded, grabbed a few slices of meat and bread, and hurried off.

"Enjoy the food and then rest. Your journey has been a

long one, and I am grateful for your courage and determination in getting Ian's message to us."

William nodded, his mouth full of food.

Brianna reached out and touched William's arm. "Thank you."

He finished his food. "Ian is anxious to see you."

"And I him. Now eat and rest and I will see you later."

Royce stood and helped Brianna off the bench. He requested a light fare be brought to his solar. He and Brianna needed to talk.

She hesitated on the staircase, the babe more active than usual.

Royce was concerned. "This has upset you."

She shook her head and continued up the staircase. "I have been expecting it. I knew Arran could not be trusted, but . . ." She remained silent until they entered the solar and Royce closed the door. "I had not thought he wished me dead."

Royce took her in his arms. "I will not let him hurt you."

She eased out of his arms and rubbed at her stomach, the babe protesting. "I know that, but I also know how tenacious Arran can be. When he wants something, he goes after it with a vengeance. And what belongs to him . . ." She did not finish; she could not, for memories rose up to disturb her.

Royce went to her and took her gently by the shoulders. "Listen to me, Brianna, I understand your fear of your husband. You lived that fear every day you were with him, but you are with him no more. You are mine now and will remain so. Arran can be as tenacious as he wants, but this time he has chosen a foe who is more tenacious than he. He will not succeed; he is doomed to failure. I will make certain of it."

She smiled, for the babe gave her a hardy kick. "Your child agrees with you."

His hand went to her stomach, and he grinned at the activity he felt. "The child knows his father well."

"And makes his opinions known."

"Like his father."

Brianna grew quiet and rested her head on his shoulder. "I do not want to lose what I have with you."

He wrapped his arms tightly around her. "I have taken care of you since first we met, and I will continue to do so. We will love, you and I, forever and ever."

"Do you think that is long enough?" she asked with a teasing laugh.

"Nay, not even eternity loving you would be enough."

She raised her head and placed her hand to his cheek. "No matter what happens, always remember that I love you."

A tingle ran down Royce's spine. An omen? He had not feared battle, for loss was part of battle whether defeated or victorious. He had not feared losing his life, for that was always a possibility when entering a battle. This battle, however, was different. He feared losing Brianna and his child, and that tore at his heart. He could not imagine life without her. He would do everything to protect her, but as in any battle, the outcome was yet to be determined. He intended to be victorious, for he understood that his opponent did not play fair—and neither would he.

He would do anything, *anything* to protect Brianna.

28

STRANGERS PASSING BY OR SEEKING SHELTER IN THE
village were carefully watched, and no stranger was allowed anywhere near the keep. All of the clan was watchful and cautious, having been alerted to the fact that
Brianna was in danger.

Brianna found that the Campbell clan well protected
their own. They were fiercely loyal, but then, so was the
Cameron clan. Arran had been loyal to no one but himself
and greed.

She appreciated the clan's protection, but after a week
of constantly being followed around by two or more men
and several of the clan's women joining her for a stroll, or
her husband forever being at her side, she began to feel
imprisoned.

She ached for her freedom, but she understood the necessity of her guards. That, however, did not mean she
was always understanding.

"I do not want to do any stitching right now, Della," Brianna said a little snappishly.

Della paid her no heed. "It will be good for you to join a few of the village women and stitch. Stitching always clears the head."

Brianna was curt. "My head is clear."

Royce listened from where he sat at a table in the great hall with John and William.

Della continued to pay her no mind. "We will all have freshly brewed cider and honey cakes."

"I am not hungry," Brianna said, and though she was not tired, it seemed a good excuse to get away from everyone. "I feel the need for a nap."

"I will settle you," Della said, ready to tend Brianna's every need, though actually her intentions were to protect.

"Nay!" Brianna heard her own harshness but did not care. She wanted simply to be left alone. "I do not need settling."

Her abruptness did not upset Della. "As you wish."

Royce admired and was grateful for Della's patience. He understood how confined his wife felt and how her usual pleasant nature had sorely been tested of late.

Brianna went to leave the hall when she suddenly stopped, turned, and walked up to her husband. William and John looked as though they were ready to flee as she approached, but one look from Royce warned them against it.

"Do you think Ian may have run into trouble along the road?" she asked with concern.

"It is possible, though your brother is wise and would be prepared for anything," Royce said, hoping to reassure her.

She was not reassured. "Perhaps you should send some of your men out to see if my brother is close by."

Royce did not doubt Ian's skills and knew her suggestion was unnecessary, but he also knew that his wife was irritated and that nothing at this point would please her. He hoped to handle her with a gentle hand.

"If he does not arrive within the next day or two, I will consider it."

"He could be in trouble this very moment, and you intend to wait a day or two?" Her voice rose with each word.

It was possible her own accident haunted her thoughts, and she truly worried over her brother. But somehow he doubted that; she was simply agitated by her condition and confinement. He reminded himself to have patience, as he had been reminding himself for the last two days.

"Your brother is a skillful warrior."

"He can still be hurt."

William and John inched closer to the edge of their seats, each prepared to run if necessary.

"True," Royce said calmly. "But I am certain he brought enough men with him on the journey."

"It does not always matter how many men fight." She slammed her hands on her hips, ready for battle. "It did not with you."

Della cringed. John shook his head, and William's youthful eyes widened in surprise.

Royce took a solid breath. He told himself that this woman standing before him was overwrought with worry and had a right to be, that somewhere inside of her was the pleasant and lovely woman he had fallen in love with and that soon she would make an appearance and spare them this skirmish.

"Need I remind you that I won the battle, as I am sure that your brother would if faced with a similar circumstance?"

"I do not wish to see my brother suffer needlessly."

"He is not." Royce tried very hard not to raise his voice, but his patience was fast slipping away.

"You do not know that. I want a troop of men sent out in search of him."

"It is not necessary."

She was adamant in her demand. "I say it is and Ian is my brother; therefore, it is my decision."

He could not help but chuckle—not a wise reaction.

"You will not laugh at me; you will do as I say." She all but stamped her foot in anger.

Silence filled the great hall and not a movement was made. All waited for Royce's reaction.

He stood slowly in front of his wife. "You do not command this clan. I do. And while I understand your concern, I tell you there is nothing for you to fear. Your brother will arrive soon without mishap."

"You will not do this for me?"

"It is not necessary."

"I feel it is," she insisted.

"I know it is not."

She looked at him with fiery blue eyes, but it was the hint of a tear in the corner of her eye that caught him off guard. He stepped forward.

She stepped away from him.

"Brianna," he said softly.

"You are cruel!" she shouted at him and fled the hall.

Royce followed, leaving a relieved William and John to themselves.

With her extra burden she was not as quick on her feet as she once was, and that only caused her more upset and caused her to try harder, tiring herself with each step she climbed.

"Brianna, slow down!" Royce called out.

It was meant with concern, but it sounded like an order Brianna intended to ignore. She kept climbing.

"Brianna."

He warned her with a shout of her name, and she grew even more determined to have her way, as foolish as it was. Besides, was she not good at being foolish?

She was not far from the top of the stairs and thought victory close at hand when she heard his footsteps rushing up the stairs. Instincts would tell her to run, but she knew that was an unwise choice, she would never outrun him, and besides, her legs began to ache. She decided to stop, turn, and face him.

"Do not dare touch me!"

He stopped abruptly, never having heard those words from her.

The words surprised her as well, for there was not a time she did not wish him to touch her. She enjoyed his touch. It was gentle and caring and ever so pleasing. He never raised an angry hand to her or caused her pain with his touch; he only gave her pleasure.

She was being irrational and temperamental. She was striking out at him, for she had no control of the situation, no control of her life, and the thought terrified her.

He made no move to touch her, though her words wounded. He understood her anger, and he only wished to ease her worry. At the moment the best way was to allow her her way and remind her . . .

"I love you, Brianna."

Her bottom lip quivered and she fought to control her emotions. She acted a fool and now she felt foolish. Words failed her but Royce did not.

"I want to love you, Brianna." He reached out his hand. "I want to take away your hurt and fear. Let me love you."

Guilt assaulted her. "You are too good to me. I do not deserve you."

"You deserve much more, and I will strive to see that you get it."

She shook her head, and he approached, slowly reaching the step beneath the one she stood on.

"Do not think of what life was; think of what it will be between you and me."

She held her tears, refusing to cry. She had shed too many senseless tears. "That is the problem. I fear there will be nothing between us because I foolishly wed a madman. Now he will punish me as he always did, and I will be denied my love for you."

Royce took the last step to stand beside her. "Nay, you will not be denied my love, nor will I be denied yours. We are meant to be together and we will be."

He had reassured her many times, and he would reassure her as many times as necessary. She needed to hear him repeat it over and over and over, and he would do so if it made her realize that it was the truth. They would be together; nothing would stand in their way.

She rested her head on his chest, needing to hear the steady beat of his heart. "I have strength, so why, then, do I fear this?"

"In battle no one knows for certain who the victor will be. We pray for the strength to face our adversary and the courage to accept the outcome. You fear the outcome."

"And rightfully so," she said, her blue eyes focused on him. "I cannot be certain of the outcome."

"The outcome is you and I together forever. It is the road in between we must travel that presents the difficulties. If we travel it together with confidence, then the journey will be less hazardous."

She stared at him for a moment. "Now I know why you are a legend. You are wise beyond your years. You understand what most do not, and you accept what must be done and do it without doubt or fear."

He smiled and looked as though he was about to laugh.

"And," she said with a thump to his hard chest and a smile of her own, "you find humor in it all."

"When all else fails, a smile is your best weapon."

Her smile grew. "Then we are well armed."

He leaned down and nuzzled her neck. "Now that you feel secure, will you let me love you?"

She loved when he teased her neck. It sent the shivers racing through her before igniting her passion. "Do you need to ask?"

"You seem to have little choice of late. At least in this the choice can be yours."

Her laughter was a soft ripple that echoed along the stone staircase. "The choice is that I always want you."

"This is good, for I feel the same of you." He scooped her up into his arms.

"I grow too heavy for you to carry." She protested with another laugh.

"Do not insult me. You weighed little before, and the babe adds little to you."

"You do not think me unattractive?"

He stopped for a moment before entering their bed-chamber. "What nonsense is that? I think you beautiful."

"But I have grown—"

He interrupted her as he kicked the door shut. "More beautiful."

She giggled. "I do not care that you are blind."

"I can see perfectly well, and I will see your beautiful body perfectly naked very soon."

With her stomach ever expanding, she had of late attempted to avoid being naked in front of him. He of course had dissuaded her attempts and made her feel more secure with her appearance. He was an unselfish man and an unselfish lover.

It never took them long to undress, both of them always eager to touch and taste each other, though this time Royce took charge, showering her with such ardent attention that she melted to his intimate touch.

He had a way with his hands that surprised Brianna, for who would think that a fierce warrior whose rough hands caused such destruction in battle could touch with gentleness and sensitivity?

He lay beside her on the bed, his hard body warm and her soft body cool to the touch, but not for long.

"I love the feel of you," he said, his fingers tracing a delicate path over her chest and around her breasts. "Your skin is rose petal soft and smells just as sweet."

She sighed, his grazing fingers warming her flesh and spiking her passion, and his thoughtful words touching her heart.

"You are a tender warrior."

He placed a finger to her lips. "Shhh—someone will hear you, and my secret will be out."

His hand returned to working its magic and she whispered, "Your secret is safe with me."

"I know that." He kissed the tip of her nose. "That is why I confide in you, for I know without a doubt that I can trust you."

Trust.

She had longed for it and finally found it. She said the few words that meant so much to her. "I love you with all my heart."

"I know." He smiled and stole a quick kiss. "Since I tell you every day of my love for you, now let me show you how much I love you."

She giggled softly and shivered with anticipation.

"You respond like a woman in love, and that makes me want you even more."

"Then let us not waste a moment. Let us love now."

"Aye, I do not want to waste a moment. I wish us to take our time and enjoy the pleasure of loving."

She sighed at the thought, for they often took their time making love, and it was precious memories she had of those times and anticipation of the times had they yet to share.

Her sighs turned to soft moans, his fingers tracing delicate circles over her warming flesh. Her body responded, squirming to inch closer to his touch, yet he kept it faint and teasing.

His fingers traveled down her body, lingering over her rounded stomach, then lightly touching the moist heat of her. His lips descended over one hard nipple and nipped at the tender bud while his fingers brought her intimate pleasure.

Her moans turned to groans, and her body moved in a frantic rhythm. She grabbed at his muscled arm and squeezed tightly.

"Please," she said, "I do so want you."

He kissed her like a man ready to explode, and she in turn reached down and grabbed hold of him.

"Now," she demanded.

"Aye, now," he agreed.

He moved between her legs, ready to satisfy them both, when a pounding shook the door.

Della announced with a strong voice, "Ian of the clan Cameron has arrived."

29

~⊱⊰~

"LATER WE FINISH WHAT WE STARTED," ROYCE WHISpered in Brianna's ear as they entered the great hall to greet her brother and Moira.

Brianna smiled at seeing her brother, and also because it was the third time Royce had told her that, and she much agreed with him, for her brother's timing was poor, though she was happy to see that he and Moira had arrived safely.

"Ian," Brianna called out and hurried to her brother.

He hugged her and then stepped back, his hands hugging hers. "You look beautiful."

"I feel wonderful. Royce is very good to me."

Royce joined them, greeted Moira with a kiss on the cheek, and gave Ian a hardy handshake before he walked behind Brianna and slipped a protective arm around her, his hand resting on her stomach.

"My sister flourishes with you; this is good to see."

"She is well and safe and will remain that way," Royce said, wanting Ian to know he need not worry.

Brianna sensed that the two men wished to talk, and she doubted that they wanted her present, but she did not wish to be kept ignorant of the situation.

Moira stepped forward. "I am famished and there is so much to tell you about Duncan and Anne. Anne is with child."

There was excitement in her voice but there was something else there as well, and Brianna was wise enough to understand that Moira wished to speak with her alone.

"That is wonderful. I wish to hear everything. Let us leave the men to talk. I will have food brought to my stitching chamber, and you can tell me of all the news," Brianna said, eager to be alone with Moira.

"I will see to it," Della said, not standing but a few feet away from Brianna.

With a quick kiss on the cheek to both husbands, the women hooked arms and walked off.

"Why do I feel they are up to something?" Royce asked.

"Because they are, and if you tell yourself that, then you are never surprised by their actions."

Royce smiled. "You have learned well how to deal with your wife."

"When a woman is as intelligent as Moira, it is necessary for a husband to be well aware of her words, actions, and definitely her whereabouts, for she can get into the damnedest situations."

Royce laughed.

"Do not laugh," Ian warned with his own laugh. "She taught Brianna well."

Royce raised a brow. "Sometimes I think it is easier facing battle than dealing with a woman."

Ian slapped him on the back. "Are you only just discovering that?"

Royce shook his head. "It is time for a drink."

The two men sat down at a nearby table that held a full pitcher of ale to drink and to talk.

THE WOMEN SETTLED THEMSELVES IN THE STITCHING room. Comfortable chairs sat around a fireplace, a small fire burning to chase the damp chill away. Night was near to falling, and while spring warmth had dominated the days, a chill continued to settle over the night.

Hot cider and a platter of meats, cheeses, and bread sat ready for them, and while they enjoyed the cider, the food remained untouched. They were much too engrossed in their conversation to pay heed to the tempting fare.

"I know you have things to tell me," Brianna said with a sense of excitement. "But tell me of Anne first. I am thrilled for her. I know how much she wanted a child."

Moira hugged the tankard of cider and smiled. "Anne still marvels at the thought that she is to be a mother. The babe is expected with the winter and Blair is"—she paused as if in search of a fitting word—"stunned and proud, and he refuses to allow Anne to do a thing. She suffered terribly from the morning sickness for two straight weeks, and your brother and I thought Blair was going to die watching her."

Brianna laughed. "He will make a good father."

"If Anne does not kill him before the child is born. He follows her around, watching her every move, and Anne does love her freedom. That is one of the reasons she wed Blair—he understood her spirited nature."

"They will do well I am sure."

"They are at least entertaining the keep and the village.

Everyone is placing a wager on whether or not Blair will survive the birth."

The two women laughed, and when the laughs faded, the conversation turned serious.

"I felt that your brother and Royce wished to protect you from the truth, especially with you being with child. Men feel the need to constantly protect. They do not seem to understand that women have strength and courage of their own. That is why I wished to speak with you alone. There is much for you to know."

Brianna nodded. "I am grateful for your insight. I would fear more and feel more vulnerable if I was not informed of the details. Tell me all you know."

"I must first tell you that it was Anne who discovered most of the information. Ian was stingy in regards to the matter, knowing full well I would supply you with all I knew."

"Then please extend my appreciation to Anne and tell her I will pray for a safe and easy delivery for her."

"Let me start with what Ian told me. He learned that Arran had formed a group of men. Men who had no faith or allegiance to a particular clan."

"Men of little virtue," Brianna said.

"Their virtue is coins, which is what Arran promised them."

"But he had no coins of his own. It was a false promise."

Moira seemed reluctant to continue, but her hesitancy passed quick enough. "Arran planned to return to the clan, beg your brother's forgiveness, speak of his duty to you, his wife, and win Ian's approval for a second chance. Whether he was granted it or not made no difference. He intended to kidnap you and demand ransom from Ian for your return."

Brianna sat silent for a moment. "He will not stop until he has what he wants."

"That is what Ian believes, and that is why he sent William here as soon as Arran had escaped." Moira paused to sip her cider. "Anne learned that when Arran discovered that Royce had taken you away, he grew furious."

"Because I had spoiled his plans."

"Aye, now he had to devise an alternative plan, and he certainly had not considered having to face a legendary warrior."

"Royce frightens him," Brianna said with pride.

"And for good reason; the man would put fear in the devil himself."

Brianna was quick to defend Royce. "But he has a gentle soul."

"I have no doubt. Love often tames the wildest beast."

"Not so with Arran," Brianna confided.

"Love only tames when love is shared. Arran loves nothing but himself."

"Why could I not see that?" The thought that she was blind to Arran's obvious flaws continued to torment her.

"We do not always make wise choices in life. It is not a sin; the only sin is if we do not learn from them."

"You make sense of the senseless. I envy you your knowledge."

"Everyone has knowledge," Moira said. "It is easy to remain ignorant, but with a little effort knowledge is yours."

"How do I use my knowledge to combat Arran?"

"First, do not give in to your fears; that is the one thing he counts on."

Brianna nodded. "You are right. After a while in my marriage I feared everything."

"And he used that fear to control you. As it is easier to

remain ignorant, it is easier to remain fearful. You are strong; use that strength."

"How?"

"You must be ready for anything. Arran is devious and will stop at nothing to have what he wants."

"As was his way," Brianna said.

"Aye, and you know he has not changed, so you must be prepared. Do not take chances. Do as Royce tells you: make certain a guard remains with you at all times."

Brianna winced.

"I know it is not easy, especially after a taste of freedom, but this is very necessary. And now you not only have yourself to think of, you have your child."

"You are right; I have been selfish in my thoughts."

"It is difficult to have someone constantly following you about."

"I forget it was the same for you," Brianna said with regret. "I am so sorry my husband caused my family so much distress, particularly you."

"It is not your fault. You have nothing to apologize for. You need to concern yourself with you now. You know Arran will attempt to take you from Royce."

Brianna nodded. "I have no doubt he will make an attempt. Royce has prepared well for any intruders. The whole clan has."

"You sound doubtful."

"If Arran penetrated my brother's defensives, why could he not penetrate these?"

"That is why you must be vigilant to all that goes on around you. Pay special heed to your senses, for they will alert you to possible problems."

"The question is what if Arran succeeds? What then is my fate? Royce believes he wishes me dead."

"The ransom would only be exchanged when you stood in front of Royce or your brother."

"Much can happen in between that time," Brianna said and shivered.

"Then build your strength and your confidence. It may not be needed, but it will be ready if necessary. Arran will be expecting the weak woman who once was his wife. He will not know how to deal with you if you show him strength and courage."

"I had not thought of that, but you are right. If I do not cower but defy him, he will not know how to respond to me."

"It may never come to that. He could be discovered and his plans thwarted."

"But it is better to be prepared, and it will help to chase my fears."

"That it will," Moira agreed with a smile. "Now I am hungry; shall we eat and speak of more pleasant things?"

"Aye, I am famished and feeling much better. Thank you yet again for your help. It is wonderful to finally have a sister."

The two women hugged and set about enjoying the food.

The men continued their talk in the great hall. Ale flowed freely and food was brought out in intervals.

"There is no more to do but wait. A game I do not favor," Royce said, dusting crumbs off his hands from the bread he had enjoyed.

"I have sent men out to see what they could discover, but Arran has a way of disappearing." Ian refilled his tankard.

"I attempted the same, and you are right, the man does have a talent for disappearing without a trace."

"It frustrates, but know for sure he will surface again."

"I do not doubt it," Royce said.

"He is a determined man."

"Nay, he is a greedy man, and greedy men make mistakes."

"You expect Arran to make a mistake?" Ian asked.

"He has already made it."

Ian waited in silence.

"He has challenged me."

Ian had heard endless gossip about the legendary Royce Campbell. He thought most a myth until he had met him a few years ago and had seen with his own eyes the man's fearlessness and his extraordinary skills and the respect given him.

Arran had chosen an opponent far beyond his meager skills, and Ian had no doubt that the man would be sorry.

Ian addressed his one concern. "My sister—"

"Is stubborn," Royce finished, raising his tankard in a salute.

Ian laughed and raised his own tankard in agreement. "That she is, and it could prove troublesome."

"Add to that being with child, and you have explosive."

Ian's laughter rumbled through the great hall. "It is good to see that her courage has returned."

"Courage, aye, but she is not invincible."

"She has been vulnerable too long."

"I understand that," Royce said, "and there is still a part of her that is. There is a deeper part that fears that her husband will forever haunt her and that she will never be strong enough to fight him. I wish to help her change that."

"I think you have. When she returned with you in tow, she looked different; she looked full of life. She defended herself as she once did when we were young, and it was good to see."

"Your sister had a courage that was undeniable when she was with me at the cottage. I was a badly scarred stranger seeing to her every need, and she showed not an ounce of fear, though I knew it was there; she just refused to allow me to see it. I can only imagine how difficult it must have been to rely on a strange man for her every need. It took courage."

"Aye, it did, and I am grateful it was you who found her."

"I had thought of that often myself, but then, I thought our meeting was meant to be; we were meant to be."

"It was fate, for it obviously intervened."

Royce raised his glass for another salute. "I was destined to love your sister. She is mine, and no one else shall have her."

Ian half raised his glass and teased, "Are you certain you want her? She is stubborn."

"Stubbornly beautiful."

Ian had to drink to that.

Their tankards clinked and moved to their lips when the hall door flew open and William and John rushed in.

"Strangers have been spotted in the woods."

30

NIGHT FELL FAST AND PROHIBITED THE MEN FROM
thoroughly searching the woods and surrounding area.
Extra guards were posted around the village and in and
around the keep. Brianna could not take a breath without
someone being aware of it. She was constantly watched
and she did not protest.

Royce was relieved by her change of heart, though her
calmness troubled him. She looked and acted as though
nothing concerned her. She smiled, laughed, teased her
brother, and chatted endlessly with Moira at the evening
meal.

Royce leaned over to Ian, who sat beside him on the
dais, to ask, "What did your wife do to my wife?"

Ian was pleased that Royce thought of Brianna as his
wife, though another ceremony, when the time was appropriate, would be necessary to make it official. He looked
from Brianna, who sat next to Royce, to his wife, who sat

on his sister's opposite side. They were laughing and chatting and looked to be having a delightful time.

Ian shrugged. "Seems to me that she made her see reason. Moira always makes people see reason."

"You have learned this from experience?" Royce asked, his smile much too wide.

Ian winced. "Aye, I did and ask me no more."

A commotion at the double doors drew their attention and brought Royce and Ian instantly to their feet.

William approached the dais in a hurry. "One of the guards in the village has been wounded, an arrow in the chest. He does not fare well. The healer tends him."

Moira stepped forward, placing a hand on her husband's arm. "Ian, perhaps I can help."

"It is better you remain with Brianna," Ian said.

That remark brought Brianna to her feet, though a bit slowly. She had grown tired from the busy day. She approached her brother. "Nay, if Moira can help save the man, she must go to him."

Royce settled it. "Ian, go with your wife and take extra guards. Brianna will be safe here with me."

"Thank you," Moira said to him and turned to Brianna. "You will be fine."

"I know I will." Brianna hugged her sister-in-law and watched her and her brother hurry off. Then she turned to Royce. "He is close by."

Royce slipped his arm around her waist. "You would make a good warrior, for your senses are strong."

"I am a good warrior, for I intend to fight for what I want and I intend to win."

Royce could not hide his pride in her nor did he wish to. "You make a worthy opponent."

"Aye, that I do."

Raised voices again drew attention to the door. This time John hurried in with several men following.

"Several of the livestock have been slaughtered," John said as he approached Royce.

Royce did not leave his wife's side. His arm remained firm around her. "You know what to do."

John nodded and most of the men in the hall followed the group out. The remaining men took guarded stances around the hall and a few walked off to join others already on guard throughout the keep.

"He plays with me and he will be sorry."

Brianna shivered, having never heard the cold hardness in Royce's voice before.

"Are you all right?" he asked, his deep green eyes filled with concern.

She felt the need to apologize. Arran was causing such grief, and she was partly to blame for having foolishly wed him. "I am sorry for—"

He silenced her with two fingers to her lips. "Do not apologize for him. The blame is his, and he will suffer the consequences."

"He will cause others to suffer needlessly."

"Do you hear anyone complaining? This is their home, and they will defend it against intruders."

"But I brought this intruder with me."

"Nay, you did not. His greed brought him here, and it is his greed that will mark his end."

"Then I wish for a speedy ending so that no more suffer," she said before resting her head on his shoulder.

He rubbed her back, hoping to soothe her worries. "Fear not, it will end. I will see to it."

"I fear it will be a night of endless concerns."

"He will do no more this night, his attempts to take me away from you having failed. He will now seek other means."

She trembled.

"You are safe." His arms tightened around her.

The doors to the hall opened again, and Ian and Moira entered, followed by William and several other men.

"Your man does well," Ian informed Royce.

"Your healer is remarkable. Brianna will do well with her when her time comes," Moira said.

Brianna stepped away from her husband to stand next to Moira. "Martha is wise in her ways, but I had hoped that you would be here for the birthing."

Moira smiled. "I had hoped you would ask me."

They hugged and the two men smiled, for a moment of sanity had finally intervened.

Brianna raised her hand to cover the yawn that attacked her as she returned to her husband.

"Time to retire," Royce said and took his wife's hand. "Ian, join me early in the morning; there are some things I wish to discuss with you."

"And I with you." Ian looked to his sister. "Rest well. You are safe."

Brianna smiled a lazy smile, for that is how she felt: lazy and wanting nothing more than to seek her bed.

The keep seemed exceptionally quiet as she and Royce walked to their bedchamber. They passed several men who acknowledged them with a nod, and it amazed her that the paired guards remained silent, not exchanging a word. She recalled their quiet departure from her brother's land and had to inquire about it.

With the close of the bedchamber door she turned to Royce. "Your men keep silent when they travel and guard. Is this something you expect from them?"

He began to disrobe. "I learned when I was young the wisdom of remaining silent. In silence you are more aware and hear much more that goes on around you. When traveling the roads the silence alerts us to unwanted company, the same in the keep. If the men talked, they would not hear an intruder's approach."

Brianna removed her garments slowly. "It must take practice to remain silent."

Royce laughed. "It takes patience, and patience is an acquired skill in itself."

"So first they learn patience and then silence."

Royce walked naked over to her and pushed her hands aside and finished undressing her. "They practice both together."

"That must be difficult."

His hands were gentle, his touch intimate, and even though weary, Brianna responded with her body, warming to his touch.

"A *determined* person can accomplish it without much difficulty."

"Is that a challenge?" she asked.

"Only if you accept it." His hand swept down to cup her naked bottom.

She gasped lightly, her hands grasping his shoulders.

"See, it is not always easy to remain silent."

His grin was more of a challenge than his words, and her hand swept down to cup him in her hand.

It was his turn to gasp, and he did louder than she had.

Her victory laugh was gentle; however, it still irritated him.

"I forget how tenacious you are."

"Determined, dear husband, determined."

His hand slowly moved away from her bottom, caressing her soft flesh as his fingers searched out the heat between her legs. "Aye, but then so am I."

She bit at her bottom lip, preventing the long, heavy sigh that begged to escape when his fingers began to tease her. She kept enough wits about her to slide her hand over him and pleasurably torment him as he did her.

His mouth moved to hers, nudging her teeth away from her lip so that he could kiss her senseless, and he did. It did not take long before she completely surrendered to his touch. Her body grew impatient for more intimate contact, and she ached with the want of him.

Her moan was barely audible at first, but as he continued to caress, tease, and taste, it grew until the sound filled the bedchamber.

He scooped her up into his arms and carried her to the bed. It was mere moments before he entered her, and they joined as only eager lovers could. Their combined moans filled the room, and for a brief second Brianna wondered if the guards heard them, and then she realized she did not care.

They lingered in their loving, enjoying every kiss, every touch, every moment of intimacy. He was gentle and caring with her, making certain she was comfortable in any position he placed her in until finally they shared a powerful climax that left them breathless.

They each lay on their backs, their bodies damp and their breathing heavy.

"We need practice," Brianna said when her breathing calmed.

"Aye, we should practice as often as possible," Royce agreed, his breath still heavy.

"I am available whenever you are."

He turned on his side with a laugh. "Be careful what you say, for I will see that we practice night and day."

She turned on her side, her protruding stomach resting against his. "Is that all? I thought more practice time would be required."

He laughed again and rested his hand over her soft belly, where his child lay comfortably nestled. "You are tenacious."

He expected her to remind him that she was determined; she did not.

"Nay," she said softly, her hand covering his. "I love

you and love making love with you. I sometimes think I want you too much, and I do not tell you of my desire for fear of being too demanding."

"Never think that, for I want you with as much tenacity and I love you with the same tenacity. And do not fear discussing anything with me. I wish us to talk of everything. There will be no secrets between us."

"Then you will tell me what it is that you will discuss with my brother tomorrow?"

He did not hesitate to answer. "Arran's options and possible tactics."

"You wish to know your opponent."

"I know that he is a coward, for only a coward treats a woman the way he treated you. And a coward also attacks the way he did this evening. He foolishly alerted me to his presence; now what does he do?"

Brianna shivered. "I do not know. I only know that he had a way of appearing when I least expected him to. After a while I found myself constantly looking over my shoulder or around me, for I feared he would appear out of thin air."

"He was on familiar ground, his own home. That would be easy for him."

Brianna shook her head. "Nay, he did it wherever we went. My brother's keep, the woods, the village. He always lurked in the shadows."

He slipped his arm around her. "He cannot lurk here."

"I tell myself that I am well protected—" She hesitated.

"Tell me," he said, caressing the curve of her back.

She waited a moment more before answering. "I feel most protected when you are with me, and yet I know that it is not possible for you to always be by my side."

"You think Arran will come out of the shadows when I am not with you?"

She nodded. "It is his way. These things he did tonight

are but diversion. Be sure that he has other plans, for he intends to have his way."

"Diversions to take me away from you."

"Aye, then I am alone and vulnerable."

"There are guards."

"I know, but somehow he will find a way past them."

Royce shook his head. "Never."

"You said the magic word," she said with a soft laugh. "I once said *never*, and Arran showed me how wrong I was."

Royce tensed, hearing the hurt in her voice. "This time I will show him that he is wrong."

He hugged her to him, and she settled in his arms after he reached to pull the blanket over them.

"I am glad that Moira will be here when you give birth."

"You attempt to change the subject and divert my worried thoughts," she said, snuggling her face against his chest.

"Aye, I do but I am honest when I say that I am glad Moira will be with you. I do not like to think of you in pain."

She laughed. "Birthing a babe is painful; it cannot be helped."

Royce grimaced. "I do not want you to suffer."

"You should have considered that before making love to me."

"You told me you could not bear a child."

Her hand went to her stomach. "I thought I could not. Wed four years, I had expected to conceive a child, and when the years passed and I produced no heir, Arran told me that I was barren. I believed him."

"He is the one—he is unable to father a child."

"Which probably infuriates him, for it makes him appear less of a man."

"He is less of a man," Royce said.

She shivered and wrapped her arms tightly around him. "What suddenly troubles you?"

"The babe, I had not thought—" She stopped as though fearful to speak her thoughts.

He suddenly realized what caused her fright. "You think he would harm the babe?"

"If by chance he captured me and demanded ransom, he would need to return me before coins exchange hands, but that does not mean he would treat me well. And knowing I did not conceive a child with him but did with you would infuriate him to the point of rage. He might then strike out at me and purposely cause me to lose the child."

His hand instantly went to rest upon her stomach. "No one will hurt the babe and no one will hurt you. Do not worry."

"For myself I do not, but how do I protect the babe if necessary?"

"You will not need to." He attempted to reassure her. "You will remain safe here with me."

She felt safe in his arms and wanted to believe she would remain so, but she also realized that there was the possibility that he could capture her.

Prepared.

Moira warned her to be prepared for any possibility. She was right, and tomorrow they would talk and she would prepare.

Prepare for battle.

31

Royce did not let Brianna out of his sight. The next morning when they woke, he remained abed with her until she was ready to rise, and together they went down to the great hall. He had sent a message to Ian that he would be delayed and that Brianna would be with him and could Moira come to keep her company while they talked.

He had thought Arran dangerous, but after last night and his discussion with Brianna he realized that the man was far more dangerous than he had thought. Arran was actually deranged.

There was a chill in the great hall, so a fire had been lit, and Moira and Brianna sat at a table near the fire. Royce and Ian sat at the dais, and six men were positioned around the hall. No one could enter without being noticed.

Brianna and Moira talked in hushed voices, not wishing anyone to hear their conversation.

"I realize now that I must prepare," Brianna said. "If Arran should happen to succeed in capturing me, I must be able to keep the babe safe from harm."

Moira frowned. "You are right. The only life precious to Arran is his."

"In his fury he lashes out, and I never had any means to stop him."

"So you surrendered to his brutality."

"I did not know what else to do," Brianna said, "and after a while I acted accordingly; it became a habit."

Moira placed a comforting hand on her arm. "Habits can be broken. It takes strength, courage, and—"

"Tenacity," Brianna said with a laugh, recalling last night with Royce.

"With all the protection that surrounds you, you still fear Arran will succeed in abducting you?"

"Habit," she answered. "I am reacting out of habit. He always had his way, so I assume he will do so again."

"Then if you wish to be prepared, do not act out of habit. You have changed; you are no longer that young woman he could dictate to. You gained your freedom and independence and the strength to do as you must."

"But he thinks of me as his wife, his property, and I am, so how then can I be free?"

Moira squeezed her arm. "No one but you can own your thoughts and many times our own thoughts can help set us free. If you continue to think fearful, you will react fearful. Think with courage and tenacity and you will demonstrate it. Arran would not know how to respond to a woman of strength and intelligence."

"You are right. He feared you; I could see it in his eyes."

"Then he will fear you if you are to meet, for you are much like me now."

Brianna looked surprised. "Truly, you think so?"

"Nay, I know so."

"Then it must be so." Brianna laughed and Moira joined her.

Their husbands glanced their way.

"It is good Moira is here with her," Royce said, relieved to see his wife happy.

Ian nodded, slowly staring at the two women.

"Why do you not seem pleased with their laughter?"

"They are plotting," Ian said with a firm nod. "I know my wife and she plots."

"I have enough to be concerned about; now I must worry about plotting women?"

"I would make it your top concern."

Royce rubbed his forehead. "What could they be plotting?"

Ian scratched his head and gave the question thought. "Knowing my wife and her independent nature, I would say she is attempting to help my sister be ready in case Arran should succeed in abducting her."

Royce stared at him.

Ian nodded. "I know the feeling; Moira leaves me speechless at times."

"Arran will get nowhere near Brianna, and even if he did, what could she do to protect herself? She is a mere woman and with the burden of child."

"I have no answer for you, though it might be wise that she be prepared in case she is faced with the situation. Warriors always prepare for battle. Why not Brianna?"

"She is not strong enough to defend herself."

"Not physically, but we both know that a battle is often fought with one's wits."

"This is difficult for me to comprehend," Royce said. "My thought is that I must protect Brianna."

"And you do, but as in battle, being prepared for the unexpected could mean the difference between victory and defeat."

"I have learned this well. That is why I am always prepared, and I feel Brianna need not worry."

"What would you do if Arran succeeded in abducting her?" Ian asked.

"That will not happen." Royce refused to believe it even possible. He would protect her and keep her safe.

"But if it did," Ian insisted. "What then?"

Royce was just as insistent. "It will not happen."

"You are as stubborn as my sister."

"Determined," Royce corrected with a laugh and a slap to Ian's back. "Besides, the women make plans. Though it is not necessary, at least they enjoy themselves."

Ian shook his head. "You have much to learn about Brianna."

"Do you not have much yet to learn about Moira?"

Ian looked to his wife, her smile wide, her cheeks flushed, her dark hair in a thick braid that fell down her back. "I am forever learning about her."

"Then we will never be bored, will we?"

"True enough." Ian shifted his glance to his sister. She looked radiant, her dark hair pinned up, her hands resting protectively over her rounded stomach and her smile precious. "My sister means much to me."

"I know this."

Ian was honest with Royce. "When Arran returned, I would have much preferred to run a sword through him for all the pain he had caused so many. Unfortunately that was not possible."

"Had you decided what you intended to do with him?"

"It was only a matter of time before he did something

himself. His words of regret and forgiveness meant nothing. He meant to charm and misdirect so that what he truly planned was not suspected, and that would give him the freedom to accomplish his true intentions."

"Abducting Brianna," Royce said, glancing at his wife, who was deep in her own conversation with Moira. "But I feel there is more to his intentions than just Brianna."

"Brianna serves a purpose to Arran. She will bring him a fat purse so that he may start over someplace else, perhaps farther south or to the outer Isles. There is nothing left for him here, and he is wise enough to know that. So once again he uses Brianna for his own means."

"Not this time." There was a conviction to his words that could not be denied.

"We should not underestimate him," Ian said. "He is a troubled man and that can make him dangerous."

"Far too dangerous, which means he will stop at nothing to accomplish his goal."

"I think him anxious and that could cause him to make a mistake."

"Aye, I agree his patience is running out," Royce said.

"Then he will make another move soon."

"I do not doubt it, and I expect it will be as foolish as his last attempts."

Ian sat back in his chair. "There is nothing to do then but to wait."

To everyone's surprise several weeks passed and not a word was heard from Arran. The surrounding countryside was quiet with a stranger passing through the village now and again. Guards remained posted and watchful, but daily routine once again became common, and soon many gave the threat of Arran not a thought.

Moira and Ian began to miss their son, and Brianna thought it unfair that they should remain when there was nothing they could actually do to help the situation. It was nice having them there, but their presence was not necessary.

"It is time for you to leave," Brianna announced one day over the morning meal.

Ian seemed surprised; Moira did not.

"I was thinking the same myself," Moira said. "I miss my son and all at the keep."

"You are throwing us out?" Ian asked with a laugh.

Brianna shook her head slowly. "I enjoy you both here, but there is no reason for you to stay. Your son probably misses you, and your life is there with him as mine is here with Royce." She reached for her husband's hand where he sat beside her at the long table.

"Brianna is right," Royce said. "Go home to your son and worry not. All will be fine."

"I will return in two months' time for the birth," Moira said.

Brianna rested a hand on her protruding stomach. "I cannot believe that in such a short time the babe will arrive. I am relieved to know that you will be here with me."

"I would not miss it, and I know if Anne is well, she will insist on helping as well."

"Since the decision of our departure appears to have been made, we will leave early tomorrow morning," Ian said.

"I will have some of my men accompany you," Royce said.

"I have enough men, I do not think that will be necessary."

"I do," Royce insisted. "At least until you leave Campbell land."

Ian knew it was senseless to argue. He shrugged. "If you wish."

"Come, Brianna," Moira said, standing. "We have this

one day together to discuss final preparations for the birthing, then all will be ready upon my return."

Royce helped Brianna out of the chair. Not that she needed help, but he was an attentive man, and she had grown accustomed to his attention. He did not follow the women, though two guards did without any objection from Brianna.

"Are you certain that you do not require my presence?" Ian asked with the women gone. "I feel Arran is playing a game."

"Then he plays with the wrong man, and aye, I am certain. You have spent enough time here. I have a force of men well able to handle the situation."

"If necessary, you will send for me?"

"Immediately," Royce assured him and leaned closer to Ian as if about to impart a secret. "Now tell me, what do our women really discuss?"

Ian laughed. "You are finally learning."

BY LATE AFTERNOON THE WEATHER HAD TURNED stormy, and if it continued, Ian and Moira's departure would be postponed.

The two women along with Della had decided that the kitchen was the perfect place to spend a stormy afternoon. Della had joined them earlier to discuss the birthing preparations, and then Brianna had suggested they all bake a fresh berry pie and enjoy it.

They baked an extra one for the two guards who stood silent by the two entrances of the kitchen and then decided that their husbands would probably enjoy one, too. They laughed and had much fun, and soon the room began to fill with a delicious aroma, and the two guards sniffed the scented air with appreciation.

They began to clean off the table they had worked on,

and Della grabbed a bucket to step outside and retrieve fresh water from the rain barrel outside the door. Moira and Brianna continued cleaning the table so that there would be room for them to sit and enjoy the pie.

Della called out for help with the bucket, and one of the guards went to her aid. When a few minutes passed and they had not returned, Moira and the guard glanced at each other.

"Take her out of here," the man said to Moira and moved toward the door, that the other guard had disappeared through only moments before.

Brianna glanced up from the task of wiping the table and noticed the alarmed look on Moira's face.

"We need to leave here," she said, hurrying to Brianna's side.

Brianna dropped the cloth and grabbed for Moira's outstretched hand.

"Stay where you are."

The familiar voice caused Brianna to freeze in her steps.

She and Moira turned to see Arran holding a knife to Della's throat.

Both women remained completely still.

"No smile for your husband?" Arran asked, applying pressure to the knife at Della's throat and forcing her farther into the room. "I knew with patience I would find you in the kitchen baking berry pies. You always had a penchant for them when the berries were in bloom."

Moira held firm to Brianna's hand.

"Did you think I would not come for you? Did you think I did not miss you or know how much you missed me?"

Two men entered behind him, rough and dirty in appearance.

Brianna reminded herself that she had prepared for this

possibility, and she was ready. Though her legs trembled and fear rippled through her, she demonstrated not a sign of her fright.

"I care not that you come for me. You mean nothing to me, and there was not a day I missed you."

Moira squeezed her hand, showing her support and confidence.

A malicious grin spread across his face. "You mean more to me than you know, dear wife."

He motioned to the two men, and one quickly took Della from him while the other hurried over and wrenched Moira away from her. In seconds a knife was placed again at Della's throat and to Moira's throat.

"Now, dear wife, the choice is yours as to whether you come with me or not." He raised his hand, and the two men pressed the knives more firmly to the women's throats.

She surprised herself with her answer. "You have never given me a choice before, Arran. Why should this time be any different?"

Moira did not hide her grin.

Della choked getting the words out. "You tell the bastard!"

Arran turned his fury on Della. "I have no trouble cutting your throat, old woman."

Brianna stepped forward. "But I have trouble with it. Let her be."

"You think to give me orders." He raised his hand to her.

Brianna stopped herself from cringing as she had often done. "I think you foolish enough to stand here and waste precious time arguing with me."

Before he could strike her, one of the men spoke.

"She is right. We waste time with this nonsense. Take her and let us be gone from here."

Arran reached out and grabbed Brianna by the arm. "You have forgotten about obedience. I will remind you." He shoved her toward the door.

She turned and looked to Moira. "Tell Royce I love him."

Her words infuriated Arran, and he grabbed her by the back of her hair and pushed her out the door but not before saying to Moira, "Tell Royce she *belongs* to me, and he will pay a dear price to own her."

32

AN UPROAR ROSE THROUGHOUT THE KEEP AS NEWS
spread of Brianna's abduction, but it was the thundering
roar that caused all to shiver and cross themselves, for the
leader of the clan's fury had been unleashed, and the devil
himself could not match his wrath.

Several guards had been injured, one seriously, and
Della sustained a minor cut to her throat, her assailant
hasty in his departure and not caring where his knife
touched. Moira suffered no injuries, though she felt foolish for not being more aware of the obvious.

"When Della did not return immediately, I should have
whisked Brianna right out of there." Moira paced in front
of the large fireplace in the great hall. She was chilled and
stopped often to warm her hands.

Ian kept a constant eye on her. He knew she was not
shivering from the cold, for the hall was warm; her chill
was caused by her ordeal, and while he wanted to hug her

to him, he realized she needed to walk off her agitation and concern.

Della, with a bandage wrapped around her neck, brought Moira a hot cider.

"I told you to rest," Royce said.

"I am rested and intend to do what must be done—" Della paused and tears filled her eyes. "As will you do so that she is returned to us safely." Della left the hall, wiping at her falling tears.

Royce looked to Moira. "Tell me what you have not."

"You are observant," she said and moved to stand beside her husband. Ian slipped his arm around her waist.

Royce waited. He had learned the power of patience when in battle. Sometimes it was better not to charge ahead but to first learn your opponent's intentions, and then a wiser choice of tactics could be determined.

Moira took a sip of cider and inched closer to her husband. "Arran told me to tell you that Brianna belonged to him and that you would pay a dear price to"—Moira paused, knowing the words would affect him and Ian— "own her."

Ian spoke up. "He thinks to sell my sister to Royce?"

"Did he not always think of her as his property?" Royce asked, not as upset as expected. "He treats her as he always did, and that will be his mistake."

"Aye, you are right," Moira agreed. "Brianna is not who she once was. She spoke up to him when he raised his hand to her, and he did not like it."

Royce looked ready to kill. "He raised his hand to her here in her own home?" The thought drove him to the edge of rage. He had promised Brianna that he would protect her. He had given her his word, and here she was threatened in her own home and then abducted when he had repeatedly assured her it would not happen.

"He never struck her," Moira said, hoping to diffuse some of his anger.

"He has raised his hand to her enough; she need not feel it again," Ian said, his own anger evident in his heated eyes. "We need to reach her as soon as possible."

"The men gather now. I leave as soon as I finish here."

"I go with you," Ian insisted. "There are enough men here to protect Moira and the keep, and he will not be so foolish as to return here."

"But he will send the ransom demand here."

"I will see that it reaches you," Moira said, knowing her husband could not sit idly by while a search went on for his sister. It had troubled him the last time this had happened, and he could not go, for she was giving birth to their son. Now, however, there was nothing to stop him, and she certainly would not.

Ian squeezed her waist, letting her know he appreciated her support and understanding.

Royce did not wish to waste time arguing. "I will send men back periodically so you are aware of our whereabouts and so that you may send along any messages received."

"Then we leave now," Ian said, removing his arm from around his wife and stepping forward.

Royce stayed him with a raised hand. "Nay, there are things we need to know first, or we ride senselessly."

Ian was impatient. "Arran disappears fast. We can lose the trail if we do not hurry."

"If you hurry and ride without thought and purpose, we will solve nothing. And if Arran disappears as quickly as you tell me, then he has already done so and we will follow a worthless trail, which is probably his intention."

Royce made sense, so Ian asked, "What do you need to know?"

"Brianna mentioned something about land that once

belonged to Arran but was in disrepair. I had a few of my men discover where this property is, but I wonder if he would take her there. If so we can easily locate them."

"You sound doubtful that it would be his destination," Moira said.

"It seems too obvious, and he might suspect that Brianna had mentioned it to someone. I do not think he would take the chance, though I could be wrong."

"He cares not if he provides shelter for her. Perhaps he intends to remain in the woods. The denseness of trees and such would provide concealment," Ian suggested.

"A possibility, but he is a man who observes and waits for people to react out of habit or anger. He knew Brianna would eventually spend time in the kitchen and give him a chance to abduct her. He thinks to anger me enough to ride off immediately after him and follow a senseless trail he has others ride while he goes another way. And of course he suspects that her brother will advise me how he is not an easy man to track, and therefore time should not be wasted but immediate action taken. All will divert us from his true destination."

"Then where does he go?" Ian asked.

"Perhaps the better question would be where does he not go?" Moira said.

Royce nodded. "He goes where we would least expect."

Ian nodded knowingly. "There is only one place for him to go."

"Where?" Moira and Royce asked.

"Home," Ian said. "He is returning to what is familiar to him and where we would never look."

"The keep where he and Brianna lived," Moira said, agreeing with a firm nod.

"I have not assigned anyone to reside there since

Arran's betrayal. I had hoped that Brianna would one day wish to return," Ian said.

"With a new husband?" Royce asked.

"I had hoped."

"She will have a new husband before she leaves there," Royce informed him. "Gather what you need. We leave within the hour."

"We will be ready," Moira said, realizing they would be close to home and missing her son.

The two men glared at her.

It was Ian who spoke. "You may go as far as our home."

Moira did not protest. It was where she wished to be. "You will take care, the two of you, and see to bringing Brianna home safe."

"That I promise you," Royce said with a strength that sent a shiver through Moira. Within the hour they were gone, their pace steady and their destination known.

"No complaints, dear wife?" Arran asked, riding beside her.

Her back hurt, she was tired and concerned for her unborn child, but she had no intentions of telling him. "None."

He looked disappointed. "Good, then we will continue to ride."

They would have continued to ride no matter her response, so she paid him no heed. Silence had always been her ally when dealing with her husband, and she expected it to remain her ally. Besides, her mind was preoccupied with thoughts of Royce. She knew he would search for her, and it was only a matter of time before he found her. Until then she had to remain strong and courageous for herself and the babe.

"You were not a proper wife."

She knew he intended to torment her, so she refrained from responding, though she had to bite her tongue. That gave her courage, for she had never before thought to disagree with him.

"Instead of mourning me, you found another man."

Very much a man, she wished to say. Instead she shrugged. "He found me."

"And you expect him to find you again?" He laughed. "I think the babe will arrive before he does."

His remark startled and frightened her. What if Royce could not find her? Soon after they left the keep, Arran's band of men divided, their intention to divert Royce away from Arran. She did not think it would work; he was too much a seasoned warrior to be so easily misled. And she would not allow herself to believe otherwise, which was what Arran intended.

Royce would come for her; she was certain. Until then she would be patient and keep herself safe.

"Tell me of my funeral," Arran asked. "Was it well attended?"

She stared at her husband for a moment, wondering what it was that she had found so attractive about him. He was selfish, arrogant, and cruel, and his features were far less appealing to her. She must have been blind when she thought herself in love with him. Now he was simply repulsive to her.

"I asked you a question," he said, reaching out to grab her arm.

Her reaction was quick, and she moved out of his reach. "I did not attend your funeral."

His face grew scarlet. "You dishonored my death?"

"You dishonor yourself."

He attempted to ride closer to her, but he had forgotten what an excellent horsewoman she was, and she skillfully maneuvered her horse away from him with little difficulty.

"I am an honorable man and do what is necessary when others refuse to."

"You are deceitful and selfish."

"How dare you speak to me with such insolence," Arran said, his fury on the edge of erupting.

Brianna wisely bit back her response. She was all too familiar with the consequences.

"Why did you not attend my funeral?" he asked. She did not answer fast enough for him. "Answer me before I beat the answer out of you."

Her hands began to tremble, for she recalled the brutal beatings and she feared for her unborn child's life. Then she recalled the conversation with Moira, reminding her that Arran preyed on the weak and defenseless. It would do her no good to show him fear. She had to remember she was in battle, and in battle a warrior did all he could to defend himself.

"I did not want to attend your funeral. I did not care that you died. I was grateful that you were dead."

He stared at her utterly bewildered and then shook his head. "You have grown brave since our parting."

"Nay, I have always been brave. I simply allowed you to rob me of my bravery."

"If I did it once, dear wife, I can certainly do it again," he said with a smile that had once charmed Brianna and now simply disgusted her.

"I am not a naive young girl anymore."

He laughed. "I made certain of that."

He certainly had and the thought turned her stomach.

"So tell me, did I teach you enough so that you pleased this barbaric warrior who you spread your legs for?"

"You think him barbaric? His deeds are so great that they have made him a legend."

"He is a ruthless warrior who kills for fun and profit."

She knew Royce too well to fall for Arran's lies. "And you think you can get more coins from him for my return than you can from Ian?"

"You are quick witted. A quality I despise in a woman." He grinned. "But Royce Campbell will pay a hefty price for your return, that I am sure of. I saw the way he looked at you when I interrupted your wedding celebration. He loves you, that is obvious, and he will do anything to get you back."

She spoke with courage. "Royce taught me what true love really is, and I am grateful the good Lord sent him to me, for I love him with all my heart and soul."

Arran sneered. "You were always a fool, and love is for fools. He uses you. He wishes an allegiance with the Cameron clan, and what better way than through marriage. He tolerates you in bed and probably seeks fulfillment with other more talented females."

"As you did?"

He seemed pleased when he said, "You were an inadequate lover. You gave me no choice."

Her temper took hold. "I was an innocent young girl. I knew nothing."

"And you learned nothing."

"You taught me nothing but pain and humiliation," she said, her temper flaring. "Royce taught me differently. He taught me about the beauty of love and the pleasures in sharing that love." She bit her tongue, for she wished to scream out at him that Royce was truly a man and he just a shadow of one.

"Then if this man loves you so dearly, why was he not successful in keeping you safe from me? And where is he now? Why has he yet to rescue you?"

He meant to demean Royce in her eyes and fill her with fear, but his tactics were worthless. She was far too secure with Royce's love, and her response proved it. "He is not far away. He waits for the right moment, and then you will taste his wrath."

She was convincing enough that Arran cast a hasty glance around him.

"He will come for me," she assured him. "He will definitely come for me."

"He will come for you with a pocket of coins."

"If he must he will, though love is priceless, Arran, and you never understood that."

"Everything has a price, even love."

"You are right," she said with a nod. "Everything does have a price. You demanding a ransom from Royce will have a price. Are you willing to pay that price?"

"You talk nonsense."

Her words had the effect she had hoped for: he squirmed in his saddle.

"I speak the truth. Do you think a man with Royce's reputation will pay a ransom and seek no retribution?"

"Do you think me a fool? Do you think that I am not prepared for that?"

Her skin prickled.

"I see you are worried." He grinned. "You know me well, and you know I will do what is necessary to survive."

She knew she should not ask, but she needed to know. "What do you plan, Arran?"

"I plan on returning you when the ransom is paid." His grin widened. "I see that surprises you. I had thought to kill you, but that serves me no purpose, and besides, I need to guarantee my escape before Royce can retaliate."

Fear ran her skin to gooseflesh.

"Ask me, dear wife. Ask me what it is that I will do to prevent the great warrior from following me?"

She feared asking the question, for she thought she knew and that thought gave her a horrible fright.

"You cannot bring yourself to ask—or do you already know the answer?"

She did not want to play his game. He had always played frightening games with her, and she would no longer be a willing partner. "Speak your intentions and have done with it."

He laughed, enjoying the control he had over her. "Perhaps I will make you wait."

This time she laughed. "Nay, you wish to see my reaction when you inform me. You ache to see it. I would not be surprised if you were hard from the thought of it."

His face exploded a bright red. "You will suffer for that and—" He intentionally paused, making her wait and wonder, letting the fear build inside of her and diffusing his own anger. Then calmly he said, "I will turn you over to Royce but keep your child."

33

⚜

FEAR RACED THROUGH BRIANNA. SHE SHIVERED AND sent a silent prayer to the heavens for Royce to hurry and rescue her.

"I inquired as to your birthing time, thinking that it might prove beneficial to me, and it certainly has. It is one of the reasons I waited to capture you. And do not think he will find us quickly. He would not think to go where I take you," Arran said, pleased with the fear he saw on her face.

The babe remained safe inside her. He would not take the chance of injuring the child if he felt he needed the child. It was a relief to realize that, at least, but his intentions still frightened her beyond all reason.

"I will treat the child well until he is returned to you." His tongue charmed, and most would believe him, but she knew better.

"Nay, you will not, and Royce will not let you take his child."

"He will have no choice, unless of course he wishes to forfeit one life for the other. Who would he choose to live—you or his child?"

She would gladly give her life for her child and knew that Royce would do the same, but she wished for them all to live and share a long life together. She would not allow her husband to rob her of any more dreams.

She turned her startling blue eyes on him. "Royce will come for me before the babe is born, and then the problem will be yours."

He forced a laugh, though Brianna could see she had cast doubt over his plans.

"Think what you wish," he said, and having grown tired of tormenting her, he rode ahead.

Brianna took a comforting breath. She needed to keep her wits about her, and as much as it frightened her to consider such a horrible possibility, it was necessary.

Prepare.

She had to prepare for the possibility that Royce would not reach her in time. If so, she needed to have a plan of escape. She did not know where he was taking her, but when she learned of their destination, she would better be able to formulate a plan. The plan would mean an escape, and provisions would be necessary.

She began making a mental list of all the things she needed and what things to look for. Her first thought was their destination. Where could he be taking her? Her mind listed the various possibilities, adding to that Arran's devious mind.

A sudden thought came to her, but she disregarded it. He would not be that foolish. Then it struck her and she slowly shook her head. He would send his men to the keep, and he would take her to the cottage, where Royce had taken her to recover from her wounds. And the men who had first divided off from them would circle back to the cottage and be his protection.

By the time Royce discovered his error, it would be too late. He would never be able to reach her before she birthed the babe. Now she realized just how much she truly was on her own.

Her hand went to her stomach. "It is all right, little one. I will protect us until your father comes for us."

Royce would find them. He would hunt for them no matter how long it took. He would not give up until he found them, and she would be patient and do what must be done to survive.

ROYCE SAT BRACED AGAINST A LARGE ROCK STARING at the night sky. Hundreds of stars sparkled against the darkness, almost as if each wished to prove their own brilliance. He wondered if Brianna looked on the night sky at this moment.

He shut his eyes tightly, opened them, and cast a silent prayer to the heavens that she was well and safe. He had done that every day and night for the last two weeks. They had found the one trail, and as thought, Arran was headed for the keep where he and Brianna had resided when together.

Every day had been a torture without her. He was aware that she had become an important part of his life, but now he knew just how essential she was to his life. He missed sleeping beside her at night. She would cuddle against him, and oftentimes he would feel the babe kick and marvel at the tiny being their love had produced.

In the morning she would slowly stretch herself awake, and he would slowly caress her until she purred like a contented kitten. Throughout the day they would seek each other out to talk, walk, or share a needed kiss.

But most of all he missed hearing her tell him how much she loved him. A day did not pass without her saying, "I love you." He had enjoyed hearing those words over and over, though he had not realized how much until he had not heard them.

"Do you wish solitude, or may I join you?" Ian asked, walking up to him.

"Join me," he offered. "I have dwelled on my problems long enough."

"With good reason; you miss my sister and worry over her safety." Ian sat opposite him a tree trunk as his backrest.

"More than I ever thought possible. Her safety was my concern, and I should have been more diligent. I failed her." It had tormented him that Arran was able to abduct Brianna from the keep. He had arrogantly assumed that any attempts would be met with defeat. He rarely underestimated his opponent, and it would not happen again.

"I felt the same when my wife's life continued to be in danger in our own home. If I could not protect her there, how then could I protect her at all?"

"Perhaps it has to do with love," Royce said, attempting to understand.

"Love? What would that have to do with it?"

"We love our women. Arran loves no one and can therefore make decisions based on logic rather than emotions, which is how a skilled warrior handles battle."

"Are you saying our love blinds us to the best course of action?"

Royce nodded. "If I thought more like a warrior than a man in love, my course of action would have been different."

"How so?"

"If someone wanted something I had, I would have

used it as bait to draw my opponent out instead of hiding it away."

"But you could not use Brianna as bait because you loved her and worried over her."

"Exactly," Royce said. "I would not dare risk her life, and yet by not risking it, by not doing as I would normally do, I risked her life even more. And now she is on her own with no one to protect her."

"The thought plagues my mind, for I feel as guilty as you in failing my sister."

"I was so concerned with my own guilt, I had not thought about you."

"I have thought much," Ian said. "I failed in protecting her after learning how her husband treated her, I failed again when I assumed him dead, and now for a third time."

"This was not your fault, it was mine," Royce insisted. "She belongs to me now and is my responsibility. I was the one who should have made certain of her safety."

Ian shook his head. "Say what you will, it was my fault. I should have made certain Arran was dead and not have accepted a ring and burnt corpse as the only evidence to his demise."

"I think what troubles us is that Arran has managed to outsmart us both."

"That does irritate me."

"I agree. The man irritates me more than I care to admit."

"Arran deceives with charm and character. He confuses his opponent, giving him ample time to attack or escape."

Royce frowned. "Then he does not often make mistakes."

"If he makes mistakes, he is often prepared with another plan. He never seems to be caught unprepared."

"So he prepares for every possibility."

"Moira believes so. That is why she spoke of being prepared to Brianna."

"She did?" Royce asked with surprise. "Tell me what they spoke of."

"Moira was educated by a monk who taught her many skills. The one skill she found the most useful was preparation, preparation in all her studies and writings and experiments. Without such preparation she believes she would have no success. She took that knowledge and applied it toward life. This is what she discussed with Brianna. She convinced Brianna that while she felt safe with your protection, there was always the possibility that Arran could succeed in his attempts to abduct her. What then? What would she do?"

Royce slowly shook his head. "You tried to convince me of this."

"I know my wife well, and I knew she was concerned for Brianna. She had made instant friends with my sister upon meeting her, and she was aware, for a stranger sees with clearer eyes than a family member, that Arran did not treat Brianna well. She helped her to regain her self-esteem and self-confidence after Arran's hasty departure."

"Moira did an excellent job. Your sister's strength and courage saw her through the accident and helped her deal with a complete stranger she was entirely dependent on. Not an easy task for any woman."

"Moira has done well with Brianna, which is why she wanted Brianna prepared for any possibility."

"I am confused," Royce admitted. "How could Brianna be prepared for her husband abducting her? I would like to think it was possible, but how?"

"I wondered the same myself. Arran ingrained my sister with fear. How could she possibly be prepared for facing a man she feared?"

Royce shook his head as if the answer finally dawned on him, and he found himself an idiot for not realizing it. "By showing the man no fear."

"I felt as foolish as you for not realizing it myself."

"That takes much courage."

"You doubt Brianna has enough courage?"

"Nay," Royce said, "she has the courage and more. I just feel foolish for being an arrogant fool and in believing I was her only defense."

"Moira was raised in a convent since she was twelve and realized that while other women were there, she basically had herself to depend on. After all it became habit, and she looked to no one but herself to do what needed doing."

"And she attempted to instill this in Brianna?"

"Aye, and I am grateful to her for it."

"So am I," Royce agreed. "It gives Brianna an edge over her opponent."

"And it gives us time knowing she will defend herself. Arran found my wife offensive with the way she spoke her mind. When Brianna does the same with him, he will not know how to react. He did not know how to react to Moira, and it was obvious he was uncomfortable around her."

"But Brianna was once his wife. Will that not make a difference?"

"Arran preys on the weak, those unwilling or unable to defend themselves. Those with strength he cannot tolerate."

Royce gave that thought. "Yet he leads me to his destination."

"He thought you would follow the other trail."

"Did he?" Royce grew silent.

"One trail was meant to divert."

"Was it? Or were two trails meant to divert?"

"Two? Where, then, would Arran go?"

Royce grew uneasy. "I do not know, but suddenly I feel we are being led astray and Arran has gone in another direction."

"But where? Where could he go? Where would he go? Brianna is heavy with child. He wishes to ransom her and be rid of her so that he may have his freedom." Ian grew quiet for a moment. "Something is not right."

"Aye, I feel the same as you. Something is wrong with this whole situation."

"Arran often deceived. I think he deceives us now."

"Purposely," Royce said. "He purposely wants to keep us from finding him, and he purposely sends no demand for ransom yet."

"He requires time."

"Aye, but for what?"

Royce knew but feared voicing his concern. "He wants the babe born."

Ian's blood ran cold. "He cannot mean to harm an innocent babe."

"You said yourself that Arran loves no one and therefore can do what is necessary. Two hostages are always better than one."

"So he sends us on a false chase while he waits somewhere else with Brianna and waits for the birth of your child."

Royce nodded, his hands forming fists and squeezing tightly. "We go where he wants us to, but he will not be there."

"Brianna must realize this by now."

Royce did not want to think of how frightened she must be. He wanted to know that she was strong and would do what was necessary to survive and give him time to reach her. He grew furious thinking of her giving birth to their child alone. He had told her he would be there with her, and he had wanted to be there with her. He could not take away her pain, but he could hold her hand and help her bear the pain.

"We need to think of where he would take her." Royce stood and paced in front of the rock. He was annoyed with himself, anxious to amend his destination and adamant about confronting Arran. The man had consequences to face.

"It could be anyplace," Ian said, standing and pacing beside Royce.

"Tell me more about Arran."

"What more is there to tell?"

Royce was insistent. "There must be something that would help."

"He charms, he is deceptive, and we have determined that he loves no one—"

Royce interrupted. "And he does not care to appear the fool."

"I would agree with that. He thought himself wiser than most, and I suppose he makes choices others would not."

"Brianna and I made a fool out of him."

"Aye, he would see it that way."

"And he would want revenge."

"But he gets revenge by abducting Brianna," Ian said.

"But his pride has been damaged, and that does not sit well with him. So what does he do?"

"He attempts to make you look like a fool."

"Right, but how?"

"He diverts you to a bogus destination."

"That is not enough for him," Royce said and stopped pacing, though he ran his fingers roughly through his long hair. "He wants to humiliate me."

"He does that to you by sending you to the wrong destination."

"I might look foolish, but not humiliated."

Ian shrugged. "How could he humiliate you? He has already abducted Brianna and leads you astray. Anyone would feel a fool. I did."

"As do I," Royce admitted. "A seasoned, legendary warrior such as myself being unable to deal with one single man."

"But you do, you go after him, track him, and find him—that is inevitable."

"He leads me on a chase, the destination being my final humiliation."

"Your keep?"

Royce shook his head. "It would be known the moment he set foot on Cameron land. There is no way he would slip past again."

Ian rubbed his chin. "He wants to humiliate you, he wants enough time to pass so that Brianna will give birth, which means that he must make certain you are drawn away from his intended destination."

"Which means we are going in the wrong direction."

"What if we are wrong and this is the correct direction?"

"That is solved easily enough," Royce said. "I send men one way and I go another."

"It means you go alone. You will need help." Ian could see that Royce paid him no mind, but he was insistent. "I know how you feel about finding Brianna, but do not allow your anger to make foolish decisions. Arran will be heavily guarded. He is not stupid, and he probably hopes that you will be."

Royce laughed. "You are as good as your wife in making someone see reason."

"I learned well from her."

"And I should have learned by now that you intend to remain beside me until your sister is found."

"I am glad you finally realized that, though I still advise a group of men to go with us."

"I agree, but give me your word that Arran will be left for me to deal with."

Without hesitation Ian said, "You have my word."

"Good, then in the morning we divide and change direction."

"That is fine, but do we know what direction we go in?"

"To know where Arran goes, one must think as Arran does."

"Think like a madman? I have come to realize that Arran is not only devious but—"

Royce finished. "Deranged. I have already reached that conclusion."

"So where, then, does a deranged man take his wife to hide her from the man who loves her and whose child she carries?"

"Back to where it all started. Back to where I upset his plans. Back to where I humiliated him."

Ian shook his head confused. "Where it started? Upset his plans? What are you talking about?" Then it dawned on Ian, and his eyes widened and his voice rose with his temper. "Arran was responsible for my sister's accident?"

Royce nodded. "Aye, I believe he was, though the accident did not go according to plan. The men he hired probably caused a worse accident than planned, and when my presence became known they were frightened away."

"You think he knew you were at the cottage?"

"I think he discovered our whereabouts the same time Blair did."

"Then he waited after that, but why? Why not appear right away?"

"It is beneficial to wait at times, especially if Arran thought he could fatten his purse."

"After hearing there was to be a possible wedding, he thought to get more coins from you than from me."

"He was in no great hurry. The coins are what matter to him."

"So he is patient again and takes Brianna to birth her babe where the babe was conceived."

"And memories born. I only hope those memories of our time together keep her strong in her resolve and courage. I hope she remembers all I told her when we were there; if she does she will know that I come for her. She will remember how very much I love her."

"So he returns to the scene of his crime."

"Aye, he returns to the cottage and we will follow."

34

THE DAYS WERE WARM, THE SKY A STUNNING BLUE, and all around her flowers bloomed brightly and Brianna planned. Her time was growing short, and if Royce did not arrive soon, she would have no choice but to leave and seek safety in the woods.

Day by day she had gathered the items necessary for her escape and items necessary to birth the babe. Her delivery time drew near, and the thought of giving birth alone frightened her, but the thought of Arran taking her child away from her frightened her more, so she had no choice but to accept and prepare to deliver her child.

She had hidden the gathered items in the woods each time she scavenged for branches and twigs to fashion baskets. One basket she had made would help her carry all her items, and she would soon stock it and leave it in the woods.

Surprisingly Arran had not bothered her, at least physically. His remarks were meant to torment and hurt, and at one time his words would have inflicted damage. Now, however, they had no effect on her.

She was much too busy to pay him attention, though it appeared that she did little but collect material needed to fashion a variety of baskets. While her hands created, her mind plotted, and she felt secure that while it appeared that she sat idly by she was actually busy planning.

"You sit here every day making those stupid baskets," Arran said, walking up to where she sat on a blanket beneath a tree, her hands busy bending and shaping the branches into place.

"What else have I to do?" She shaded her eyes from the sun that glared from behind his shoulder and then slowly stretched her arms, moving her head from side to side, pretending to ease her neck muscles when actually she watched the men who guarded the surrounding area. She had been able to determine when they switched places and what men were less vigilant than others.

"You were always lazy," Arran said with disgust.

"Did you think I would change?" While rubbing the back of her neck, she watched two men busy talking and laughing and not paying attention to their duties. She had watched them before and decided the two would serve her well when she made her escape.

"Nay, I did not and that is why it irritated me so to think that I required you in exchange of coins."

"I am curious, Arran."

He sneered. "A strange concept for one who never questioned."

She did not bother to remind him of the consequences she was made to suffer if she had dared to question him. She simply wished to settle her curiosity. "Why did you wait so long to abduct me?"

"Your ignorance astounds me."

She looked at him as if he were the ignorant one. "What does my ignorance have to do with it?"

"You are ignorant of the truth. You always have been and you disgust me as much now as when we were married."

"You will be rid of me soon enough."

"I would have been rid of you by now if the idiots I sent to bring you to me had done a proper job of abducting you."

Brianna digested his remark, and the realization fired her temper. She did not, however, display her anger. That would have pleased Arran, and she had no intentions of pleasing the repulsive man.

"So it was you who caused my carriage accident and the death of the two men."

He seemed proud, raising his chin in triumph.

She deflated him fast enough. "You must be accustomed to failure by now."

He turned bright red and his hands fisted at his sides. "Will you think me a failure when you must leave your child in my care?"

His words stung her heart, but she would not give him the satisfaction of knowing his target had suffered a direct hit. "That will not happen."

"You are so sure, and yet the great Royce Campbell foolishly follows the wrong trail. By the time he realizes he has erred, the babe will be born and the wee one will guarantee my safety."

"You are the fool if you believe that." Mentally she called to Royce, told him where she was, and prayed that he heard her silent plea.

"Is he here?" Arran asked, spreading his arms wide. "Do you see him?"

Brianna defended the man she loved. "He would not be so foolish as to walk straight into your camp."

"Why not? He is a legend; legends cannot die. What has he to fear?"

"Royce fears nothing."

He rushed toward her, leaning over so that his nose nearly touched hers. "He will know true fear by the time I get done with him."

She wisely remained silent, and besides, a dull ache had begun in her back a short time earlier, and at first she had paid it no mind, but it had continued, and she feared the babe might have decided to arrive sooner than she had thought.

If that were so, she would need to make a hasty escape and find a place in the woods to birth the babe. This being her first, she would be wise to leave as soon as possible.

Arran had stepped away from her, and she made an attempt to stand, her extra burden making movement slow for her. Arran ignored her need for assistance and watched with a smirk as she struggled to stand on her own.

She was about to tell him she was going to gather more branches when to her shock her water broke and flooded the ground around her.

Arran laughed. "The babe arrives, and where, dear wife, is the father?"

She wanted to scream in frustration. What now was she to do? A pain stabbed at her stomach, and she realized that at the moment the only thing she was going to do was to birth her babe.

"Go and deliver the little bundle who will guarantee my safety."

He would not even extend a helpful hand. She walked off on her own, the pain subsiding, but she knew not for long. She barely reached the cottage door when another pain struck.

Arran called out to her when she bent over from the pain. "You are on your own, wife, there is no one here to help you."

Tears stung her eyes, but she refused to let them fall. With difficulty she made it into the cottage, shutting the door behind her. "Please," she cried softly. "Please, Royce. I need you."

Having been present for several births and having discussed the birthing process in detail with Moira, she felt comfortable that she understood what needed to be done. She had gathered twice the necessary items, having left half in a bundle in the woods and the other half in the cottage. She thought it wise that Arran should see her prepare for the delivery, or he might grow suspicious. Now she was relieved that she had done so, for all was ready for her.

She placed the items she needed close by the bed and filled two buckets with water. Carrying them near the bed was the most difficult, but with slow steps and much effort she succeeded.

When another pain hit she was next to the bed, and she sat, her hand resting where the pain struck. It was then she realized that her birthing pains were close together and that there was a good chance the delivery would be fast and she hoped safe. If she grew too weary from the labor pains, she would have difficulty tending the babe.

She managed to slip off all her clothes but her shift, then lay on the bed ready to face the birth alone.

The pains continued on into the night and Brianna did not have the quick birth she had hoped for. Arran had ventured into the cottage now and again to complain that she took too long and that she should have done with it.

She tried not to fight the pain, but at times she wanted to scream. Instead she gripped hold of the sheets and bit down on the thick stick that she had purposely broken down to size for just this reason. She had no intentions of letting Arran receive any pleasure from her screams. No matter how difficult, she would not cry out.

The night wore on and into morning. She thought she would not have an ounce of strength left to tend the stubborn babe, for it seemed that he did not want to be born. She ached from the endless hours of pain, and when finally she lay back and told herself no more, the babe arrived.

It was past dawn when Brianna finally settled herself and her daughter down to rest. She was a beautiful little girl, full in the face and with a thatch of dark hair. While she gave her mother hours of suffering, when she was ready she had slipped into the world without a problem and with much less pain than her mother had expected.

She gave a cry but settled quickly against her mother, and even when Brianna washed her clean and tucked her in a warm blanket to lie beside her, she barely made a sound. She seemed content and fell fast asleep.

Brianna had little strength left to see to her own needs but did what was necessary, and though she wished for a thorough cleaning, it would wait until she was stronger.

Arran entered the cottage and looked upon the sleeping babe and Brianna pale as death and barely able to keep her eyes open.

"You could not even birth a babe," he said with his usual disgust. "Now what am I to do?" He shook his head, then quickly nodded. "You look as though you will not make the day. It will be up to the babe to get me my coins. Aye, this will work."

He spoke to himself, and while he made little sense, she realized he thought she was dying. If she could rest for a few hours, perhaps then she could make an escape. If she could just manage to get into the woods, grab her bundle, and find a safe refuge, she and her daughter would be fine.

She was strong; she could do it. She had to or else Arran would take her daughter from her, and that she would not allow. She would rest and keep her daughter safely by her side, and when the time was right she would make her escape. She had to, no matter how much she ached or how tired she felt; escape meant her daughter's life.

Arran watched her eyes drift shut and shook his head. "Worthless."

She would be gone soon. His only hope now was that Royce cared for his child as much as the mother. New plans would be necessary all because his wife was a weak woman who had no birthing strength in her.

He wrinkled his nose at the disorder in the cottage. Bloody towels lay on the floor and blood stained the sheets. It was a disgusting sight and he wanted no part of it. As soon as Brianna died, he would have her body dumped in the woods for the animals to feast on. Hopefully he could keep the tiny bundle alive. For now he wanted no part of either of them, and he fled the cottage.

Brianna heard the door shut and her daughter stir. She rocked her gently in her arms. "It is all right, little one. I will rest and then we will leave here and wait in the woods for your father. He will come for us. I know he will."

She fell into a light slumber, but the birthing had robbed much of her strength, and she could not stop the deep sleep that her body needed to heal from grabbing hold of her. She and the babe fell into a contented and much needed sleep.

Arran paced in front of the cottage. He had to devise new plans. With Brianna close to death, the babe would not survive long on its own unless he could find nourishment for it. He needed to keep the child alive until Royce parted with a substantial amount of coins, then it mattered not to him if the babe lived or died.

He silently cursed Brianna. She never did anything right. She never had the strength nor was she woman enough to be his wife. He would not mourn her passing; she had not mourned his.

He would make his escape to the outer Isles and start anew. No one would know of him there. He would become someone else and find a clan that was deserving of him. He looked around at the men he had gathered. They were a motley bunch deserving of nothing, and as soon as he was done here, he would make certain to part ways with them quickly enough. They were not worth the coins he had promised them, and he certainly had no intentions of sharing any coins with them.

He rubbed at the pain in his neck. He would send a ransom demand to Royce immediately, not telling him of Brianna's death, but informing him of the child's birth.

He laughed. He did not know whether Royce had a son or daughter, and he did not care, though he thought that a son would bring more coins. Knowing Brianna's inadequacies, she probably gave Royce a daughter. Nonetheless, the demand would be sent, and Royce no doubt would answer.

Arran raised his head when he heard shouts and someone cry out as if in pain. His eyes widened and he took several steps back.

Royce walked out of the woods bare-chested, sword in hand, and his deep green eyes enraged with fury. He swatted the men who approached him out of his way as if they were mere insects that disturbed him.

His men and Ian kept their distance at the edge of the woods, but remained alert and ready for battle. When

Arran's men caught sight of them, they fled without a thought.

Arran stood alone.

Royce drew his sword and stopped a few feet in front of the trembling man. "I have come for *my wife*!"

35

ARRAN WATCHED HIS MEN FLEE LIKE FRIGHTENED rabbits. He was left with no choice but to face the mighty Royce Campbell. He needed to keep his wits and think quickly. There had to be a way to make the warrior more vulnerable, giving him a better chance at defeating him.

Royce's voice thundered with demand. "Where is Brianna?"

It was a quick decision for Arran, and one that could go in his favor or against him, but he made it with hopes that it would work to his advantage. "Brianna birthed your babe early this morning. She did not survive; the child barely clings to life. They lie together in the cottage."

Royce stood silent, trying to comprehend the news.

Arran hoped his first thought would be to go to Brianna and the child. Then he could easily slip away before Royce's men could reach him. He took a step aside as if offering Royce entrance to the cottage.

Fury raged in Royce's eyes and he threw back his head and let out a tremendous roar that had the animals scurrying in the woods, the birds taking flight, and Ian and the men shivering.

Arran feared he misjudged the situation and attempted to convince Royce to go to her. "She called for you repeatedly, and even now I know she would wish you by her side. She loved you more than she could ever love me. And she begged that you see the child safe."

His words worked the opposite of what he had hoped. Royce grew enraged and drew his sword.

Arran held up his hands. "This will solve nothing."

"A coward to the end, Arran?" Royce asked with a calm fury. "You think to take the woman I love from me and cause her death, and there will be no consequences? You are not only a coward, you are a fool."

Arran did not care for this remark. "Who is the fool? Am I not the one who took her from the great Royce Campbell?"

Royce advanced on him slowly. "And are you not the one who is responsible for her death?"

Arran knew then there was no escaping him. He would have to fight, but he did not have to fight fair. He drew his sword. "You were the one who followed the wrong trail, so are you not the one responsible for her death? Did you not promise to keep her safe—and did you not fail her?"

His accusation pierced Royce's heart, and he knew that when all was done, he would suffer as he had never suffered before, but right now at this moment he would make Arran suffer for all he had done to Brianna and for robbing him of her.

"I am about to rectify that," Royce said and swung his sword.

Arran raised his sword to deflect the blow but was driven to the hard ground from the force of the powerful strike. The idea that he should be on the ground beneath any man infuriated him, and he lashed out, swinging his leg to catch Royce with a heavy blow to his knees.

Royce stumbled but righted himself quickly enough, giving Arran time to lurch to his feet and hold his weapon firmly in hand.

Metal clashed with metal, fists flew, blood poured, and the two men continued fighting. Arran was confident with his swordsmanship, though his strength was nowhere near equal to Royce's. But he had no wish to die and no intentions of dying.

Royce gave thought to nothing but striking out at Arran, blow after blow after blow, and he was prepared for anything, not trusting Arran to fight fairly. Therefore, he was not surprised when in desperation Arran pulled a knife from his boot and lunged at his chest.

Royce grabbed for his hand, twisted the knife away from him, the end hitting him hard in the nose, and tossed it to the side. "You fight like a coward."

"I fight wisely," Arran said, wiping away the blood that spilled from his nose.

Royce raised his sword and edged him on with a wave of his hand. "Come on, then, and fight me like a man."

Royce's men and Ian had moved in closer and watched the fight with interest. Arran knew that he could not win; his only chance was to escape. He had grown tired, and Royce looked enraged with revenge, and that would provide him with the stamina to fight all day. He had to end this and quick.

Arran raised his sword and moved so that he was nearer to the woods and as their swords clashed, he maneuvered them closer and closer to the edge of the woods. His chance came when he fell to the ground, and Royce was about to lunge at his chest with his sword.

He grabbed a handful of dry dirt and threw it in

Royce's face, blinding him and giving himself enough time to attempt an escape. He ran straight for the woods with the speed of a frightened rabbit.

Royce cleared his eyes in seconds and followed him. Arran was fast and Royce feared losing him. He stopped, raised his sword, and with two hands on the handle and all the force he could muster, he flung the sword at Arran.

Arran turned at that moment and with wide, horrified eyes, he watched the sword descend and pierce his chest. He fell on his back, hitting the hard ground and gasping for breath.

Royce reached him as his last breaths slipped away, and it was with a smile he said, "Brianna joins me."

An agonizing roar echoed throughout the surrounding area, and Royce pulled his sword from Arran's chest and rushed to the cottage. He stopped Ian from entering, handing him his sword.

"This is for me to do."

Ian tensed. "My sister?"

Royce did not answer; he turned and entered the cottage alone.

The smell of blood stung his nostrils, and the scene in front of him tore at his heart. How she must have suffered birthing the babe alone with no one to lend a helping hand, and here of all places. Here, where they had shared so much love.

He tensed from the pain and desperately fought the tears that threatened. He would be strong—he had to be—if not for him, then for Brianna, for she had been strong. He could tell she had worked hard giving birth and had fought to the very end.

And he had not been there for her.

The pain in his heart was like none he had ever felt, and he knew he would feel more before his time in the cottage was done.

He approached the bed, a sheet covering most of Brianna's body. She lay on her side in a protective huddle, and he could see why when he stood beside the bed. A small bundle he thought at first was a pillow lay beside her, her arm draped over it. It was the babe wrapped in a blanket and lying there lifeless.

Brianna was pale and lifeless; not a move and not a sound.

A tear fell and he did not care. She had once told him that it was not a sign of weakness but strength to cry for the one you loved, and he loved Brianna like no other.

He leaned over, needing to touch her one more time, needing to feel her soft skin even if it would be cold to the touch. He needed very much to touch her again.

He reached out and touched her face, and to his shock she stirred.

He was so startled he jumped back and with wide eyes watched as her eyes fluttered open slowly. He fell to his knees beside the bed, draping his arm over her arm that protected their child.

"Oh, Lord, Brianna, can you ever forgive me?"

It took a moment for her mind to clear and to recall recent events. She smiled when she thought of their daughter. She could not understand why Royce was upset. He had come to their rescue. She did not have to worry now, he had saved them and all would be well. So why was he upset?

At that moment the babe turned fussy and began to squirm and cry.

Royce was once again shocked senseless. He simply removed his arm and stared at the squirming little bundle who opened her mouth and let it be known that she wanted nourishment and she wanted it now.

Brianna smiled and laid a tender hand on Royce's arm. "Your daughter Breda makes her wants known."

"Daughter?" he asked, a smile spreading as he gazed at the squalling little girl. "She is beautiful like her mother."

Relief suddenly ran over him, and he reached out to pull Brianna and his daughter into his arms. "Never again will I see either of you in harm's way."

Brianna gave Royce a slight shove so that she could settle the babe at her breast to feed.

"Let me help you," Royce said, standing and holding out his hands, not knowing what to do but wanting to take care of them both.

"Sit," she said with a gentle laugh.

"You need help."

"Right now I need you beside me." She patted the bed.

He sat and stared at the feeding babe and again felt the need to apologize. "I am so sorry that it took me so long to find you."

"You came just in time. As soon as I rested I was going to attempt an escape to the woods, and there I intended to wait until you found us. I had no doubt you would find us."

He shook his head, not believing what he heard. "You birthed a babe and planned to escape shortly afterward?"

"I had hoped to escape before the birth, but your daughter insisted on arriving early and upset my plans, so new plans were necessary."

"You remained strong through this all."

She reached for his hand. "I remained strong because of our love, and I knew our love would bring you to me as swiftly as possible. I waited patiently and prepared patiently. I love you, Royce Campbell, and I always will. And I thank you with all my heart for giving me such a lovely little girl."

She wiped at the single tear that fell from his eye. "That tear means more to me than any words, for now I know the depth of your love for me."

He leaned down and kissed her gently. "I love you, Brianna, and I am so very grateful for your strength and courage, for you saved our daughter's life."

She laughed. "I am reluctant to tell you the names I called her at the time I was birthing her."

Royce grew concerned. "You had a difficult birth?"

She shook her head. "It was long and tiresome, and I swore several times that I would have no more children."

"If that is what you wish." He was anxious to please her and ease any worries.

"Nay, it is not. I wish for many brothers and sisters for our little one."

Royce grinned. "That is a relief."

They both laughed and the joyous sound echoed through the cottage.

The door creaked open slowly, and Ian peeked his head in.

Royce waved him in. "I forgot you waited outside."

"I was worried—" Ian stopped when he saw the tiny babe at Brianna's breast. He hurried over.

"A daughter," Royce announced proudly. "I have a daughter."

There were handshakes, hugs, and kisses, and Royce was soon cleaning up the cottage while Ian went off with a few men to hunt for the evening meal. He then tended to Brianna, and when she was fresh from her washing, he settled her and his daughter to rest on clean sheets and blankets.

The two females napped, and Royce sat watching them. It gave him pleasure knowing they were safe and he was here with them.

Ian shared the evening meal with them, and when it was done, Royce stepped outside with him for a moment.

"Does she know of Arran?" Ian asked.

"Nay, I have not told her yet."

"She has not asked?"

"Nay, she has not."

Ian placed a hand on his shoulder. "Tell her and be done with it."

Royce nodded and entered the cottage. His daughter was sound asleep tucked in her mother's arm, and Brianna looked about ready to fall asleep.

"Come join us," she offered. "It will feel good to sleep in your arms again."

He shed his clothes and joined her beneath the covers, wrapping his arm over both of them.

They cuddled and kissed and Brianna said, "Tell me, Royce, I need to know."

He knew she spoke of Arran, and he told her the truth. "I took his life."

She sighed. "Then it is done and over."

He did not wish her to feel guilt or sorrow for a man who caused his own demise. Arran was where he deserved to be, and he would trouble no one ever again. "For him, aye, but for us it just begins. Will you marry me, Brianna, and spend the rest of your days with me?" He smiled. "The choice is yours. It has always been yours."

Her smile bordered on a soft laugh. "You have always given me choices, now I give you one. Aye, Royce, I wish to marry you. Do you wish to marry me?"

He wrinkled his brow. "I need to think about that."

She poked him in the ribs.

He laughed. "Aye, I wish to marry you, and I wish for you to love me forever."

She kissed his lips softly. "Your wish is granted."

Epilogue

Eight weeks later

THE CELEBRATION WORE ON WELL INTO THE NIGHT, but the bride and groom sneaked away without anyone noticing. Anne eagerly took Breda for the night, allowing the newlywed couple the entire evening alone.

It had been a joyous wedding. Breda snuggled in her mother's arms and watched her mother and father wed without a cry or protest. The little girl actually smiled when her parents were proclaimed husband and wife.

The ceremony and celebration were held at Royce's keep with many of the clan Cameron attending. The two clans got along well and shared happily in the merriment.

Royce was happy when he finally shut and bolted the door to their bedchamber and with swift hands undressed himself and with slower hands undressed his wife.

He had missed the intimacy between them and was eager to make love with her, but first there was the touching. He loved to touch her, to feel her soft skin, to have her respond to his caresses, to hear her sighs and moans, and to feel her surrender.

He expected all of it, and he got more, for she was just as eager as he to touch, and the shared intimacy had them both sighing, moaning, and surrendering.

Once, however, was not enough for them, and they pleasured each other over and over before they both settled exhausted in each other's arms.

"I am still amazed by true love," Brianna said, rubbing her cold foot against his warm one.

He sounded as though he was making a wise statement. "Love is allowing your wife to warm her feet on you even when it chills you to the bone."

She rubbed her chilled foot up his warm leg. "See how truly amazing love is."

He shivered. "I am trying to make sense of it."

She cuddled against him, and he wrapped a firm arm around her. "Do you think love will ever make sense?"

"I think most worry over love too much. It is wiser to simply love."

"I think I understand that now. We cannot force love or bend it to our rules. We cannot blame love for our decisions or problems, and we cannot say love is blind. It is we who are blind. And love is not just words; love is action. You rescued me, you gave me choices, and you let me be me."

"And you accepted me with all my scars."

She giggled softly. "After I screamed."

He nuzzled her neck. "Now I make you scream for a different reason."

"And I enjoy every scream."

"As do I," he said and continued to tease her tender neck. She in turn began to touch him.

His mouth found hers. "We will never stop loving, you and I."

"Never," she promised. "I will love you forever."

Clan loyalty forced her to marry...
but can it force her to love?

ISLE OF LIES

Donna Fletcher

**Tricked into marrying an enemy of her clan,
Moira Maclean finds herself pregnant
with his child, and unable to suppress
her growing love for him.**

"Donna Fletcher's talents are unfathomable."
—*Rendezvous*

0-515-13263-2

Available wherever books are sold or
to order call 1-800-788-6262